**Fog wreathe...**
**speeding pa...**

Melinda's hands clutched whitely on the steering wheel; she fought vertigo at the unnatural sensation of sitting perfectly still and simultaneously moving at high speed, nothing but foggy clouds on which to orient in the unnatural silence

Just as soundlessly, she abruptly stopping moving. No transition, no slowing . . . In an instant, the fog stopped speeding past to freeze in a standstill just as unnatural—no shifting currents in its patchy gloom, not so much as a muffled sound coming through the closed windows. Just silence, silence all around . . .

*The explosively loud screech of brakes and scream of terror and grind of metal glass breaking guardrail groaning—*

Melinda screamed at the shock of it, jerking inside the Outlook as something slammed into the vehicle from behind, and all the outrageous noise of it exploded into her senses. A guardrail loomed in her vision as the vehicle tipped and she grabbed around for purchase—the seat belt, the dashboard, the steering wheel—and inexorably slid sideways anyway. The guardrail gave way . . .

There was nothing beyond.

*Nothing.*

**Also available from Pocket Books**

*Ghost Whisperer: Revenge*
*Ghost Whisperer: Plague Room*

# GHOST WHISPERER

based on the hit TV series created by John Gray

# GHOST TRAP

Doranna Durgin

POCKET STAR BOOKS

New York   London   Toronto   Sydney

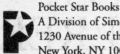

Pocket Star Books
A Division of Simon & Schuster, Inc.
1230 Avenue of the Americas
New York, NY 10020

This book is a work of fiction. Names, characters, places, and incidents either are products of the author's imagination or are used fictitiously. Any resemblance to actual events or locales or persons, living or dead, is entirely coincidental.

First Pocket Star Books paperback edition April 2009

POCKET STAR BOOKS and colophon are registered trademarks of Simon & Schuster, Inc.

For information about special discounts for bulk purchases, please contact Simon & Schuster Special Sales at 1-800-456-6798 or business@simonandschuster.com.

The Simon & Schuster Speakers Bureau can bring authors to your live event. For more information or to book an event contact the Simon & Schuster Speakers Bureau at 866-248-3049 or visit our website at www.simonspeakers.com.

Design by Richard Yoo

Manufactured in the United States of America

10   9   8   7   6   5   4   3   2   1

ISBN-13: 978-1-4165-6014-2
ISBN-10:      1-4165-6014-9

*To Adrianne, for the Positives*

*With thanks to my editor Margaret, for letting me play in the fun fictional universe, and to Lucienne for knowing I'd want to, and to Kim Moses on the television side of the force for making sure things stayed true to the vision.*

# GHOST TRAP

# 1

*Sleep my child, and peace attend thee,*
*All through the night;*
*Guardian angels God will send thee,*
*All through the night . . .*

*All through the night . . .* Melinda Gordon opened her eyes into bereft sadness. A sob filled her throat; her lashes stuck together with unshed tears. She lay in the silent darkness, struggling to separate the wash of inflicted, outside feeling from her own inner self. *I'm in my wonderful bed with the cast-iron headboard,* she told herself. *I'm in my gorgeous old home, renovated by my amazing husband.* The same husband who lay beside her, a warm, strong presence in the cool of this spring night, with a breeze from the barely cracked bay window blowing pale curtains into dancing shadows and drawing out a chill on Melinda's skin.

The tears spilled over anyway, even though they weren't quite hers; she let them run down to the pillow, but couldn't stop her sudden intake of breath, or the sniffle that came afterward.

Jim's voice was quiet in the night. "Again?"

She laughed—a weak thing, not meant to convince either of them. "Looks that way."

He shifted up to his elbow, looking down on her. After a moment, he used his thumb to wipe away the tear lingering in the corner of her eye. "Still don't have a handle on this one?"

She shook her head, even so slightly. "Honestly, I'm not even sure this is a ghost reaching out to me. It feels more as though . . ." She hesitated, and shook her head again. "It's hard to explain. It feels as though I'm on the edges of something. As though . . . I'm coincidental."

He laughed, and it was a lot louder than hers had been. "Trust me," he said. "You are anything but coincidental." And he gathered her up into his strong arms and kissed the damp edge of her eye, then rested his face against her hair and pulled them both back into sleep.

*Late, late, late!* Melinda gave her reflection a dissatisfied look, leaning forward at the drop-front dresser across from the foot of the bed. Her eyes—almond, long-lashed, and expressive—were normally a morning routine no-brainer. A little soft mascara, a little smudgy liner, maybe some earth-tone shadow. "The puffy look," she informed herself, "is not in. It will *never* be in." And she dabbed on a little more concealer.

But only a little more, because really, it was a lost cause. She set the little pot of makeup aside, stood up, and gave herself a critical inspection. On this spring day, the outfit would just have to speak for her—sky blue top with spaghetti straps and a wide ribbon gathering the empire waist, snug jeans with slim legs that showed ankle above strappy sandals. Long, dark hair drawn up in an offset ponytail and falling in waves, a jeweled-clip accent perfectly matching the blue of the top. Cheerful, bright energy—and maybe it would be enough to fool her way through the day.

And maybe tonight she would get the sleep she needed, after so many days of imposed sorrow brought her awake in tears that had at first been so obviously someone else's but now seemed more and more like her own.

Determined to think of better things—for there was nothing she could do for this unhappy spirit until she had more information—Melinda smoothed down her top, turned on her sandaled heel, and put energy into her step as she skipped down the stairs and snagged up her big satchel of a shoulder bag—going for practical today, a decision that might or might not have anything to do with the fact she was running late, late, late.

Uh-huh.

Out into the bright, early morning, out to her jaunty red Saturn Outlook, and the remnants of the spirit's sadness slipped away. She slipped a CD into the player, sang along to the chorus of "Can I Go Now," and headed out from Hazen Street into Grandview. Delia had no doubt beat her to SAME AS IT NEVER WAS, Melinda's antique store, but she had keys, and Melinda would grab them coffee on the way in to make amends. And since she was running a little late, the line at Village Java wouldn't be as long. *There, see?* Everywhere, a bright side.

Of course, she didn't find quite the parking spot she wanted, but a walk on a fine spring morning wasn't to be spurned. Especially a walk through the carefully tended town square, with its impressive war memorial, plentiful flower beds, and lush green grass—not to mention the smiles greeting her from those hustling along the sidewalks who were obviously just as late as she. She carefully didn't look at the charming old clock . . . it still carried memory shadows of the doomed Flight 395, and she didn't need to face those today.

*Shine, little glow-worm, glimmer!*

Okay, *that* perfectly suited the day she was trying to make. Perky and cheerful, with tones so round and full she expected to find musicians just around the memorial. But so many years of experience let her know . . . no matter how close it sounded, no matter how clear and true the harmony, it wasn't coming to her through her ears. Not really. And no one else heard it at all.

Wait a moment.

She stopped. She closed her eyes. She let her head tip back slightly.

> Lead us, lest too far we wander,
> Love's sweet voice is calling yonder!

Perfect.

Four part.

Barbershop harmony.

She said, "Oh, you must be kidding." And then, because she just had to, she turned around to find them.

> Shine, little glow-worm, glimmer—

Four of them. Four of them, beaming and delighted at the recognition in her eyes—and apparently oblivious to the startling trauma wreaked upon their bodies. Broad red vertical stripes on their blazers, red bow ties, white pants with a crease pressed into the center of each leg, straw boater hats atop their heads. One of them—of course—had a handlebar mustache. One tall, one stout, two somewhere in between; two pale, one swarthy, one rich brown. They doffed their hats, held them before their chests as if readying for the big finish—and then disappeared, just an instant of surprise presaging their abrupt departure.

"Kidding," Melinda informed the spring air, "would have been okay, too."

She made it into SAME AS IT NEVER WAS with coffee in hand, her mind's ear still echoing with the ringing harmonies of the old-time song, her thoughts racing ahead—already picking at the puzzle of how she'd learn more about the four men with so little to go on. All four of them had died at one time . . . they had died in their barbershop quartet outfits. But that song . . . it was old, she was sure of it. Classic. As was the tradition behind the outfit. The men could well have died a century earlier.

So she needed to know more before she went poking around. Not to mention she needed to admit to herself that this sudden impulse to go straight to Penthius was an equally futile attempt to evade the effects of one ghost by burying herself in the needs of another. Or in the needs of four of them . . .

She pushed through one of the double doors, expertly employing her elbow as she kept the two coffees steady. "Good morning!"

Delia looked up from the counter where she multitasked: a cell phone at her ear, a tangle of tarnished jewelry at her fingertips—delicate old stuff that contrasted with Delia's chic clunky look of the day, bracelets and earrings and necklace all colorfully suited to her bold blouse, with its fitted upper bodice and flowing sleeves. "Melinda! I was just calling—"

Within her purse, Melinda's cell phone rang. Delia snapped her phone closed; Melinda's silenced. Melinda said, "Ah-hah."

Delia's eyes narrowed slightly. "You all right? You look—"

"I know, I know . . . tired. Sorry about the time . . ." She assessed the morning so far by an expert glance at the counter contents—the jewelry, which meant there'd been time for make-work. There were also several sticky-note messages clinging to the counter beside the low-profile register, and otherwise . . . gleaming marble, with the leather pen holder off to the side, the trinket box at the corner, a small notepad and pen set neatly off to the side. "I brought amends." She pushed one of the giant Village Java cups across the counter toward Delia.

"Tired? I was going to say stunned. But that coffee looks as though it has my name on it, so who am I to argue?"

*Stunned?* Melinda couldn't help a glance over her shoulder. "I suppose you could say that."

Delia got it right away—*a ghost moment.* And she changed the subject right away, too. Melinda could see it coming in her expression—the instant of discomfort, the slightly too-cheerful moment that followed with her next determined intake of breath. "So what's keeping you up at night? Or shouldn't I ask?" Her voice grew more natural—and more wicked. "You and your honeymooning hubby . . ."

Melinda laughed a protest. "The honeymoon was over ages ago!"

Delia shook her head, patently unconvinced. "That's what you *say.* . . ."

"Hey!" Smiling, Melinda shook her finger. "We will now talk about something else."

"Fine," Delia told her, and swept away from the counter with drama, coffee in hand. "*You* choose."

"Oh my God, are we in third grade?" Melinda burst into true laughter, and Delia followed suit, and together they untangled jewelry until a van full of retirees who had seen far too many public television antiquing shows came in and haggled over pennies, eyes gleaming.

Melinda helped them load up their purchases while Delia bagged the last-minute item—brand-new bags, they were, complete with hang tags printed with the same antiqued *S* set against a three-leaf clover that adorned the bag. Tasteful earth tones, a modest spray of flowers beneath the *S*, the store's name scripted across the top within a peach border . . . Melinda loved them. Nonetheless, as the van pulled away from the curb, she joined Delia in the doorway with a sigh of relief. "Okay, *that* was stunning, in a scary kind of way."

"What's that?" A voice a little deeper than it had been only a few months ago spoke out from down the sidewalk—Ned approaching. "Another ghost?"

Delia's good humor vanished at her son's question; she turned to him—tall, filling out into heart-throb material, backpack slung across his shoulder and his grin fading into uncertainty—and Melinda took advantage of the moment to make an exaggerated wincey face at him. For if Delia hadn't quite gotten over the whole I-see-dead-people thing—hadn't truly accepted it—she *really* hadn't gotten over the fact that Ned had known of Melinda's gift months before she did, or that he'd accepted it unconditionally. So before Delia could say anything, before Ned's expression fell any further as he realized his error, Melinda stepped up. "No, the scary-fervent antiquers who just drove away. They've seen every *Antiques on the Road* show ever made, been on eBay, and they were so very certain they would find some cheap hidden treasure that they could flip for big bucks."

Okay, that got Ned's attention pretty quickly, too. He slipped the backpack off his shoulders, letting it slump to the sidewalk beside his feet and next to Melinda's flower boxes; his maturing features took on the little-boy look of any young man secretly thinking *pirate booty!* "And did they?"

"Are you kidding?" She dismissed the thought with an airy wave of her hand. "We've got plenty of treasure in here, but I'm afraid I've already found it. And half of it even came complete with undeniable provenance." Well, undeniable if you could see and hear the former owners explaining the history of the thing. Not so much, otherwise.

Delia held the door open for them all, but her gaze narrowed down on Ned. "Aren't you supposed to be at that reading program?"

"Reading program?" Melinda said, deliberately oblivious to Ned's grimace. "Do tell."

"Not for *me*," he told her, quick to get that part out of the way. "It's one of those buddy reading programs. You know, like the Paws to Read program. Some kids get to read with dogs, and some kids get us."

"Us, who?"

"From school." He dug into the backpack and pulled out a brochure, which he held up without looking up; once she took it, he dug further until he came up with a thin coil-bound notebook with a colorful cover that struck Melinda as—

"Whoa," she said. "They're trying just a little too hard, aren't they?"

"The whole thing makes me want to grind my teeth," Ned admitted.

"Oh, no, you don't!" Delia said. "We paid good money for those teeth!"

Melinda flipped through the brochure. "'Teen Reader Leaders.'"

"Yeah." Ned squirmed a little—something he did less and less these days as he grew into himself and his confidence. "Like you said . . . they try too hard. But it's a good program. It pairs us up with little kids who aren't reading so well."

"*And* it gets you out of gym class," Delia said, going straight to the bottom line—but not without a smile that was both understanding and proud.

"Gym?" Melinda sent him a puzzled look. She might have understood it before, when he was clearly still a boy, slight and a little gawky. But little of that remained, and Ned's interest in school teams had grown right along with his bones. "I thought you liked—"

"*Sports*," Ned said, seeing her question coming. "I like *sports*. That's not anything the same as gym class, really."

"Ah." She smothered a smile at this earnest explanation. "So you go to the elementary school after classes once a week and work with the at-risk readers?"

"Right. It's not so bad. The kids are cool, mostly. Though today . . . okay, *that* was scary. Don't you guys have anything to eat around here?"

"Us *guys*," Delia said, "are in a place of business, not a cafeteria. But I happen to know there's a plate of homemade granola crunch cookies waiting at home. If you can last that long."

Ned straightened, striking something of a heroic posture. "I'll wait," he declared.

"And the crowd cheered!" Delia said, making mock cheerleading-spirit finger gestures.

Melinda smiled at them and their mother-son silliness, her fingers running across the glossy brochure. "What happened today?"

Ned sobered quickly. "The kids, that's what. I mean, they're just kids. Second grade, mostly. So it's not like they were *grrr*, tough-scary. They were—" He looked at her. "Can I use the word *spooky* around you?"

She laughed. "Sure, why not?"

"Well, that's what they were. Spooky. They all looked drugged or something, and out of nowhere, they'd start humming the same tune together. I mean, seriously—we had them split up into groups, and they weren't talking to each other, but then all of a sudden they were all humming the same tune."

"They heard a radio," Delia said, matter-of-factly. "Sharp little ears."

Ned gave her an impatient look. "There was no radio," he said. "And they weren't pranking on us—they were trying to be good. I mean, get real. One of the guys is on the football team, and all the boys want to be just like him. And the little girls all suck up to Amy."

"Goth must be in for the tender set," Delia observed drily, apparently familiar with the Amy in question.

But when Ned would have protested, Melinda shook her head. "No, I get it," she said. "The kids try to impress you, not pull tricks on you. And they weren't in a position to pull this particular trick on you anyway."

"Right," he said.

"Can you hum it?" she asked him, on a sudden impulse.

"Hum it?" Delia asked, though in truth she looked no more puzzled than Ned. "Why?"

Tricky, this. "Aren't you even the least bit curious what song a classroom full of kids would suddenly start humming together?"

Delia shrugged. "Whatever they heard on the radio."

"That no one else could hear. Right."

Ned shifted uneasily. "Hey, never mind, it doesn't matter—I can't give you the tune." And when Melinda turned to him in surprise, he grinned. "What, you think a bunch of zoned-out kids sound like a school choir? They weren't very good. It was hard enough to tell they were humming the same thing."

"Well, there you are, then," Delia said, satisfied. "They probably *weren't*."

Ned struggled visibly with the impulse to turn sullen at this blatant doubt. "Whatever. They let us go early, anyway. Said the kids weren't in a place to learn." With perfect timing, he waited until Delia bent to straighten the shelf of disarrayed bags and still-flat gift boxes behind the counter, whereupon he made a face at Melinda. *They were spooky,* that face said.

Melinda widened her eyes slightly, an all-purpose response that meant both that she understood him and also that he was playing with fire. Out loud, she suggested, "Maybe you'd better go get those cookies before it gets any closer to dinnertime."

"Yeah, wouldn't want to miss out on the cookies." He returned to his grin, the one that would no doubt shortly be driving young women quite mad, and shouldered his pack. "See you at home, Mom."

"Pull the chicken out to thaw, will you?" Delia called from behind the counter.

"Got it," he said, the door already closing on his voice.

"That kid," Delia said, standing to flip long,

sleek, dark hair back behind her shoulder. "Too much imagination."

"Hey," Melinda said, a verbal poke. "It's a good thing he's doing. The reading." She didn't mention that the teacher had been the one to let the class go—that whatever had happened there, Ned hadn't been the only one to observe it.

"You know, you're right. Definitely a good thing. A good kid. As long as he doesn't ruin his appetite with those cookies."

"Hey, we could have kept him here and put him to work. Those antiquers cleaned out enough of the small stuff. . . . I think I'm going to consolidate that corner over there and bring up the washstand I've almost got cleaned up. It might make a conversation piece if I worked on it right here . . . but still, it's mostly done."

"Sure, and if someone wanted it, you could finish it up in no time. Get Jim here tomorrow afternoon, and I'm sure Ned would be happy to help."

"Great!" Melinda flipped her offset ponytail back over her shoulder, surveyed the store with hands on hips and narrowed eyes, and began the process of mental rearrangement. This here, that there . . . It would fit.

And if most of her attention lingered on the weird juxtapositions of her day—of the spooky kids and the jaunty barbershop quartet, the grief-stricken spirit brushing up against her dreams and the determined, overinformed shoppers of the day . . .

Well, the lost-in-thought narrow-eyed look covered more than just how to shift the stock around.

> *Sleep, my child, and peace attend thee,*
> *All through the night.*

Melinda woke with familiar tears drying on her face, lilting melody lingering in her mind. She didn't hesitate this time; she slid out of bed and grabbed the oversize shawl at the bedside, wrapping it tightly around herself as she padded out into the hall—far enough from the bedroom so Jim wouldn't wake, not quite so far that she ended up going down the stairs.

"I hear you," she said. "I'd like to help you. Won't you talk to me?"

Sorrow whispered in the hallway, a cold breeze coiling loosely around her. A *shush*ing noise changed from tender to harsh, a hissing demand with an edge to it. Melinda's skin tingled, then prickled; she drew back, pulling the shawl closer, searching the hallway for any signs of the spirit herself. "Please," she said. "I want to help."

Nothing. No emotions, no warnings . . . no prickling breeze.

"Mel?" Jim's sleepy voice filtered out into the hall, a tinge of alarm to his question.

And because he had good reason—because there had been plenty of nights when she'd welcomed his willingness to leap from the bed to be with her, to comfort her, or offer himself as a sounding board, or take her back to bed and hold her into sleep—she was quick to say, "It's nothing. I'll be right there."

But as she looked at the empty hallway, she knew it wasn't nothing. She just didn't know how long it would take before it became definably *something*.

As if Jim Clancy didn't know what was still going on. As if he hadn't known even the night before, when he'd woken to that empty bed, just as much as now, when that distant expression drifted over Melinda's features—clean, classic, Audrey Hepburn mixed with sexy, twenty-first-century girl next door, and always a balm to his eyes.

But not so much when they held that particular look to them. "You okay?" He sat down on the park bench with the meatball sub he'd brought from the fire station, a dripping concoction with giant meatballs sliced in half, smothered with sauce and cheese. "Because I'm thinking that face isn't completely about how much you want my food."

"Not completely," she admitted, sitting beside

him with her chef's salad fresh from the seasonal market just down the square—but not without looking around, and not without frowning. Jim looked around with her, but he knew enough about that expression that he didn't expect to see anything—just as he didn't doubt that she would.

The square was its usual gorgeous self, in spite of the veiled nature of the sky—thin clouds dulling the sun's light without obscuring it completely. It wasn't as warm as the day before, and she'd worn a cute little cable-knit cardigan with a scoop neck and snug bodice, all full of flatter and flow. Jim thought quite highly of the sweater, in fact, and of the way the lowest button, placed so high just under the bodice, let the breeze catch the light-weight knit and expose pale skin.

"You don't hear it, do you?" she said.

"Hmmm?" he said, the meatball sub in foil untouched at his side.

"I didn't think so. I'm not even sure *I*—" She realized, then, where his attention had gone, and drew herself up, rather primly at that, folding her hands to pin down the wayward sweater at her trim waist. "Did anyone ever tell you that it's insulting to be considered nothing more than a belly button? Especially when you're trying to have a conversation?"

"A conversation about something that no one can hear, maybe not even you?" But he drew his gaze up to her eyes, trying to gauge if they were laughing or held true annoyance in the deep brown beneath the sweep of those dark lashes. *Some of both*, he thought. *That's not good.*

She sighed. "I thought . . . maybe I heard the melody I've been hearing in my sleep. You know. The one . . ." She hesitated, but he didn't need to hear the rest of it. *The one that makes me cry* were her unspoken words, and he knew it clearly enough. She looked away, over into the square. "I was kind of hoping you could hear them. Because I hate to think that they might be coming from inside my head."

That startled him. "What, you mean that she's gotten to you? Planted that much of herself there? Does that happen?"

Her shrug was rueful. "It never has. But I don't take anything for granted these days."

Not since Romano and his Laughing Man side-kick had shown up. Not since a whole planeload of people had died in a field outside of Grandview, and that dark spirit had lured so many of them away. Not since before then, when the lines between living and dead seemed too thin somehow, affording spirits an access to Melinda—to her home, her shop, her *life*—that they'd never had before.

To Jim's life, too.

She took a deep breath, flipped the plastic lid

from her salad, and tore open the packet of dressing. "Let's eat," she said. "This one's going to come to me in her own good time . . . I don't even have enough to start research yet."

"Eating," he proclaimed, "is a good thing. Now tell me you aren't going to try to weasel a bite of this sub from me."

"*Weasel?*" she repeated, and he knew he was in trouble—if exactly the kind of trouble he'd gone looking for. The kind that lit that particular fire in her eye. The kind that would carry over until they got home and would lead to a certain amount of chasing around the living room, complete with growling and helpless giggles and eventually tangled limbs.

Except at just that moment her gaze went distant, and this time she seemed to be looking *at* something, and he couldn't help himself—as much as he expected to see nothing, he turned his head to look. And saw, in fact, something. *Heard* something, a woman's voice rising across the distance as she turned to the five- or six-year-old child sitting beside her in another section of the square. "Eileen!" the woman said, and the edge in her voice sounded like panic and not anger, even as she took the child's arms and gave her a little shake. "Eileen, what's wrong?" And shook her again, a little harder this time—enough so Jim found himself on his feet and cutting across the grass to reach that sidewalk and that bench, with Melinda only half a step behind him.

He might have warned the woman; he might have asked if she needed help. He didn't need to do any of those things. She looked up as he approached, the perfect picture of a harried caretaker—too young to be this girl's mother, but not too young to be her nanny. Face flushed against a coffee-and-cream complexion, curly strands escaped from caramel-black hair classically gathered at her nape, eyes a little wild—but not so wild they didn't instantly take in Jim's paramedic uniform. "Oh, *good*," she said. "She won't answer me—she's just *sitting* there—"

"I'm right *here*," the little girl piped up, her voice full of bossy querulousness, her frown making it clear that the grown-ups were being annoyingly incomprehensible *again*. "I thought we were going to get ice cream."

"But—" the young woman said, looking at the girl with confusion, and then back to Melinda and Jim, baffled and embarrassed. "I swear, I mean, I was really frightened. There's no way I would have shaken her—" She stopped short, looking at them with an entirely new kind of fear. "Oh, this must look really bad."

The little girl took over a moment fast turning awkward. "It *is* bad," she said, standing up on the bench to stomp her foot. "I *told* you I heard some-

one singing, and you got that look on your face
that means you think I'm making it up, and then
you said we'd get ice cream, like it would make me
forget what I was talking about. That means you
owe me ice cream! You owe me ice cream *twice*—
because you said we would get it and then for not
believing me! And I want *Smurf*!" But at the tail
end of that spoiled-sounding demand, Eileen cast
her nanny a quick, michievous look; the woman
gave the child a gentle poke in her tummy, the affection—and the game between them—obvious.

"Well," Melinda said, and although she smiled
at the girl, Jim thought he saw a sadness there.
"She certainly looks fine now. In fact, she looks like
a little girl who thinks she should have ice cream."
She lowered her voice slightly. "Don't worry. It's
obvious you were looking for help."

Relief washed over the woman's features at their
understanding . . . if a relief tempered by worry. "I
just don't know what happened."

"She's probably fine," Jim said. "But you should
have her seen. There are certain kinds of epilepsy
that can present the way you describe."

The woman thanked them, but didn't linger—
her hand, in fact, had been claimed by the little
girl, who already tugged her toward the end of
the square that offered ice cream. And while Melinda stared after them, Jim watched Melinda—
her thoughtful expression, that little bit of tension

around her ever-expressive mouth. He moved closer, one hand landing gently on her shoulder. "Well?" he asked, and they both knew what that meant. *Was it a spirit*? The influence, somehow, of a troubled Earthbound Spirit trying to find his or her way to the Light?

But she only shook her head. "I don't know," she said, and briefly met his gaze with troubled eyes before returning her attention to the retreating girl and her nanny. "I just don't know."

He didn't say it out loud; he didn't need to. If it was a spirit, they'd find out soon enough.

# 2

MELINDA FLOPPED BACK against the living room couch, letting all the air out of her lungs in a *whoosh*. A ghost haunting her nights but not actually trying to reach her, a little girl in the park who had gone blank even as Melinda thought she heard that same sorrowful song in the bright sunshine of daytime, and four barbershop singers off to the side—and what could she come up with in research?

*Nothing, that's what.*

"That good, huh?" Jim hesitated at the foot of the stairs, headed for the shower with a hand towel draped over his shoulder and sweat dampening his gray muscle tee. He'd definitely given those basement weights a workout this evening.

Melinda responded with an inarticulate sound of frustration and made a vague gesture at the computer on the low table in front of the couch, not bothering to look at the screen.

"Hey, it's early yet," Jim told her. "You don't have much to go on."

"Well, that's certainly true." She let her head fall back, watching him from that weird, nearly upside-down angle. A clear invitation if there ever was one. *Come talk to me. Distract me.*

"You really don't want me over there," he told her. "I am so not fresh."

That was worth a brief pout. "Shower, then," she told him. "I could use some company."

"Hey," he said. "This isn't like you, Mel. You're the one who tells me . . . these things happen in their own time. That the ghosts sometimes have to sort themselves out before they can communicate well enough for you to help."

She chose not to hear him. "The guys are singing the classics. I pretty much guessed that, but now I know. So far they haven't come up with anything past 1920. But that doesn't mean *they're* that old—maybe they just like singing the oldies. And the woman!" She threw her hands up. "I can't even pin that one down yet . . . mostly because I can remember the melody perfectly, but the words slip away as soon as I wake up. Truth is, I'm not even sure she sings words."

"In their own time, Mel," he repeated, coming

over to the couch in spite of his warning, blotting his face and chest with the towel. "What's up? You haven't really been yourself since we saw that little girl at the park a few days ago."

"That's ridiculous," she grumped at him, crossing her arms over her stomach and looking away, giving the kitchen entrance a good scowl. "Whoever thought of that saying, anyway? How can I *not be myself*? Trust me, there were plenty of times when I was growing up that I *really* didn't want to be myself, and it didn't do me a bit of good. There I was anyway."

"Hmm," he said, silent for a moment after that, leaning on his elbows at the back of the couch. "Not really about the ghosts, is it?"

She didn't answer right away. What was she thinking, marrying a man so perceptive? Finally she said, "You're not just going to let me snit about this, are you?"

He snorted. "If it means turning the word *snit* into a verb, definitely not." How casual he was, moving the accent pillow out of her reach. "C'mon, Mel. What's eating at you?"

This time, her silence was more thoughtful . . . if grudgingly so. Finally she leaned forward and closed the laptop, giving up on the ghosts—he was right; it was too early. "You know how I am," she said finally, as if that explained it all.

"I do," he said. "And gladly so. But you

know . . . just for the record . . . which part of you are we talking about?"

At that, it simply burst out of her. "The part that knows what it's like when you're so young and vulnerable and adults don't believe you!"

"Ahh," he said, his voice deeper with sudden understanding. "The little girl in the park . . . you think she heard something, after all. And her nanny didn't believe her."

"And look what it got her," Melinda said, though even she was surprised at the anger in her voice. "That music almost took her away, somehow."

At that, he hesitated. "We don't know that," he said carefully. "You weren't even sure you'd heard anything there—and there *are* possible medical explanations. Even if the nanny had believed Eileen, what could she have done about it?"

He made perfect sense. Of course he made perfect sense. And yet her temper flared, beating against the inside of her chest like a wild thing clamoring for freedom. "Something!" she said. "Anything! How will we ever know?"

"Ahh, Mel," he said, that deep understanding back again. He shifted closer, putting his head against hers. "I'm sorry no one believed you. They should have, and it wasn't right, and it wasn't fair to the little girl you were. But this is now, and I'm here, and *I* believe you."

"Oh," she said, a small voice. Within her, the

wild flare evaporated, mist gone in the sunshine.
"Well. So much for a perfectly good snit."

He kissed the top of her head. "My work here is
done," he said, in his deep superhero voice.

*Tap, tap, tap.*

Not a tapping at the door. Not a noise Jim
could hear at all. Something ghostly. Something
altogether new.

"Ha," she muttered. "Looks like *my* work is just
beginning."

Buffered moments in the store basement, time slipping past unheeded, soft humming drifting past
Melinda's ears and through her mind . . . capturing
her . . .

"Melinda?"

Delia's voice reached Melinda, but only distantly, even the second time. "Melinda?"

Darkness around the edges, the damp scent of
earth and concrete, the chill of underground . . .
all wrapped in sorrow, with tears slipping steadily
down her cheeks, her face otherwise blank and her
eyes blind to the outside world . . .

Until Delia came all the way down the stairs
to stand directly beside her and say, "*Melinda,*"
sharp and concerned, and Melinda quite suddenly
blinked and came back to herself—once more
perceiving the ornate, hand-painted wooden dinner bell she'd been cleaning at the worktable. Or

at least, preparing to clean—here in the basement of the store, with antique furniture waiting for repair and cleaning, goods piled in loosely organized groupings, and the original foundation structure of the building and, indeed, the town, enclosing the room and every bit as interesting as the room contents themselves.

As casually as possible, Melinda drew a finger along her lower lashes, wiping away the accumulating tears. *No more of* that, *thank you very much.* "Delia? What is it?" As if nothing was awry, indeed, to be sitting down here like a zombie. A *crying* zombie.

"I . . ." Delia started, then stopped—at first startled, and then to reassess. "You've been down here awhile. I thought you might need a break. But then I thought you'd probably actually gotten something"—she hesitated, looking around the immediate work area, before finishing with a note of question in her voice—"done?"

Melinda mustered her dignity. "I'm thinking deep thoughts."

"Uh-huh. Deep enough to have struck water, I see." She tilted her head slightly, concern evident; the neat row of diminutive hoops lining the outer edge of her ear all shifted in unison. "Seriously," she said. "What's going on? And can I help? Because you haven't been yourself for days, and now . . ." She gestured vaguely at Melinda. "Now this?"

Was it in her head, then, that echo of a song? *Shake it off, Melinda.* Time to get some token work done. "It's a passing thing," she said. "I'll be fine." *And you really don't want to talk about it anyway.* "Tell you what. Give me ten minutes to finish this, and I'll come up and spell you on the floor. It's a beautiful day out"—beautiful enough that they'd propped the door open—"and didn't you say something about getting a good walk in today?"

"I did." Delia's face lit at the thought. "And I can grab some fresh lettuce at the market—and oh! Herbs for the lemon chicken I want to make tonight."

"Then it's a plan." And then, when Delia didn't quite leave, Melinda made a fingers-walking gesture at the stairs. "Go. Ten minutes. I promise." She picked up the bell, blowing off the dust and reaching for a cloth to dip into the dilute cleaning solution in the small roaster pan off to the side.

"All right," Delia said, her voice a warning. "But now that you've promised me fresh air and shopping, I'm watching the clock."

Good. It would keep her focused—keep her mind away from that faint echo of song. Melinda picked up the baby's toothbrush from the neat row of tools beside the pan, gently scrubbing the accumulated grime at the top of the bell.

*"HELLO, MY BABY!"*

She couldn't help it; she gave a little shriek, fumbling the bell and barely managing a wild catch before the delicate piece hit the ground. Four-part harmony, full-bodied voices at full volume . . .

"Indoor voices!" she told them, for there they were, all four of them in their red-striped trauma-damaged splendor, hats in hands, expressions most earnest . . . comprehension, nil.

"*HELLO, MY DARLIN'!*"

Melinda winced, reminded herself that no one else would hear it regardless, and then went for what they'd understand. "You know, the acoustics down here are really bad. Can't you just hear that echo? If you were to tone it down a little . . ."

Ahh, comprehension. Much more moderated, now. "*Hello, my ragtime gal . . .*"

And really, they were good. At this volume, she was tempted to sit back and simply enjoy them. They certainly seemed to revel in putting on the show, with their stage expressions and their choreographed gestures, clustered together in their stage grouping.

But she had a bell to clean, and they wouldn't be here if they didn't have a need.

"*Send me a kiss by wire, baby, my heart's on fire!*"

She held up her hands in a choir director's all-stop, and silence fell. "You're wonderful," she said. "But can you tell me something about yourselves? Can you tell me why you're here? What happened to you?" Surely they hadn't died on stage—not all at once.

They looked at one another as if just now realizing *here we are*—and the realization startled them right out of themselves and into a shimmering uncertainty.

"Please," Melinda said. "I know I can help you. But I have to understand what you need—"

Back they came, solidifying into stark detail: crimson blood slashed across the smart red stripes; an arm hung useless; half the mustached man's face disappeared into a blurred mix of gore and darkness, bone showing through . . . white cloth turned torn and charred. The black man's face held horrible burns; smoke rose from his charred outfit. An acrid odor bit at Melinda's nose—flesh and cloth and rubber.

*Rubber. That's probably not turn of the century.* A first clue.

"Okay," she said. "You were all in some sort of accident? Do you remember—"

The mustached man opened his mouth as though to respond, looking astonished when no sound emerged. The others jumped in to fill the gap—and they, too, made no sound. Finally, after several false starts, they managed a faltering and uneven "*Hello, my baby . . .*"

"You *can't*," Melinda said, startled. And then, less certainly, "You can't talk to me, can you? You can only sing together—"

A distant scream reached her ears; she froze. Had that been real-time? *Now*-time? Or part of this quartet's manifestations?

"Melinda!" Delia's alarm answered that question without a doubt.

Melinda put the bell on the table and cast her work apron aside, running for the stairs—and by then the barbershoppers had disappeared, leaving only the lingering burnt-flesh-and-rubber stench.

Melinda left it behind, running into the bright daylight of the store, to find Delia already crossing the street to the square, moving with hustle. Another gorgeous day, another pair of strappy sandals not meant for running, but Melinda nonetheless caught up with her friend as another scream—loud and clear—cut the air.

"There," Delia said, still moving out strongly— she'd found the screamer, all right.

Melinda's stomach went cold and tight. *The nanny.* Days earlier, Jim had given her that questioning look, that slightly wary look . . . wondering what it was he couldn't see or hear as this same woman panicked over a zoned-out child. But even she hadn't been sure . . . just thought maybe she'd heard . . .

Maybe now she knew. Because mere moments earlier, she'd been captivated by that same music— might still have been there, if Delia hadn't interrupted, if the quartet hadn't stepped in and taken over the airwaves. And while she'd come back to this world . . .

The little girl hadn't.

"Your phone," she said to Delia, although they were only two of several people now rushing toward the distraught young woman, and now it was easy enough to see her charge—the little girl, her head slack, her arms slack, her body slumped. "Do you have your phone?"

"My—" But Delia cut herself off as she understood Melinda's intent, slipping a hand into the offset pocket of her belt-wrap blouse and slapping the phone into Melinda's hand even as they reached the bench. No more screaming—the young woman had seen them coming, and even though she wasn't all that much younger than Melinda, she reached for her, clung to her.

"You saw us the other day," she said. "I took her to the doctor, I swear I did. He checked her blood and he scheduled some tests, but he didn't say anything like this could happen!"

Delia, the mom among them, already crouched by the child, checking her forehead, the pulse at her slender wrist, gently patting her cheek. "C'mon, honey," she said. And then, to the young woman, "Did she eat today? Did she say anything about not feeling well?"

Melinda flipped the phone open, dialing a number she knew by heart. *Jim's phone.* "Pick up, pick up," she muttered at it. He'd be there, she knew—she hadn't heard the engines go out. A glance down the block confirmed it, revealing the shiny red noses of the trucks through the open station doors. Still, it seemed to take forever, a forever during which she couldn't take her eyes from that pale, still face, the unruly ashy-auburn curls, but still . . .

Faster than calling nine-one-one.

"Delia?" Jim's voice, puzzled and a little out of breath—she'd caught him hauling gear or cleaning the rig, right in the middle of *something*.

"No, it's me. I'm in the square—that little girl needs help. *Run,* Jim—"

"Be right there," he said, and cut the connection. Within moments, he emerged from the station, sprinting their way with a basic kit in hand.

Melinda returned Delia's phone, and all the while the nanny kept repeating, "She seemed *fine;* we were just out to get ice cream and I was telling her no way, not that Smurf flavor, and she just . . . she just *faded,* and now I wish I'd just said, 'Whatever flavor you want, Eileen . . .'"

By then Jim was there, already crouching beside the bench, and Melinda gently drew the young woman back. The paramedics' rig pulled out from the station, lights flashing, to take up position at the nearest curb; Jim's partner, Bobby, emerged with another, heavier kit, and as the crowd grew, drawing both customers and proprietors from the shops surrounding the square, the two quickly had the little girl stretched out on the bench, assessed and prepared for transport.

Not once had little Eileen responded to them. Not to blink, or flinch from the unfamiliar touch, or turn from their questions.

"Tell you what," Melinda said, looking at the worried faces and knowing that *she* certainly wouldn't be able to return to business as usual. "Coffee and muffins at my store, for anyone who wants to stop by." She caught Delia's eye, who came to quick attention—for there certainly weren't coffee or muffins to be found in SAME AS IT NEVER WAS at the moment. Village Java would come to the rescue, she had no doubt. A little community cooperation.

The crowd stirred, but Delia was the only one who moved, easing off to take care of those details as Melinda offered a fleeting smile of thanks. The others wouldn't leave, she knew, until the rig drove off. Even now Bobby carried the little girl away, the nanny trailing; Jim made quick work of snapping the medical kits closed and stood, lingering briefly beside Melinda. "Any clues, here? Because let me tell you, we got nothin'. Her blood glucose is normal, her pupils are normal, her BP is . . . well, you get the picture. And this is far beyond any petit mal seizure."

Melinda gave the merest shake of her head, too aware of the crowd around them. "I heard . . . well, but it doesn't make sense. I was in the store basement and I heard . . . well, what I've been hearing. Right before . . . but then the barbershoppers came in—" At his puzzled expression, she shook her head again. "Let's just say I've got nothin'. Not yet. But I'll keep looking."

He glanced at the rig. "I'll call."

She nodded, discovered she was hugging herself in spite of the spring warmth, and deliberately dropped her arms to her sides as he jogged away to the rig, lugging the hefty kits as though they were weightless. Within moments, the rig pulled away from the curb, lights flashing and siren winding up, heading for Mercy General. Melinda turned back to the uncertain gathering. "Coffee," she said, her finger at her shoulder to tip at the store. "Muffins. Seriously." And then she headed for the store herself, to clear surfaces and set aside fragile things.

*Tap, tap, tap.*

That noise again. She made absent note of it, distracted, and checked both ways before setting foot into the street. Automatic, that—a glance and a glance. She'd almost reached the other curb when the screech of brakes startled her into a squeak, goosing her the rest of the way across. She took the last section in a little leap and whirled from the sidewalk, turning to see . . .

No one. Nothing. The street was clear.

"Okay, then," she muttered. "We've got clues—we just don't have any idea what they mean."

She hoped they had the time to find out.

But the news didn't come fast *or* good.

"Nothing?" Melinda said, crossing the spring-green grass of the Driscoll County Park, picnic basket in hand, hope in heart. No better place for hope than here, with the happy activity—a man romping with his dog, completely unaware that Homer the ghost border collie romped with them; a pair of cyclists cruising the bike path; a young mother with her two children, toddler and infant; a couple long dead, strolling quietly together under the shade of her parasol. Those two would have fit perfectly in a Seurat painting.

And Melinda meeting her hunky fire guy for lunch, fresh off a run to the hospital and signed off for the day. He knew what her query meant—that she was still thinking of Eileen from the day before. He shook his head, a regretful gesture, and held out his hand for the basket while she cased out the perfect spot—beside a freshly budded tree, in the edge of the shade. Just enough sun, just enough shade on this unseasonably warm day.

She shook out the blanket she'd had tucked under her arm and spread it there, catching her flirty spring skirt so it tucked neatly beneath her legs as she folded down onto the clean surface. "They haven't been able to figure it out?"

"Not a clue." He put the basket off to the side and lifted out the chilled plastic container, passing it over—and in turn, the plates, thermos, glasses, and napkins. "They're not saying it in so many words, but . . . the MRI, the CT scan, the blood work . . . it's all perfectly normal. She seems like a healthy little girl."

"Except for the fact that she's dying." Melinda's mouth went tight.

"Except for that," he agreed.

For she was. For all that she seemed to have done no more than mysteriously fall asleep in the middle of the day and failed to wake, she also seemed to be falling deeper and deeper asleep. Her brain activity, he had told her on the phone, was diminishing. She was scheduled for a special brain scan later that day.

And Melinda . . . "I got nothin'," she muttered.

"You've got lunch," he said firmly. "And you'll figure it out. You won't give up, and if this is something ghostish, you'll figure it out."

"Ghostish," she said, and wrinkled her nose at him. "I like that."

"And I'm going to like *this*." He peered into the lunch container with appreciation. "Have you been into my mom's recipes again?"

"What, you think I can't come up with a recipe

on my own? Just because you're the dabbler of the family . . ." Fightin' words, those, and she said them with a wicked gleam.

"*Dabbler?* I do not *dabble*. I *cook*. I *create*."

He was winding up, all right. Melinda laughed. "And I eat, happily, whatever you feel like creating. And no, this isn't your mom's. It's chicken-strawberry salad. I found it on the Internet, and it looked good. Orange and lemon marinade, all those strawberries and oranges . . ."

Jim stole a strawberry. "I'm convinced," he said. "Diversion tactics successful. Let's eat."

Melinda laughed. "I might say the same to you. Diversion tactics successful. I'll think about Eileen later." She dished out their portions and handed him a plate. But as he reached for it, she withdrew it—impish impulse overriding maturity—and when he reflexively withdrew his hand, offered it again, until he finally snatched her wrist and drew her in to set the plate aside altogether. "Why, Mr. Clancy," she said, offering no resistance whatsoever. "Don't you think we'll become a cliché, making out in the park?"

"Why, Ms. Gordon," he said, "what makes you think I care?"

But eventually they ate the chicken-strawberry salad, and found it good; they drank the wine, and found it just as good. Stomachs full, they lay back on the blanket; Melinda rested her head on

Jim's shoulder and listened to the grin in his voice as he told her of Bobby's most recent adventures in the firehouse kitchen. Eventually the warm sun and her sleepless nights proved irresistible; her lids drowsed closed.

> *Hill and dale in slumber sleeping,*
> *I, my loved one's watch, am keeping,*
> *All through the night.*

Beautiful the voice, beautiful the melody, so low as to be subliminal. So subtle as to draw her in without alarming, without alerting. Not here, speaking to her personally, but everywhere—humming through the earth itself, sinking into her bones. Absorbing her. Comforting her. Enfolding her. Examining her . . .

And if that last didn't quite seem to fit in, if she somehow felt looked at from the inside out and discarded as all wrong, the enfolding song none-theless made it all right. She grew heavier, drawing the notes around her as though they were a beloved quilt.

> *Midnight slumber close surround thee,*
> *All through the night.*

It seemed so very natural to stay there in that place. Even though she was vaguely aware of a familiar voice speaking to her, a deep and beloved voice tight with concern, she couldn't quite bring herself to respond. She merely drew the quilt of music more closely around herself and sank into its deep beauty.

Sank . . .

Deeply . . .

Jim didn't realize there was any problem, not at first. To be honest, he was pretty much too full of satisfaction to realize anything had gone amiss—sated with this time stolen from their busy days, sated with good food, sated with PG-rated, park-public kisses.

Okay, maybe R-rated at moments. But just barely. Because the park-public part, that was real enough. And then to top it all off by lying here in the warm sun together, Melinda in that sundress with faint blue stripes evoking days past and spaghetti straps very clearly the fashion of the day, snug bodice and swinging skirt, toes with pink pearl polish peeking out from sandals adorned with little blue flowers . . .

Yeah, it felt right. No ghosts, no fires or accidents, just Melinda tucked up on his shoulder, fitting just right. Delicate size two, her equally petite hand resting on his chest, the perfect weight to follow along as his ribs rose and fell with his breath.

Until he stretched and murmured something

about her lunch hour being gone, and she didn't respond. Until he propped up on his elbow and she didn't wake, slipping limply into the crook of his arm, head lolling on a slender neck. "Mel," he said. And then, "Melinda." And even then, "*Melinda!*"

But that hadn't worked, and now he found himself leaning over her, checking her pulse on that same slender neck, gently knuckling over her breastbone as if she were one of his diabetic or drug-overdose patients. No, not as if—much more gently, and yet with a welling concern he'd never felt on the job.

He wouldn't let himself think the word *panic*.

He wouldn't let himself think of the little girl, of her normal pulse and her normal pupils and her absolute unresponsiveness.

"Melinda," he said, and drew her up into his arms, his cheek next to hers. Was it his imagination, or did her lashes flutter at his breath across her skin? But she only sagged against him, as limp as . . .

*Eileen.*

As the little girl who'd never woken up. Who now lay in ICU with her brain activity slowing down for no good reason, with her metabolic rates slowing . . .

"I don't think so," he muttered. His fingers found the ice water she'd turned to after the meal—a big open wineglass. Plenty of ice cubes. He found one, brought it dripping to her neck, ran it up and down that tender skin. "Not like this. Not *you*." He shifted the ice to the other side of her neck; melting water ran into her hair. She sighed a breath, but nothing more.

Quite suddenly he found himself grown fierce. He took her face between his hands and bent over her, and he let the fierce through to his voice. "Melinda. Come back to me. *Right now.* You don't belong there. You belong here with me. *Right now.*"

For a moment he thought it was for nothing, his best shot used up and nothing but desperation left. He had the wild impulse to upend the entire glass of ice water on her, the entire quart cooler of it— but that was panic again, and he wasn't allowing himself to panic. Not yet.

Any minute now, but . . . not yet.

A definite flutter, and he couldn't stop himself. He kissed those responsive eyelids, one at a time, and he kissed her cheek and her chin and her nose and her cold wet neck. Quick, hard, desperate kisses, and when she said, faintly but full of bafflement, "Jim? What—?" he drew her in close and tight, burying his face in her hair and breathing as heavily as if he'd just lapped the park several times instead of sitting here on this quilt in the park on a warm spring day with his lady love in his lap.

After a moment, he forced himself to ease

back—far enough so he could look into the confusion on that beautiful face and make some token attempt to smooth the disarray of her hair. "You—" he started, and had to clear his throat. Jim Clancy, the calm one. Always in control. The professional, the paramedic, used to handling a crisis.

Yeah, right.

"You went away," he said. "Just like Eileen, you went away. I thought—" No, he wouldn't say that out loud.

"I heard music," she said, sounding as dazed as she looked. And maybe she still heard it, for she picked up the melody, her voice sweet and true. "*Sleep, my child, and peace attend thee, all through the night . . .*"

"It's an old lullaby," Jim said, startled. "My mom used to sing it to me—"

"Faith? Faith sang to you?" That seemed to get her attention; relief lightened Jim's chest as she took closer note of her surroundings, sat up on her own.

"Believe it or not, yes. That very song. It's from . . . what, a couple hundred years ago?" The ramifications were obvious enough . . . the spirit involved could be from last month or last century.

"I'll have to look it up. Now that I have some words, I mean . . . and why am I wet? And cold?" She ran her hand along her neck, looking at the gleam of water on her fingers.

"Because I was desperate." He tried to keep his voice light. He failed utterly; it all but disappeared on the last words.

She understood. Of course she understood. She slanted him a quick, sharp glance.

"You need to find out more about this ghost," he said. "Mel . . . you need to do it fast. And not just for that little girl."

She turned to him, her brown eyes big and nigh irresistible. "Eileen . . . that poor little girl doesn't have a chance. If she's in that place, that same place that just took me . . . she's just a *child*. She doesn't know about ghosts and their effects on people. If *I* got sucked in, how can she possibly escape that place on her own? She doesn't have a *you* . . ."

"She has parents who love her, and the nanny who loves her," Jim said firmly, not about to watch that guilt trip settle in without interfering. "Maybe they just need some encouragement in reaching out to her."

The dazed effect disappeared completely, replaced by determination. "I can do that. I don't even need to blow my cover. Not yet."

"First things first. Let's get lunch packed up and *you* back home—"

"Ohhh, no." She reached for her sandals, which had somehow left her feet during that extended public display of affection, toes tickling right up his calf right under the cuff of his pants.

Okay, that was a much better frame of mind to end a picnic. Jim shook off the remainder of the *desperate,* and by then Melinda had climbed to her feet, putting the picnic basket aside so she could tug the blanket out from under him. He rolled to his own feet and took it from her, shaking it out and folding it in quick, efficient moves. "Mel—"

"No," she repeated. "Go back home and what? Sleep? I don't think that's such a good idea right now. Delia's expecting me at the store, and that's where I'm going to be."

Right. Big strong paramedic, helpless before Hurricane Melinda.

No, not helpless. But affected. "Mel," he tried again.

"No," she said, quite brisk as she put a few final things in the basket and smoothed her dress down, checking the placement of the narrow straps. But when he just waited, she stopped fussing with details and gave him that look, the big brown almond eyes again, taking a single, deliberate step right up to him. "I really can't," she said, searching his gaze to see if he understood. "But why don't you come in with me? I've got more stuff in the basement to move around."

He narrowed his eyes. "Uh-huh. And this sudden need to move furniture doesn't have anything to do with the equally sudden need to appease me? Because that doesn't work so well for me, the whole pretend-to-need-me thing just so I'll feel like I'm doing some good."

"Oh? Well, okay then." She turned on her heel, giving the picnic basket a carefree swing as she looked over her shoulder. "I shouldn't be late tonight."

Well, crap. Outmaneuvered again. So, two big steps and he'd caught up. "Though I could use exercise. It was a slow shift."

"Uh-huh," she said. But within the next step, she'd taken his hand, and they walked together to their vehicles—her GM Outlook, his truck, where she let her fingers slip through his and gave him one of those smiles, the one that looked up from beneath long lashes and managed to look sleek and shy at the same time. "See you there."

Not that he broke the speed limit getting there, but he might just have bent it a little, intent on arriving before Melinda. He parked the truck behind the store to leave space for her customers out front and casually sauntered into the store—to Delia's surprised expression from where she took inventory of the lotion and soap corner, Melinda's favorite corner of modern luxuries that evoked fine things of the past.

"Hey," Delia said, attempting a smooth recovery. "You two kids have a good picnic?"

"Promise me you'll never say that in front of Tim," Jim said, not hiding his wince. "In fact, I think it should just never be said at all."

"You," Delia said pointedly, "are but an egg." But she gave him her charmingly off-sided smile, and he knew he'd been had. "Where's Melinda? Because, you know . . . the whole picnic thing . . . pretty much implies being together."

"We were. Are. I've been recruited for more furniture moving."

"Oh, hey, want me to call Ned?" A frown lingered at her brow. "He may have that reading session after school today, though."

"No problem. I don't think anything's coming upstairs . . . just shuffling around down there." He hesitated, glancing out the door to see Melinda's Outlook arriving. "Listen . . . keep an eye on her this afternoon, will you?"

Delia, too, lowered her voice—as if Melinda would hear through the closed doors and closed windows of the red SUV. "What's up?"

He made a face, gave a little shrug. "She's just not quite herself."

Delia's eyes narrowed. Lately she'd gotten pretty good at detecting the ghost-avoidance factor. Too good, for someone who didn't really want to talk about it in the first place. For someone who now and then could wrap her head around a particular incident, but—in spite of herself—then defaulted back to just-can't-go-there mode. "This isn't just bad picnic food, is it?"

Jim checked out the window. Melinda was gathering herself inside the Outlook, taking a bit longer than normal. So he took the plunge, and he did it quickly. "Whatever affected the little girl at the park . . . it's trying to get its hooks into her." Possibly not entirely accurate—he had the impression that Melinda just happened to be vulnerable to what she just happened to be able to hear.

The little girl, he wasn't so certain. Because children sometimes saw things . . . sometimes not. So was this a haunting, or was it coincidence . . . he didn't have a clue.

Delia wasn't concerned—or even aware—of such nuances. "*What?*" she said. "Is she all right? What can we do?"

From unbeliever to protector in seconds, and here came Melinda. Jim gave her a cool-it gesture—but held low, and hidden by his body as Melinda pushed through one of the shop's double doors, smiling a somewhat wan greeting at Delia.

"Hey," Delia said, arranging her face into into a don't-know-nuthin' expression that made Jim wince. Melinda was no fool—and indeed, she slanted him a knowing look, one eyebrow raised. But fearless Delia charged forth. "How was lunch? And oh—that professor friend of yours called. Twice. Rick Whatsisname."

"Payne," Melinda said automatically, and shook her head. "I don't know what that's about. But not today."

"And look!" Delia took a step back, and revealed a box from behind her flowing slacks.

Melinda's expression brightened. "Our luxury soaps! Lavender and citrus and cocoa—"

"Piña colada," Delia said. "Peppermint!"

*Diversion tactics successful, indeed.* Score one for Delia. Jim cleared his throat. "I'll just head downstairs and wait for direction."

"Ah," Delia said wisely. "The mere mention of colorful, luxurious soaps . . ."

"And they say men are the strong ones," Melinda said, and this time when she glanced at him, she had that sparkle back in her eye, and he relaxed a little.

"Go ahead," he said. "Make fun. As long as I make it out of here still smelling like a guy." He turned sideways to ease past them to the stairs with exaggerated care, heading into the spacious basement, where he would pretend to be engaged with moving furniture while he really kept an eye on Melinda.

And what worried him most was that she knew what he was up to . . . and she was letting him do it.

Being awake wasn't the problem.

But Melinda really didn't know what she was going to do about the sleep equation. She couldn't go without it—not indefinitely—and she was nowhere near figuring out what was up with this spirit. She didn't know what the woman wanted; she didn't know how the woman had died; she didn't have any common ground, any site of known importance that would draw the ghost out for conversation.

So she sat on the stairs, her knees and ankles tucked together beneath the lacy spring skirt, and directed Jim in the process of getting dirty, grimy, and sweaty while coincidentally shifting the furniture stock around into a much more logical arrangement. The pieces she meant to get to soon, within easy reach. The bulky stuff farther in the back. And one formerly clean husband, stripped down to his stretchy tank top, muscles gleaming and ripe for an admiring gaze.

She should have been right in there with him, helping as she could. At the least, she should be on her feet, giving the decisions a closer hands-on approach—a more thoughtful look here, a pondering moment there. But her thoughts were stuck back in the park, on the hauntingly beautiful melody now running through her head. And before that, on the barbershop quartet and her first indication of what had happened to them, if nothing of what they needed from her.

Somewhere in all that rested the fate of a little girl. She'd suspected it before the park; now she knew it. The fate of a little girl whom the doctors wouldn't be able to help no matter their best efforts.

Who Melinda feared she wouldn't be able to help no matter *her* best efforts.

"You okay?" Jim asked, for approximately the one billionth time.

She sat straight, slapped her hands down on her knees in a gesture of finality. "You know, I guess I'm not. I guess I can't bring myself to believe there's *nothing* I can do right now. That I just don't know enough."

He left the furniture to sit beside her—leaving a careful distance between his grime and her tidiness, and wiping his hands on his jeans in a futile gesture. "You know more than you think. You were *there*. If Eileen's parents don't want to talk to you . . . maybe *you* can talk to *her*."

She brightened. "I could, couldn't I? If I'm not too late . . . visiting hours—"

"There are evening hours," Jim said. "Find the nanny. She'll get you in if they're being fussy about family."

Melinda gave a decisive nod. "That's a plan, then." She stood, heading up the stairs.

"Hey," he said. "What about all this? We're suddenly done?"

She sent her voice floating down the stairs behind her. "Half an hour ago, as far as I can tell."

"Hey," he said. "*Hey!*" In three bounding steps, he reached her side. "Half an hour ago—?"

"I was thinking," she said. "And watching. And

enjoying the watching. Can't blame a girl for that, can you?"

"I—" He stopped, looked down at his disheveled self, then over to Delia. "This is one of those times there's no right answer, isn't it?"

Delia, caught in decision over soap-display fine points, stood with her hands full and her expression full of meaning—brows raised, lips clamped closed, amusement in her eyes. "Silence," she said, "is a very fine tactic."

"Outgunned," Jim groaned. "Again." He trotted down the stairs to pick up his uniform shirt and returned to inform them, "I'm going home to clean up and make dinner." And, with a meaningful look, "*Call* me if anything comes up."

"Everything's fine," Melinda reassured him. She might not be happy, she might find herself challenged, but for the moment, she was perfectly free of the song that had drawn her in. In fact, before she went to see Eileen, she'd make sure she knew more about that song. . . .

The shop phone rang; Delia picked it up as Melinda gave Jim a perfunctory kiss good-bye, definitely avoiding the grime. He smudged a finger down her cheek, grinned at her exaggerated pout, and headed for the door—and the moment he turned his back, she, too, smiled. The world might well be falling apart around them, but as long as they had this . . .

*Tap, tap, tap.*

"Melinda, it's Professor Pay—"

Outside, engines revved; tires squealed against asphalt. Melinda jerked around, breath stopping in her throat, as a vehicle roared down the street. And Jim seemed oblivious, but it was so real, so full of sound and fury and rumbling ground and the stench of burnt rubber, everything but the sight of it—

She darted out of the store after him, crying his name, as unheeding of Delia's "*Melinda!*" as Jim seemed to be to his imminent danger, and she reached him just as he stepped out into the street, grabbing his elbow to pull him back hard enough that they both lost their balance, falling onto the hood of his dark blue truck.

"Mel!" Jim grabbed her arms, steadied them both, took stock of her terrified expression. "What?" He looked around, for an instant as alarmed as she was. And then, "Mel, there's nothing!"

"I know," she said, and really, she had. Truly. She just wished she didn't sound so broken. "It was one of my spirits. I don't know which . . . I'll figure it out. But it was so real . . . it was so loud. . . . I couldn't take chances. Not with you."

"Ah, c'mere." He drew her in for a stifling hug, grime and all, rocking her slightly. "It's been a hard afternoon. You sure you don't want to come home with me? Take the rest of the afternoon off? You can close the shop if Delia can't cover."

She soaked up the hug for a good long moment—but a moment less than she wanted to, because if she'd stayed any longer, he'd have known just how much she'd needed it, and then there wouldn't have been any convincing him. "I'm going to keep busy," she said. "I need to keep busy."

He smoothed her hair back, rubbing his thumb lightly over the tiny mole just beneath the outside corner of her right eye. "Okay," he said, and then repeated his enjoinder from inside. "But . . . *call* me."

"I will," she reassured him. "I promise." She kissed him lightly on the cheek—yes, grime and all—and returned to the store.

"Melinda . . ." Delia stood where she'd been, frozen in indecision over her next words.

Melinda was too tired to deal with it—trying to dance around Delia's discomfort with her gift and her avocation, so many years of helping earthbound spirits find peace that she'd long ago lost count of just how many people she'd touched, both living and dead. Better to sidestep it completely. "*Sleep, my child, and peace attend thee,*" she sang, low but clear. "*All through the night.*"

"Oh!" Delia said, one hand going to her throat in an unconscious gesture. "How beautiful! I didn't know you could sing like that—that's almost . . . *haunting.*"

Melinda smiled wryly, managed to keep the rest of her reaction to herself. "Something I heard recently. Do you know it?"

Delia shook her head, made a final, determined decision about the arrangement of soaps, and nodded at the counter, behind which sat Melinda's laptop. "Bet you can find it on the Internet."

"Is there anything *not* on the Internet these days?" Melinda went for the laptop, switched out to a fresh battery, and booted it up. Her fingers flew over the familiar URL for the Penthius search engine, and she typed in a line of the lyrics. It took only moments to find the answer, while Delia tidied up the discarded soap packaging. "Well, it's Welsh. And look, it's old—a lullaby from the late seventeen hundreds."

"That's old, all right," Delia said with appreciation, coming behind the counter to look at the screen. "Where did you say you'd heard it?"

Melinda shrugged. "Just one of those things," she said. "And now I can't seem to get it out of my head." Okay, that was an understatement. And she wasn't sure she'd really learned anything useful. Except as she stared at the lyrics in their entirety, she suddenly realized she knew them—that she knew the entire melody, knew it deeply, and had absorbed the two verses long before she saw them on the laptop screen . . . a soul-felt, sweet lullaby.

One that had been haunting her for days now.

Going on weeks, if with less intensity at first. And one that she was sure had somehow haunted little Eileen into her strange coma.

One that might do the same to her, come nightfall.

As tired as she was, she didn't know if she dared go back to sleep this night. But if not this night, what about the next? She wasn't naive enough to think she could resolve this mysterious spirit's issues within twenty-four hours. Not when the spirit behind it all hadn't ever come to her for help in the first place—hadn't made the slightest connection. Melinda was beginning to doubt she ever would, not beyond that slight, passing glance of attention the night Melinda had gone looking for her.

Still, it was all fine and good to be patient and understanding when the only price came as a few ragged nights and hard dreams. But now it seemed that a little girl struggled to find her way out of that quicksand music, just as Melinda had struggled this afternoon . . . and now, it seemed the draw of that music was stronger than ever. More demanding. Even though Melinda wasn't the target, but just, somehow, an unexpected listener.

"It turned into an earworm, huh?" Delia said sympathetically, responding to Melinda's comment of moments earlier as she finished flattening the packaging for the recycle bin. "Don't those just drive you crazy? There's only one thing for it—replace an earworm with an earworm."

"That's cruel!" Melinda exaggerated her horror, returning to the search engine page. It was a long shot, but if she searched on deaths, on the lullaby title, on singer . . .

"It's a small world after all—" Delia started.

Melinda gave a dismayed shriek, clapping her hands over her ears. "No, no, *no*! Who knew there was a wicked core behind all your deceptive kindness?"

Delia laughed and gathered up the packaging trash, heading out through the back to the recycle bin with a grin on her face.

"I don't hear you, I don't hear you, I don't hear you," Melinda muttered at the classic earworm, and hit Return to let Penthius do its thing on her search request. Not surprisingly, it returned only a few listings, none of which truly matched. She swapped words around, added the word *accident* just in case, and tried again.

No. Not yet.

She wasn't surprised. Frustrated, but not surprised. She didn't have enough information yet.

What if *getting* enough information meant going back to that place—the deep, distant place she'd gone to at the park this afternoon? What if it meant voluntarily going in so deep that only Jim could get through to her? And even then . . . only *maybe*. She shivered, made a shivery noise to go along with it. Not her first choice of investigative techniques. Maybe she'd talk to Eileen's nanny, to her parents. Perhaps the little girl had said something that they'd found odd but that Melinda would find important.

And in the meantime, she had to stay *away* from that deep, distant place.

Somehow.

She covered her eyes with the heels of her hands. *Somehow*. But she sure didn't know how.

She wasn't expecting the new music that abruptly resounded through the store, through her mind—

> *Beautiful dreamer, wake unto me,*
> *Starlight and dewdrops are waiting for*
> *thee . . .*

Her head snapped up; her hands moved away from her eyes. Yep, there they were—standing, more or less, in the middle of the old clawed bathtub piled high with glass ornaments that looked like so many ethereal soap bubbles spilling over, or nearly spilling over, from someone's bath. Now they didn't so much as stir as the quartet stood there, singing earnestly, softly—perfectly pitched, perfectly in sync. *"Beautiful dreamer, queen of my song, list while I woo thee with soft melody . . ."*

"You're kidding," she said, taking them literally—and then realizing her assumption. "You can do that? You can stop it from happening?"

Still perfectly choreographed, they stopped singing; they nodded, as earnest as ever.

She came around the counter. "But what is it you need me to do for *you*? There must be something. All four of you . . . some need you have in common. Besides the way you died, of course. Unless it's all about the way you died . . ."

They exchanged looks among themselves, silent . . . baffled. The mustached man opened his mouth as though he might say something . . . and then frowned, as if he didn't quite know how to say it. A foggy smoke passed before them, and when it faded they were again torn and ripped and tattered, bloody and wounded. They started singing again—but each took a different song, a different key, and as the discord echoed, grew, and rebounded off the walls of the store, Melinda winced. Just as she was sure it would fade away, it swelled even louder, and in the tub the delicate glass ornaments cracked and shattered, tumbling in on themselves; she slapped her hands over her ears and cried out at the inexorable cacophony of it.

The quartet looked at one another in horror, looked around them—looked at Melinda, as much in unison as their song—and disappeared as abruptly as they'd arrived, leaving behind the echoes of tangled notes and a few final ornaments crumpling into the pile of ruined beauty.

Slowly, cautiously, Melinda lowered her hands. *Silence.* Could they really come between her and the entrapping lullaby with their own music, and would they, and why did they have such awareness of it in the first place? Not to mention wondering how they'd died and what they needed to find peace with themselves.

Wondering what she would do with this bathtub full of glass shards.

"No, no, *no!*" Delia said, striding in from the back, slacks flowing, smart color-block blouse fluttering. "Earworm! I gave myself the earworm!"

# 3

THE FATIGUE OF the day settled down hard after that.

At least, once Melinda had finished cleaning out the bathtub—a mess that she had suggested, in response to Delia's significantly raised eyebrows, should probably just go without explanation for now. And then the phone had rung, and Delia, with one look at Melinda's exhaustion, had gone for it—and said, "Oh, hello, Professor," with more significantly raised eyebrows that garnered an emphatic head shake and cutoff gesture from Melinda, upon which Delia had said, "Oh, I'm sorry, Melinda's gone home for the day," followed by an additional series of comments that made it clear she was fielding persistence.

At which point Melinda thought it was indeed a fine idea to go home. It'd nearly reached closing time at that, and after taking a close look at her,

Delia had all but pushed her out the door. "Ned will be late tonight," she said. "Closing up will save me from sitting at home alone."

And so Melinda found herself driving home, Jim alerted to expect her and more than glad of it, the radio turned off for once, and her head . . . still full of music.

"Talk about an earworm," she muttered. "*Hello, my baby!*" echoed through her head—chorus, verse, and encore, but her own inner jukebox had nothing to do with it. The music had started faintly even as she put the Outlook into gear, and swelled as she headed out of town on the state road that led to the small cluster of homes where she and Jim lived. She heard enough for the words to sink in past that catchy chorus, to begin to wonder what this song was *really* about. "*I've never seen my honey, but she's mine, all right.*" That sounded worse than Internet dating! "One more thing to look up," she sighed out loud. And then, even louder and even a tad pointedly, "Supposing I'm still sane by the time I have the chance!"

But the song didn't leave her; it only waxed and waned as the road curved through the area, a beautiful drive at that—at least, on any normal day. Melinda took a deep, heartfelt breath of relief when she turned off the state road and onto Hazen, and the quartet's song drastically reduced in volume. "Not that you guys aren't good or anything, but . . . I've really had enough for the day. I'm going home to sleep, assuming you mean it about running interference."

But the song had faded into silence, leaving her—for the moment—to guess their intent for the future. Maybe she should catch a nap while Jim was still awake—surely he could find a home-improvement show or two to watch while she slept, even if she kept him from managing actual home repairs so he could keep an eye on her, make sure it was a natural sleep. But the home-repair impulse was as much habit as anything else; things had stopped peeling away from their old fixer-upper some time past. Now it was pretty much fixed-upped and even into its second round of decorating, especially in the kitchen.

Redecorating, she'd found, kept her mind off the occasional spirits who brushed past closely enough to affect her life without actually communicating clearly enough to tell her what they needed . . . disturbing, distressing, keeping her off balance and guessing. The barbershop quartet, for instance. And she might well include Lullaby Lady in that category, except she thought the woman wasn't coming through to her at all, and didn't yet intend to.

Yeah, that definitely seemed like a plan. Take a nap . . . test the waters while Jim was awake. Get a handle on what they'd have to deal with tonight.

And maybe the next night. Or the next. Or for however long it took for her to figure this out . . .

*Eileen doesn't have that long.*

"Okay, okay," she breathed, pulling into their driveway behind Jim's truck and letting her forehead rest on her hands as they curled around the top of the steering wheel. "I get it. I really do. And I'm doing my best. It would just really be nice if I had something to go on, you know?"

At least the "*Hello, my baby!*" song was gone.

But when she lifted her head, so was the driveway.

Fog wreathed the car, tendrils of it speeding past at breakneck pace—time-lapse photography in real life. Melinda's hands clutched the steering wheel; she fought vertigo at the unnatural sensation of sitting perfectly still and simultaneously moving at high speed, nothing but foggy clouds on which to orient in the unnatural silence. No lullabies, no barbershop music—even her own breath made no sound, a noiseless gasp of dismay adding to the surreal moment.

Just as soundlessly, she abruptly stopping moving. No transition, no slowing . . . in an instant, the fog stopped speeding past to freeze in a standstill just as unnatural—no shifting currents in its patchy gloom, not so much as a muffled sound coming through the closed windows. She took a deep breath, couldn't hear that either. Just silence, silence all around . . .

*The explosively loud screech of brakes and scream of terror and grind of metal glass breaking guardrail groaning—*

Melinda screamed at the shock of it, screamed good and loud and clear, jerking inside the Outlook as something slammed into the vehicle from behind and all the outrageous noise of it exploded into her senses. A guardrail loomed in her vision as the vehicle tipped and she grabbed around for purchase—the seat belt, the dashboard, the steering wheel—and inexorably slid sideways anyway. The guardrail gave way. . . .

There was nothing beyond.

*Nothing.*

And so she screamed, and she screamed—

Until suddenly Jim was there, leaning in to unsnap her seat belt, pulling her into his arms in spite of the awkward placement of the steering wheel. For the moment she clung to him, her heart pounding with the inevitable conclusion of that fall away into nothingness. As she finally took a deep breath, he released her, moving back only far enough to crouch at the open door. "Bad one, huh?"

"Bad one," she agreed. "I'm *so* glad they wait until I'm not actually driving."

He frowned. "Stop me if I'm wrong on this, but

I thought the current crop was all about the singing . . . not so much about the startling and scaring."

"I would have said so." Her hands still shook as she reached for her purse and settled it in her lap, not quite ready to get out and trust her knees. "But there was that thing in front of the store after lunch. This . . . this was a car thing, too. A major car thing. Foggy night, guardrail giving way in the mountains . . ."

"Another ghost? How many does that make?" His hand landed on her knee, gently massaging it.

She shook her head. "I'm not sure it's *another*. It might just be a different facet of someone who's already in touch with me. It's hard to tell—I know so little about any of them. Maybe it's time to dig a little harder for information." She laughed lightly, meant to be reassuring. Too bad it came out shaky. "What did I ever do before the Internet?"

"Spent too much time in dusty library archives, I'm sure." He stood, holding out his hand—probably meant for her, but she quickly passed over her laptop. "Ah-ha," he said. "Mistake. Now I have the power. And that means you eat and get some sleep before applying your formidable skills to the ghosts at hand."

She scowled dramatically. "I would point out the error of your ways, if it weren't for one thing."

"I'm not wrong?" he guessed.

"That would be it. So feed me. And then I promise I'll take a nap. Not a long one, or I'll never sleep tonight, but . . ." She bit her lip, plunged ahead. "I think the barbershoppers are going to run interference on the lullaby."

He pulled himself up with the surprise of it. "You're kidding."

"In fact, I'm not. Don't look at it too closely . . . it might just fall apart. Best thing, I think, is to give it a trial run." And hope she was right. Because otherwise, one of them wasn't going to get much sleep that night.

He watched her as though he couldn't take his eyes off her. Which any other night would be the truth, given the skimpy top she'd donned—short enough to reveal the soft skin of her stomach, snug enough to show off a petite waist, token ribbon straps leaving her shoulders bare and begging for attention.

But not this evening.

This evening, Jim draped a soft blanket over those shoulders as Melinda settled into the couch, having done no more than nibble at the peanut sauce stir-fry he'd pulled together while she showered. She rested her head on his thigh, sighed deeply, and fell immediately asleep. Too many interrupted nights, too much borderline sleep. He lowered the television volume, only half interested in the home-improvement program in the first place. Besides, he'd already been through the whole furnace-upgrade adventure.

No, tonight he watched for more important things: the difference between Melinda's face relaxed in sleep, and in that slack, empty look that had alarmed him—no, be truthful, here in the privacy of their own home, in the privacy of his own mind—had *terrified* him out there in the park. A difference that resided somewhere in the set of her mouth—lips curved even in sleep—and in her eyes, closed as they were, lashes shadowing her cheek.

A difference that tonight, no matter how closely he looked, he didn't see. Eventually he relaxed; eventually he even learned a trick or two about evaluating forced-air systems. *Too late.* As much trouble as it took to get that first system installed, it would have to last them for a while. But then, the house as a whole was finally gaining that solid feel, that *finished* feel. That house-is-a-home feel. Melinda's decorating—even if the kitchen had gone through several *looks* before they settled on something to last them awhile—and his reconstruction efforts had given them something to relax into on nights like this.

She opened her eyes. No fluttering awake, no hesitation, just . . . there. *Awake.* She sat straight up and she said, "iPod."

That took him aback. They hadn't been an iPod sort of household until this moment. "Really?"

She rubbed a little sleep from the corner of her eye. "They mean well, but really, which is worse—getting sucked in by a lullaby or going insane from endless choruses of 'Hello, my baby!'?"

He winced. "Ow."

She nodded most assertively. "Now, where's that laptop? And I don't think you need to worry about me tonight—one way or the other, I'm covered."

"It worked," he said with relief.

"It totally worked. They interrupted the lullaby every time." But she squinched up her nose and gently pounded her head with the heels of both hands. "Now, if I can only get rid of *that* song in my head . . ."

*Oh-ho. Opportunity.* "You need a distraction?" he suggested.

"*Some*thing," she said absently—and then her eyes widened, her gaze going directly to his as she realized what she'd said.

"Oh, yes," Jim told her, making his move—moving on down the couch, one hand on either side of her as she leaned back and back and finally ended up on the pillow at the far end.

"I'm busy," she said, completely unconvincing. "Very busy. Work to do. Ghosts to research, spirits to cross over . . ."

"Your *hands* are busy," he noted drily.

And she giggled, and that was the end of that.

Quiet store, quiet morning. Delia's morning off, which was just as well; Melinda needed the time for the research she hadn't done the evening before. And thanks to a night of satellite radio via the laptop and soft earbuds, she'd managed some decent sleep—without the barbershop chorus turning into an earworm, and without the risk of drifting away into the lure of that haunting voice.

*Singing a lullaby to whom?*

Not a question she could answer yet. Not without more to go on than a single late-eighteenth-century song.

The barbershop quartet, on the other hand . . . plenty of unique words for Penthius to chew on. Melinda pulled out the laptop, tucked her hair behind her ear, pushed the day's lineup of bangly bracelets back out of the way, and set to work at the front counter. Delia's careful closing notes and receipts tally from the previous day sat off to the side; Melinda pretended—unsuccessfully—not to notice them yet. Because it was time to get a handle on at least one of her visitors . . .

And it didn't take long, either. "Why didn't I hear about this?" she wondered out loud. Just a few weeks earlier—and yet a paucity of details in the archived news article. Four men on their way to a barbershop performance upstate in Otwiga Lake, deep in the Adirondacks. "You know, I could have guessed that much just from seeing you," she told the empty air of the shop . . . because you never knew when the interested parties might be lurking.

Although at least she now had a time frame. "But I still don't know what you need," she muttered. Empty store, sometimes a good thing. Because talking out loud . . . sometimes it helped.

She stared at the news article, chin in hand. Dick Berg, Craig Knoll, Jay Jones, Lee Worley. Riding in a van on the way to a big club show in which their quartet was to be featured. Little more than a traffic report.

One thing she'd learned from past experience . . . *the less said, the more going unsaid.*

"More work to do there," she murmured. Maybe even a trip to the little town where the performance would have taken place. It was spring, birdsong filled the air . . . *road trip*!

She amused herself by playing with an online mapping site and finding the perfect bed-and-breakfast. Just in case. And in the end, felt pretty good about it all. A good night's sleep, a management plan for more of the same, and a plan of action for following up on her barbershop quartet. And after work this evening, she'd head over to Mercy General and see little Eileen. Surely the doctors had found some way to stimulate her from her deep slumber, even if they didn't understand the power that gripped her.

And then Delia blew in through the door, and the rest of the world came with her. Dressed in paisley color and flowing palazzo slacks, earrings a-dangle and long, dark hair drawn back in careless, casual waves, she came in, plunked her purse du jour down on the counter, and said, "You won't believe it!"

Melinda drew back slightly, brow raised. "Try me?" she suggested, as brightly as the good night's sleep had left her.

"And don't *you* look much better," Delia said, distracted for the moment—but only the moment. "That song? I was trying to get rid of the earworm—you know, the 'It's a Sm—'"

"Right," Melinda said hastily. "The song that shall not be named."

Thoughtfully, Delia held up a finger, accompanied it with an frown. "Right," she echoed. "Excellent strategy. *The song that shall not be named.* Anyway, I ended up humming that beautiful tune you sang here last night. And Ned came home and he gave me the strangest look. You'll never guess!"

Melinda was suddenly very much afraid she could. "The same song the children were humming in the reading group last week?"

It stopped Delia in her tracks, hands on hips, the very picture of incredulous. "You *guessed.*"

Melinda shrugged, an apologetic sort of wince. She could only hope Delia wouldn't ask just *how* she'd guessed, because Delia really didn't want to know.

But to judge from Delia's narrowing eyes, she'd caught on. "Don't tell me," she said, and then, "But that would mean Ned's class—"

It was a thought she didn't get to complete, although Melinda wouldn't have called herself saved by the bell. Not when Professor Rick Payne blew in on Delia's heels, charging in with his hands already in midgesture—as if he'd been having a conversation with himself along the way. His dark blond hair was in mild disarray—which seemed to be his idea of style—and his tie had been loosened slightly over a button-down shirt with the sleeves rolled up. "About those messages," he said.

Melinda blinked. "What messages?" She closed the laptop . . . she had a very strong gut feeling that her quiet moments of research, speculation, and planning were now resoundingly over.

"The ones you didn't answer," he said promptly. "Assuming you got them. You got them, right?" He eyed Delia. "Delia, right? You gave her the messages, right? Because why wouldn't you? I'm such a charming guy on the phone, totally impressive with that whole professor-at-Rockland-U intro, don't you think?"

Delia leaned against the counter and cast a look

Melinda's way. "At what point does he pause so we get a word in edgewise?"

"Possibly never," Melinda told her. "Sometimes you just have to barge right in. Though sometimes if you stare hard, he kind of winds down . . . gets this cute little deer-in-the-headlights look."

Delia gave an assertive nod, made her choice. "We'll wait."

So Delia, leaning on one elbow against the counter in her swirl of color and cloth, and Melinda, chin in hand, waited.

"So I told my friend you were the perfect person to talk to," Rick Payne explained to Melinda—or semi-explained, seeing as he seemed to be starting right in the middle. Keep up with me, I dare you: the Professor Payne motto. "This being right up your alley and everything. And she asked me to get in touch with you, which is what I've been trying to do, but when you didn't return my calls, I decided . . . mountain, Mohammed, and here I am. To see why." And at that he did finally wind down, his gaze shifting from Melinda to Delia and back again.

"Thing is," Melinda said, after giving it that extra moment to make sure he was indeed pausing long enough for her to respond, "my dance card is pretty much full right now."

"Oh, surely not," he said. "Random things that come your way, right? You gotta know this one's good. It's been vetted by an expert."

"Professor of just what, again?" Delia said, turning to Melinda.

"Anthropology department," she said. "Professor of occult sciences, to be exact."

"Ah." Delia nodded. She might have covered a wince.

"Spreading joy wherever I go, that's my job," Payne said, entirely undeterred; he regarded Delia with a subdued version of his personal trademark smirk, now just a little quirk at the corner of his mouth. Ever ready for an expression dry and sometimes self-knowingly so. "Now, about my friend—"

"Did I not just say no?"

Payne affected shock. "You did not! Nowhere in your response did I hear the word *no*. I would have recognized it immediately."

"That'll teach me to soften the blow," Melinda said. "Try this, then—*no*. Can't. Not now."

"Ah-hah!" With a punctuating finger, Payne grabbed the promise. "Not now. That would imply *at some point*."

"*You* might infer *at some point*," Melinda said. "Not the same thing at all."

Delia looked from one to the other of them. "Are you two always like this?"

Payne and Melinda exchanged a glance. Payne said, "Yes. Yes, I would say we are."

Melinda nodded, putting a shrug into it. *What're*

*you gonna do?* "Yep," she said. "I guess so." And because Payne's finger lingered in the air, she pushed it aside. "Put that away," she said. "Because seriously. I've got too much going on right now."

"Really?" No easily discouraged mortal, that Rick Payne. He perked right up. "Anything interesting?"

"They're *all* interesting," she told him, giving him a warning eye. "And unless you can give me the details behind the barbershoppers' car accident, then no."

"You mean the one from a few weeks ago? Upstate? Guys in striped clothes and old-fashioned hats?"

Melinda put up both hands in a stop gesture. "You know what? I changed my mind. I want my trip upstate with Jim. So no. Nothing interesting. I'll just suffer through on my own for now."

Delia eyed them both with a thoughtfulness that Melinda couldn't sort out as either good or bad, and in spite of the additional chaos in this morning that had been so pleasantly contemplative until now, quick relief washed through her as her cell phone rang.

Short-lived relief.

"Hi," she said, in the tone she reserved for Jim. Payne rolled his eyes and took half a step back; he knew when he'd been outgunned. "What's up?"

"I'm here at Mercy, just came in on a run," he

said. Which wasn't the reason he called, as a day didn't pass when he *didn't* end up in the Mercy General emergency department, so she didn't do anything more than make an I'm-listening noise. "I ran by Peds ICU, and . . . Mel, if you're going to talk to this family—if it's going to make a difference—then I think you'd better do it now."

She heard it, then—the tight nature of his voice. The things he wasn't saying. That Eileen not only wasn't doing well, she wasn't doing well at *all*. "I'll be right there." She tucked the phone away, scooped up her laptop, and marched into the back room.

"But hey," Payne said, still on the floor, "what about me?"

"What about your friend, you mean?" Melinda called over her shoulder, pulling keys from her purse and pulling on the spring-weight coat that was tailored so nicely around her waist and shoulders and fell away so freely behind in the flowing lines of a cape.

"Well, of *course* my friend—and by that, I really mean my friend. This isn't one of those I-have-a-friend-with-a-problem times where it turns out to be, well, me. Because it's not. It's really her. That alone cinches it. If I was going to fake this, I'd come up with a guy friend and a guy problem."

She returned to the sales floor, flipping her hair out from beneath the coat's tidy collar. "Well, you

have plenty of time to come up with either . . .
not now." She looked over to Delia, catching her
friend's eye . . . and finding her in that state of
being pretty sure she knew what was going on but
wishing she didn't. "If I'm delayed and you need to
go, just close up. Weekday hours . . . not our high
sales point."

"I should be good," Delia said, just a little be-
mused at that.

"And *you*—" Melinda turned on Payne. "Be
good." He just looked back at her, brows raised, expression full of . . . was that some attempt at inno-
cence? "On second thought, walk me out. There's
no way I'm leaving you here to stir up trouble."

"I'll take that as a compliment," he said, and followed out on her heels, hesitating only long enough
to say, "See you later, Delia Banks," which garnered
only a wave of her hand—even if she did watch
them both until distance and the angle of the store
windows made it impossible to continue doing so.

"Don't mess with her head," Melinda warned
him.

"She's not a believer?" he said, understanding
dawning right along with one of those cocky half-
sided grins.

"She's struggling with it. It's not a joke." She
reached the Outlook, unlocked it, and slid in behind the wheel, all in a swift series of movements.
The car started smoothly.

"Where are you going? Can I come?"

"Are you shameless?" She shook her head. "Who am I even asking? Of course you are." And then she answered him. "I'm going somewhere else, and no, you can't."

He stood outside the door as she hesitated on closing it. "I really can't help?"

That stopped her. It wasn't often that he slowed down enough to let sincerity show through. "I think," she said, "that you really can't. Not unless you can find a connection between a lullaby and a little girl in a coma."

It left surprise on his face, and he opened his mouth—but she shook her head and closed the door. "Not now," she said through the rolled-up glass of the window, and pulled away from the curb.

# 4

MELINDA DIDN'T OFTEN come to the pediatric floor. She had to steel herself for it this time, standing at the elevator with her hand hovering over the Up button. She turned with relief at the familiar step coming up behind. "You're still here!"

"Barely," Jim said, and indeed he had his distracted work face on, thinking about the usual dozen things at once: the patient he'd just brought in, the state of the rig, how long it would take to right it, all with one ear listening for further calls. The expression was as much a part of his work uniform as the Driscoll County Paramedic jacket and pale blue uniform shirt beneath. "Bobby's sorting out the rig, but there's a fire out by Bayview that might pull in other units, so—"

"Gotcha," she said. The distraction didn't bother her; it never bothered her. It meant his caring was gathered up, his skills at the ready to save lives on *his* side of the line—those who still lived. She'd had that care applied to her own needs often enough; she knew the importance of it, just as he recognized the importance of saving those who walked on her side of the line. Those who needed to find the Light.

"I'm glad you could come," Jim said, and he was too serious. He shook his head, looking away. Steeling himself, in his own way. "Do what you can for them, huh? Maybe . . . prepare them."

She winced. "Don't even think it." Not if the girl had been caught up in the same song that had briefly taken Melinda away . . . there was nothing right about that, no way she could let that just *happen*. She shook her head again. "No. It just doesn't make any sense. It doesn't *accomplish* anything."

He moved a little closer, lowering his voice. "Nothing you've come across before? Not even close?"

"You think I haven't been wracking my brains since she first went under? Since *I* went under?" Her words came out more sharply than she'd meant them; she closed her eyes. "I'm sorry," she said. "It's just . . . you know how things have been lately. Nothing works quite the same for any of us. Spirits can do things that I don't expect . . . that *they* don't expect. Maybe that they don't even mean to do. If this is what almost happened to me in the park—"

"*Did* happen to you," he reminded her somberly.

"Well, I can't make sense of it. The *why* of it. And no one's come to me for help, either. So how do I fix it?"

"Wish I had the answers, babe. Just . . . go do your best." His radio spat incomprehensible static that he somehow found meaningful; he gave her a quick kiss on the cheek. "Gotta go."

"Someday you're going to tell me how you can tell what that thing is saying," she called after him.

"Trade secret," he called back, and broke into a jog.

Melinda turned back to the elevator, took a deep breath, and hit the call button. She shared the elevator up with several unidentifiable people in scrubs and a cart full of electronic gear, not to mention the young boy who reached right through the cart to push every button on the control panel—or almost every button. Melinda caught his attention in midprocess and widened her eyes most meaningfully; he was so shocked to have been caught at it that he jerked his hand back, out through the cart again.

"You see?" said one scrub person to the other. "I told you it wouldn't make any difference. They shut this thing down for hours last night while the electrician messed with it. Didn't do a bit of good."

"Oh, it's got to be *something*." The other led the

way out onto their floor. "They need to take another look."

The doors closed on them. Melinda looked at the elevator ceiling and muttered, "Oh, it's *something*, all right."

The boy giggled. He wore a hospital gown that gaped most appallingly in the back; his spine was covered with blue-black bruises, and his head looked likely to be bald under the cap he wore. His slippers were too big. "*Leukemia*," he announced.

"I'm sorry," Melinda said. "How long have you been running the elevator, then?"

The boy shrugged. "*Who knows? Who cares? No one ever let me play on them before. Now I can do it all I want.*"

"And is that the only reason you're here?" The elevator stopped at one of the bogus floors; Melinda smiled nicely at the floor nurse, who looked over in annoyance at the obviously unwanted stop, shaking her head, and the elevator moved on.

"*What other reason?*" he asked, in a voice that might well have said *duh!*

"Okay, then," she said, as agreeably as possible—especially since her floor was coming up—"is there anything I can do to help you?"

"*It would be* awesome if *you would push all the buttons on the other elevator while I do this one. I can't reach them both at the same time.*" He frowned. "*I don't know why.*"

"Another time, maybe." She'd have to check back on him; maybe he'd be more ready. "But . . . by any chance have you heard a woman singing? Maybe even humming?" She hummed a line or two of the song for him.

He snorted derisively and settled his cap more firmly on his head, positioning himself in front of the control panel. "*Nah. And you'd better get out if you're going, because I've got plans for this run.*"

Melinda didn't wait to be told twice. The moment the doors opened, she scooted out—and a good thing, too. He'd definitely been playing with the elevator long enough to get the hang of it; the doors slammed closed on her heels with quick force that would pass no safety check. She put her cheek to the seam of the closed doors and said, "You be careful!"

Laughter drifted up the elevator shaft at her.

Melinda sighed, straightened her coat, discovered that a small audience watched with experienced eyes—too many people, it seemed, came off that elevator in various unexpected ways, with various unexpected reactions. She might have asked for Eileen's room, had she not seen the nanny leaning back against the hallway, a tissue to her nose. Carefully, so carefully, she listened for that which she'd expected but hadn't yet heard . . . the music.

But there was nothing.

Okay. Clearly not understanding this thing yet.

Or had she been wrong all along? Did this have nothing to do with the music and everything to do with coincidence?

For a moment, she hesitated. If she was wrong, then what she had to say to these people might not make any difference at all. False hopes, false assurances.

*Take a breath, Melinda,* she told herself. Hope was never bad. Comfort was never wrong. She'd tread lightly; she could very well offer counsel that would help if she was right and do no harm if she wasn't.

Besides, the nanny looked up and saw her, and her face simultaneously lit up and crumpled—giving way in the manner of someone at the end of her rope who's just let the load shift to someone else's shoulders. Melinda took that breath, all right. And she went to meet the young woman. "How are you doing?" she asked. "How is Eileen?"

"I never had the chance to thank you," the nanny said through her tears, fumbling in her candy-colored purse for another tissue. Melinda quickly produced one for her. "My name is Hayley—it seems so odd that we don't even know each other, after what happened. And now—" She fought to keep her voice under control.

"I'm Melinda—I have the little antiques store on the square. My husband is Jim."

"The paramedic," Hayley said, and vigorously

blew her nose. "Pardon me. Somehow I've gotten so used to crying in front of just anyone. *Everyone.*"

"Totally understandable," Melinda told her. "How is she? What do the doctors say? I was hoping I might see her. . . ."

Hayley cast a quick glance toward the room that must have been Eileen's, and shook her head; it seemed an unconscious gesture. "I don't know if they'll . . ." She struggled with her voice again. "They don't know what's wrong. Even though I told them what happened in the square, even though I took her to the doctor's appointment her mother made . . ."

"They need someone to blame," Melinda said gently.

Mute, Hayley nodded.

"It's worth a try." Melinda smiled encouragement, gave Hayley's arm an understanding touch. "But first, I was wondering . . . before this happened, did you hear her humming? Did she say any more about the singing she heard?"

Hayley's attention jerked away from the room; she looked surprised and even a little wary. "I know I should have respected that she heard something, even if I didn't," she said. "But . . . who have you been talking to?"

It was Melinda's turn to be surprised. "No one," she said, seeing clearly the defensiveness beneath

Hayley's grief. "It's just . . . this is going to sound strange . . . it seems to be going around. So I was wondering if it was the same tune."

"You're right. It does sound strange."

Melinda smiled, stayed relaxed—because it was the best way to keep things in that no-big-deal space. "Go with it?" she suggested in a what-do-you-have-to-lose sort of way?

Hesitantly, Hayley hummed a few notes. Only a few, but Hayley had a lovely voice and excellent sense of pitch, and they were enough. Melinda picked up on them, finishing the music phrase— and Hayley gasped. "That's it!"

From the room, a man emerged; all of Hayley's confidence seemed to vanish. But it was Melinda he looked at, his grief and worry layered over with a stern nature that was supposed to make her quail. "Where did you hear that? How did you know our daughter?"

Melinda had been doing this work far too long to quail before simple stern disapproval. "I didn't, really," she said, with as much compassion as she'd give any sorrowful parent. "Though I imagine I heard the song the same time Eileen did, since my store is right there on the square where I've seen her with Hayley." Words chosen thoughtfully, those. "My husband was the one who responded that day in the square."

"And Melinda," Hayley said, though her voice

quavered faintly. "She's the one who came out when I called for help, and she called her husband."

His expression softened slightly. "We appreciate that. Travis Starcroft." He held out his hand; Melinda took it. "Forgive me, though—you're here because. . . ?"

"The obvious reason," Melinda said. "I wanted to see how Eileen is doing." She hesitated, watching his reaction. "And I suppose I was hoping I could help."

"Help?" Hayley said, though at Starcroft's expression she immediately stepped back.

"I have some experience with this sort of thing," Melinda said. "I thought maybe . . ."

His gaze narrowed in on her. She could see why Hayley tried to fly under the radar. "What kind of experience?"

"Personal experience," she said promptly.

Hayley looked away, keeping her voice low. "What can it hurt?" she asked. "The doctors don't have any answers."

"Travis?" A woman's voice came from within the room.

"Be right there," he said, and his voice changed completely as he spoke to her, softening. When he looked back at Melinda, he jerked his chin toward the room. "Come and see, then."

Odd of him, to say it as a challenge. Melinda

hesitated, then stepped forward to the doorway. Starcroft moved in behind her. "Maureen, this is Melinda . . ."

"Gordon," she finished quickly. "I have a store on the square, and I was there when Eileen took ill. I was hoping to see her . . . to talk to her."

Maureen Starcroft gave a bitter little laugh. "Good luck with that." She indicated her daughter.

Melinda took a deep breath. *So small. So frail.* Nothing like the robust little girl sitting on the square bench demanding ice cream. IV lines, EKG lines, a BP and oxygen saturation monitor . . . a respirator, the tubes dwarfing her face.

"They put her on the respirator a few hours ago," Maureen said, dabbing at the tear that slid down her cheek. "She's just not breathing on her own any longer. It's as if she's paralyzed, for no reason at all. . . ."

"That's not exactly what they said." Starcroft's voice was harsh. "They said her brain was shutting down. They *said* she was dying."

Melinda cast him an incredulous look. She strode into the room, pulled up the empty chair jammed in among the machines opposite the bed from Maureen, and said, "Eileen, my name is Melinda. Remember me from the square? You were going to get ice cream—very colorful ice cream, as I recall. And I was with my husband, Jim—he's really handsome, and he probably looked very tall to you. He *is* very tall!"

"What are you doing?" Starcroft asked—a challenge, really. "She's not there. They've told us she's not there anymore."

But Maureen looked at Melinda with a hopeful gratitude. "Stop it, Travis." She flicked a glance to her husband. "It doesn't matter what they say. If there's the slightest chance . . . *this* is what she should be hearing."

"Your love for her," Melinda agreed. "Your faith in her. Your encouragement. I wonder, does she have any favorite music?"

"She's too young to—"

"Ella Jenkins's songs," Hayley said softly. "Or Jim Gill." She perked up. "I can get them. It wouldn't take me too long—"

"Isn't there a little recreation room on this floor?" Melinda asked. "I bet they have something there."

"So now we're going to have a *party*?" Starcroft's face had a quick flush of unnatural coloring, something between pink and heart-attack purple.

"It's better than humming a death dirge right where she can hear us!" Maureen cried, half rising from her chair.

"Or arguing over top of her," Melinda said quietly. "And no, not a party. A *celebration*. Something she'd want to come back to, but also something that honors the small person she is. Something that will make her smile as she says good-bye, if that's what it comes to." She gave a clandestine pat to the pocket of her lightweight coat, where the iPod and earbuds resided. Just in case.

And yet . . . she still hadn't heard a whisper of the humming, not a phrase of a the song itself. Remarkably quiet. *Too* quiet, she was tempted to say to herself—but, in fact . . . maybe silence was just silence.

Maybe once listeners were drawn in just so far, they simply stayed there . . . even without the music to keep them there? *How am I supposed to know how this works?* she asked silently—a question out to the universe, to those in the Light, to the ghost whose side effects she now faced . . . to her grandmother, so beloved, and so long passed.

"Is something wrong?" Maureen asked, grown anxious. How quickly she'd given herself to Melinda's quiet strength—to any option besides sitting here watching her daughter die.

Melinda offered her a quick smile. "Just thinking," she said. "About someone else in my life."

"Because Eileen isn't important enough to keep your attention?"

"Travis!"

"Don't worry," Melinda told her, but she looked at Starcroft. "If I was doing this for you, I'd have left by now. But I'm here for Eileen." She looked down. "You made quite the impression on me that day we met in the park," she said. "There, I said to myself, is a young lady who knows what she wants. And more power to you! But I think you may have gotten a little lost since then—"

"Look!" Hayley stood in the doorway, CD cases splayed in one hand, a small pink clamshell of a miniature CD boom box in the other. Girly, plastic . . . it had flowers on it, and Melinda would just bet it went with something Barbie.

"Perfect!" She put her hand on Eileen's arm, careful not to tangle in the IV lines. "Now it's a celebration, all right!" Hayley came in behind her, pushing the oversize controls with the air of one long familiar with the child scale of such things. Cheerful music bounded out into the room, immediately lifting the atmosphere; Hayley sang along, full of enthusiasm.

*Please,* Melinda thought. The music had been helping *her,* had kept her safe and clear of that black quicksand place in her mind. *Please let it do the same for Eileen.*

Even though there wasn't any music here from which to protect *her,* from which to hide her.

*You see? How am I supposed to know?* She wasn't even working with a spirit. She was working with the baffling side effect of an unknown spirit with unknown issues.

"She likes this music?" Starcroft said, momentarily baffled. He looked down at his daughter with the very visible realization someone else knew his own daughter's musical preferences when he didn't.

"She does," Hayley said. "And Smurf ice cream, and looking for four-leaf clovers, especially if you get down on your hands and knees and stick your nose right in the grass. She likes concerts in the county park, and she likes to sing along. Loudly."

"I'd like to hear that sometime," Melinda said. "Loudly."

"I guess . . . I would, too," Starcroft said, and his wife could only nod.

"What do you do?" Melinda asked them. "For your work, I mean."

The sudden change of topic threw them both off stride, but only for an instant. "Order expedition at a big printing company," Maureen said. "I run the department."

And Starcroft started, "Upper management for the infrastructure department of—" before he stopped himself. "It doesn't really matter, does it? It's an important position, and it keeps me away from home. That must be obvious. But it doesn't give you the right to come in here and pass judgment on us."

"Whoa," Melinda said. "That's not what this is about."

Hayley sent the man a dark look and moved

farther into the room with the music, rendering conversation more difficult, but not impossible.

"Who do you think you are, anyway?" Angry, grieving . . . still looking for someone to take it out on.

"Someone who's trying to make this better for her—easier for all of you. This is about Eileen, Mr. Starcroft. About celebrating her life, and maybe trying to reach out to her so she can keep that life. And if not, letting her go in the best possible way, so years from now you can think of it and smile, and not be stuck in bitter thoughts about how it was everyone else's fault."

Hayley looked at her, jaw slightly dropped. Maureen looked at her husband in frozen trepidation—and oddly, something like hope. And Starcroft said, "Get out! *Get out of this room.* And don't come back here. You're not wanted, and you're not needed."

Melinda stood. "I think you're wrong," she said, and didn't fail to notice Maureen's hope flutter and fade into crushed grief. "But it doesn't really matter what you think about me. Don't let Eileen down."

She left as she always tried to leave when such things didn't go well—respectful of the request, but with unhurried calm. Hayley slipped out after her, leaving the music behind. "You're so right," she said as the hallway closed in around them, surprisingly private for such a public place. A place that acknowledged it would hear and see so many private things, as if even the walls and overhead light fixtures somehow looked the other way. "I know you're right. Maureen . . . she knows it, too." Behind them, the cheerful music cut off; the Starcrofts' voices, low and tense, filtered out of the room. "You know, I'm so glad I had that time in ER with her before they got there." She laughed, but it was as bitter as the Starcrofts' future. "I did talk to her then. I did tell her I loved her. They don't treat me like family, but Eileen and I . . ." She blinked furiously, looked away. "I just wish I had done more from the start—once they got there. I wish I'd been more insistent that they talk to her, sing to her, play her music, read to her—*anything*."

"I'm sure if anyone could make a difference to Eileen, you did." But she wasn't sure, any longer, that anyone could have. Anyone short of a determined paramedic with ice water and a fierce protective love at hand. More than that . . . an awareness of her involvement with the supernatural world.

"The thing is," Hayley said, though she had to stop to clear her throat. "The thing is, since the very start, she's just felt . . . *gone* to me. I know that doesn't make sense. There's no reason for it— but then, there's no reason for any of this. Did you know they're starting to test for weird exotic parasites? As if she's done any traveling! But still. There's something in me that never expected her to come back. I think Maureen feels the same. Travis . . . sometimes I think he just resents that she's defying him."

*Gone.* Gone where?

*Good question.* Where had she gone, after all, on a dozy afternoon in the park? From what deep place had Jim brought her back?

Dark. Muffled. Separate. Unreachable. As if the only reason he'd gotten through at all was that she'd only been caught up by the edges of something.

From within the room, a gasp—and a wail.

Hayley paled, a visible thing on her coffee-and-cream complexion. She and Melinda rushed to the doorway to find Maureen had thrown herself across Eileen's small body; Starcroft stood in apparent shock, stiff in denial. An announcement went out overhead; muted alarms sounded from the direction of the nurses' station and from within the room itself. Melinda tugged Hayley aside just in time. Medical staff rushed past them and into the room, instantly adjusting machines and IV drip, pulling out the room's defibrillator and crash cart, checking readouts and vitals and exchanging soft, staccato bursts of information.

But Melinda never took her eyes off Eileen . . . and she saw nothing. No sign of her spirit leaving her body, not even a swift blur—although from this sleeping child she would have expected a slow emergence, a confused ghost looking for guidance.

*Nothing.*

Beside her, Hayley gave a single, irrepressible sob. "They won't do anything else," she said. "They'd already decided—the doctors, the Starcrofts. There isn't anything to be done."

"Eileen?" Melinda said softly, looking around the hall, into the room. *Nothing.*

But that couldn't be. It *never* was. Even if Eileen passed quickly into the Light, she should have hesitated here; coming from a deep coma would disorient any spirit, never mind a young child.

*Nothing.*

Hayley touched Melinda's arm, shook her head. "She's gone."

And as Melinda put her arm around Hayley's quivering shoulders, she knew Hayley was right. Eileen was gone. Had been gone.

*Gone where?*

# 5

MELINDA DIDN'T LINGER. She comforted Hayley as best she could, but she'd seen enough of Mr. Starcroft to know he would look for someone to blame—someone to take out his reality on because he hadn't been able to control it. And she was troubled enough by what she'd seen—or what she *hadn't* seen.

What if Eileen *had* been caught in that same place that had caught Melinda up at the park? And . . . what if she was still there?

Melinda sat on a bus stop bench outside Mercy General and wrapped her coat more tightly closed. Trees budding around her, plenty of flitting birds, even an early bee hunting clover—but the day no longer seemed as pleasant, no longer as full of potential. A little girl gone, and Melinda had been too late to stop it—hadn't been able to work past her parents to do the few feeble things she knew to try. A little girl now missing in spirit, and Melinda had absolutely no idea why.

"*Lose someone?*" Hospital gown and socks, right out there in the street. Melinda didn't have to look twice to know that no one else would see this particular conversationalist.

"Yes, in fact," she said. "Not a wild leap, though, is it?"

The young man clearly hadn't expected a response. He flickered out in surprise, appeared on the other side of the street, and then reappeared where he'd been. "*You can see me!*"

"Also not a wild leap," Melinda said drily, crossing her legs and settling in on the bench.

He grinned. Late teens or early twenties, his face and arms flickered with wounds and exposed bone . . . motorcycle accident, she would have guessed. He seemed unconcerned; in fact, now he turned a complete circle, his arms outstretched to an invisible audience and his head thrown back as he cried, "*She can see me!*"

"Oh my God, I certainly can." She covered her eyes with her fingers, but the image of the gaping hospital gown lingered. "Turn around!"

He did—she saw it through cautiously spread fingers—but his entirely unrepentant grin hadn't faded. "*There are girls who would have paid for that sight.*"

"Yes, well, I'm not one of them." At his expression, she added, "Hey, don't pout. You've just got the wrong girl." And then couldn't help but wince when a car drove through him.

He disappeared, instantly reappeared beside her—slouched on the bench, legs sprawled. He'd certainly adapted to the fact that no one could see him in his current getup. Or else he'd never cared in the first place. A definite possibility. "*Can't blame a guy for trying.*"

She gave him a pointed look, and flashed her engagement and wedding rings at him.

"*Figures,*" he grumped, but he managed to lean a little closer.

"I take it you hang around here on a regular basis?" She gave in to the urge to smooth her coat closed where it gaped over her scooped neckline.

He scowled in response. "*Geeze, cut a guy a break.*"

"I'm sure you have plenty of opportunity to ogle," she told him. A satisfied smile crossed his face—a little disconcerting, in conjunction with the wounds flickering in and out of place, but Melinda had plenty of practice in not focusing on that aspect of her earthbound confidants. "And eavesdrop . . . and in general keep pretty good track of what's going on here."

He nodded, satisfied with that, too. "*Not much going on here that I don't know about.*"

Okay, that was probably overstating things, especially if he limited his hangout to this particular area. Waiting for someone, perhaps? But still, it was worth asking. "I don't suppose you've heard anything about unusual coma patients, or children falling asleep and not waking up, or spirits gone missing, or even a lullaby in the background? Humming and singing, very old-fashioned?"

He laughed. *"Lullaby Muzak, is that the idea?"*

"It's not funny," she told him quietly. "Lives depend on it. And it's already too late for one little girl."

It sobered him fast. *"That sucks, then. But I'm not hearing anything about it. Not chatter, not Muzak. It's been quiet here. Boring, even. I don't suppose you—"*

She shook her head, but she did it over a little smile. "Sorry, no. I just needed a moment before I got behind the wheel."

*"Something I should have thought of, not so long ago,"* he said, his expression gone wry.

But Melinda knew enough to see the sadness around the macho of him. "While I'm here," she said, "is there something I can do for you? Someone I can talk to, some message I can pass along? Something that would leave you free to move into the Light?"

Instantly, the bravado returned. *"Nah,"* he told her. He wiggled his toes within the sock. *"I guess I'll just wait around here a while longer."*

Here at the bus stop. Waiting for who, she wondered, a lifetime of ingrained habit already leading her into that puzzle. But she brought herself up short. This was a straightforward one. An easy one. A spirit who conversed with her in a straightforward manner, who knew who he was and quite probably knew what he needed. She could come back later to see if he was still here. "What's your name?"

That surprised him. "*Scott*," he said. "*Scott Wincek*."

She stood, letting the breeze tug her skirt and coat back into place. "Well, Scott Wincek," she said. "Maybe I'll see you around." She gave his insufficient hospital gown a mischievous look.

The bottom half of his body quite suddenly faded out of view; the gown remained. "*Maybe*," he said, entirely unchastened. "*Maybe next time you pay for it. Fair trade, maybe.*"

She snorted, gentle as it was. "You wish," she said, and headed for the parking lot—and though she had a faint smile as she left, it quickly faded. Whatever was going on, the local spirits didn't seem to be in the know.

A little girl was dead, her spirit missing, and Melinda still didn't even have a place to start.

Back in the Outlook, Melinda settled in behind the wheel and resolutely set her mind to the present—

to the task of driving home, where it was indeed her turn to cook dinner, and which meant stopping at the market on the way home to grab fresh fixings for the rather exotic, springtime-sandwich grilling she had planned. She had a list, she had a plan . . . she checked her watch.

Okay, time for plan B. Less exotic, still-fun, springtime-sandwich grilling.

But first she flipped her phone open and hit the autodial number for SAME AS IT NEVER WAS, figuring she might just catch Delia. "Oh, good!" she said when Delia picked up the phone, and then had to give her friend points for failing to do so much as hesitate.

"Hello, stranger," she said. "I hear that a beautiful young woman once owned this antique shop, but she hasn't been seen recently. Maybe while you're out and about, you might try to find her? And by the way, your professor friend has left about a bazillion messages this afternoon."

Melinda winced. "Not one to take a hint." And then, "I am so sorry! I swear, tomorrow is all yours. I'll be so stay-in-one-place, you won't even know me."

"Where's the fun in that?" Delia asked. "And how'd things go with your visit to that little girl?"

No way to soften this one. "She passed away," Melinda said quietly.

"No—!" Delia said, disbelief foremost. "But

there wasn't anything wrong with her! Isn't that what the doctors kept saying?"

"Nothing wrong that they could find," Melinda agreed sadly. "And I certainly wasn't able to make any difference. Her family . . . they were too torn to be receptive."

Delia apparently couldn't help a little gasp. "You didn't tell them—"

"No," Melinda said. "I didn't. There's timing, and then there's timing. They didn't need to know why I made certain suggestions about reaching their daughter. I'm pretty sure I wasn't even the first one to make those particular suggestions, even if my reasons were different. The family . . . well, some families come together in times like these. Some just rip apart under the stress. I think Eileen's parents will always regret the atmosphere in her room when she passed."

"You mean you didn't—" Delia hesitated. "Okay, I can't believe I'm saying this. You didn't do the translation thing you do? Tell the family what the little girl had to say before she went, you know . . ."

"Into the Light?" Melinda said with some amusement, completing the phrase Delia wasn't quite able to manage. But her amusement didn't last. "That's the thing. There was no sign of her spirit. I was right there, I was *watching*, but I didn't see a thing."

Doubtful, Delia said, "That doesn't sound . . . well, you know . . . good."

A hard distinction to make, no doubt, when *none* of it sounded good. "You're right. It's not. In fact, it's never happened before." *And I don't know quite what to make of the fact that it's happened now.* Melinda rubbed tired eyes. "Listen, never mind Payne. Tell him if he wants to leave any additional messages, they've got to be in the form of limericks. That might slow him down a little."

"Yeah . . . I'm not so sure."

Nor, to be truthful, was Melinda. But it was all she had for the moment. "Really, I just wanted to let you know I'll be back in fifteen or twenty minutes, and you can go early—I'll close up shop."

"No, Melinda, you don't need to—"

"I do," Melinda said firmly. "You've been more than patient these past couple of days. It's definitely time for a Delia treat." And the *really* fancy double-grilled sandwiches would just have to wait.

"Well, okay then." She tried to sound casual, but Melinda didn't miss the pleasure in her voice. Delia worked hard, stayed flexible, came through in a pinch . . . and while she never complained, she also glowed visibly at gestures and acknowledgment of her outstanding work and overall good-friend nature. "I'll be there in a few moments."

And she meant to be. She truly did.

*When the night falls silently,*
*The night falls silently on forests dreaming,*
*Lovers wander forth to see . . .*

Melinda's hands tightened on the steering wheel as she pulled out of the hospital parking lot. "Don't tell me," she said in response to those short lines of music, the exact timing, the tight harmony, the practiced enunciation. "You specialize in the classics."

They skipped straight to the chorus as if in affirmation. "*Shine, little glow-worm, glimmer . . .*"

"So what I don't get," she told them, "is why you're all coming to me as one, well, entity. You're always standing the same when I see you. You're always singing when I hear you. There's four of you, and yet . . . just one of you." She shook her head. "Just for the record, that doesn't make things very clear for me. About why you need help, or what I can do for you. But I do appreciate the chance at a spur-of-the-moment vacation upstate to look into it." She directed the SUV through an intersection and turned onto the feeder road that would take her to the state road and back to Grandview proper.

"*Shine, little glow-worm, glimmer!*"

"Okay, okay—no need to shout. I hear you. Don't you come with a volume control?" She winced, trapped inside the Outlook with sound pouring from the speakers . . . the radio off. Twiddling with the volume, however, did nothing. She turned it all the way down rather than be surprised at whatever random setting she'd found, and made the next turn.

Instantly, the barbershoppers subsided. Still singing, but muted and fading. "*Here and there, and everywhere, from mossy dell and hollow . . .*"

"*That's* my volume control?" she asked them in disbelief. "Turning the car this way and that?"

And then of course she had to know. A quick glance in the rearview, a deft twist of the wheel, and she pulled a U-turn in the middle of the road, swapping directions in short order.

"*. . . Floating, gliding through the air, they call on us to follow. . . !*" Definitely louder again, only this time in moderation. Leaving room to grow.

Melinda pulled over to the side of the road. "Okay, seriously," she told them. "So now I have a volume control. And this is something I need to explore, I see that. But you're not giving me a whole lot to work with—you know that, right? I know you were in a car accident, and I know it happened on the way to a performance." The music faded, but she still felt their presence . . . a hint of burning rubber and fabric, hot brakes and metal. "It must have been terrifying. . . . I'm so sorry you went through that. But it would really help if you would talk to me . . . if you could help me understand what I can do for you."

Oh, they were there all right. Just . . . hovering. Pregnant with need, practically vibrating with it.

And yet . . . silent.

She sighed. "Okay," she said. "I'll keep trying." She checked the road and pulled forward—and this time she was ready when they again burst into the song of the moment. "If I'm guessing right," she murmured to herself, finding a wide spot in the road to reverse course, "then you won't be so enthusiastic about this. . . ."

No, indeed. Their tone became subdued, maybe even . . .

"Are you *sulking*?" she asked, incredulous. "Because I'm telling you, you'll just have to give me more to work with. And right now, this is the direction I've got to go."

Truth was, though, the road curved and looped. And then, a thing she didn't expect—so did her serenade. Not as dramatically as with her deliberate direction changes, but just as definite, waxing and waning as she headed for Grandview . . . always increasing as she curved slightly away from town, slightly north . . . always fading again as the road curved back.

On impulse, she took a side road—a rolling, lumpy lane-and-a-half country road, one that split the difference between the directions . . . and very neatly split the difference between the volumes. "More than volume control," she guessed. "My very own GPS?" She took the turn that would intersect with the state road again; the song volume muted. "Right," she muttered. "My very own, very weird global tracking system." And then, more loudly, "Tell you what, though. I still need more clues. A real conversation would come in pretty handy."

But for now, she set herself to finally reaching the store—and after that, home to dinner, where she knew Jim would share her sadness over Eileen and her curiosity over her strange new GPS and a definite snuggle or two on the couch.

"So they didn't really need the Grandview station after all?" Melinda lifted the top of the panini press and poked at a sandwich as Jim came through the door, greeted by the most wondrous smells of toasting bread and melting cheese.

He grabbed glasses for the stout Fat Tire ale he'd freed from the basement on his way in; he was still shedding bits and pieces of the uniform and now managed to shrug off the shirt and drape it over a chair, ending up in his favorite evening crash clothes—the ribbed tank top he'd worn beneath. "Nope, we were a just in case. Even by the time we got there, it was pretty obvious we'd be turning around."

"Lucky for me," she said, and then added, "And

you! Look at these! Chicken, apples, swiss cheese, carrots . . . grate, slice, chop, mix with mayo and a little lemon juice . . . big buttered slabs of whole wheat; this is going to be *so* good. In another minute or two, anyway." She lowered the grill top. "If you'd turned right around, you would have beat me home. You must have lingered to make fire guy noises."

"What?" Jim tossed the shirt over the stair railing, startled into turning around. She wore that mischievous smile—the one that made it almost impossible to refrain from grabbing her up from behind and carrying her off, giggling wildly, until they fell in a tangle of limbs somewhere and consequently became too distracted to go back to what they'd been doing.

Except then dinner would burn, and it really *did* smell good.

"*You* know," she said, around that mischievous smile. "That's when you all stand around making noises in the backs of your throats and say, 'It's a big one,' or 'Looks to be electrical,' or 'They should have beat it down before now.' And then you talk about what you'd do if it was *your* scene, and after you've sniffed enough smoke, or whatever it is that jazzes you up about those fires, you climb aboard and come back."

Jim's eyes narrowed as he popped the beer caps. "You've been watching us," he said, exaggerating his suspicious expression. "No, wait. Don't tell me you have one of your earthbound friends keeping tabs—"

"Oh, right. Because they have nothing better to do than hold a behavioral study of a bunch of men with very big toys." She slanted him a glance, checking the sandwich again. A deliberate glance. "I meant the trucks, by the way."

He hit himself on the forehead, a dramatic gesture. "Oh, *man,* I saw that one coming, and I just wasn't fast enough—"

"You weren't," she said primly, replacing the grill again. "That means I win."

He had a bad feeling about this. No, scratch that. He had a very, very *good* feeling about this. At least, until she got that look on her face—the slight frown over her eyes, the tension in her face.

"Is that—?" she started, but she stopped herself and looked at him. "Do you hear that, or is it still just me?"

He stopped messing with the beer and listened a moment. "Your phone," he said. "Upstairs."

She made a wordless noise of dismay. "I left it on the bed! It could be Delia—Ned's got this thing going at school. Or Professor Payne—" She cast a conflicted look at the grill and finally gave it up, bolting for the stairs and snatching up his shirt on the way past. "Watch them, they're almost ready!"

"Voice mail!" he called after her. "Redial! Plenty of newfangled options for reaching my wife, who does not have to be on call to the real world twenty-four/seven, along with the earthbound spirit world!"

But the sandwiches did smell alluring at that, perfectly crispy and done, cheese perfectly melted . . . he sighed and left the beer—not much to be done there anyway, and she'd already set the table, plates blocking out bright color against the solid tablecloth—and tended the sandwiches, pulling them onto a serving plate in all their perfection. From the bedroom came an exclamation of annoyance, from which he deduced she'd missed the call anyway, and she came out onto the landing with a shrug in her voice. "Maybe he'll call back."

"Payne?"

"Payne," she confirmed.

"He'll call back," Jim said drily. He'd never quite given the man the trust that Melinda did. Having the distinct notion the quirky professor was besotted with Melinda might just have something to do with it . . . but he sure wasn't going to mention it to Melinda. Especially not on the same day when she'd nailed him for making grunting noises at a fire—not that he was owning up to that one out loud.

"No doubt," she agreed, heading down the stairs at a cheerful jog. And that's what she was doing one moment, jogging down the stairs, and the next she stiffened and her eyes went wide with terror and she didn't so much fall as fling herself down the rest of the way.

"Mel!" It seemed somehow as though he should be able to transport across the house—that it shouldn't take so long to get there, that certainly he should be there to catch her and not be spending those moments listening to her scream of terror or watching her fall spread-eagled, without any significant attempt to catch herself or prepare for that landing.

The one he couldn't reach.

The one she hit so hard, and after which she lay so very still.

# 6

*R*ight *through the guardrail and falling, falling, falling. Surrounded by thick fog, unable to see the ground, unnatural muffled silence all around . . .*

Or not so silent. "Melinda! Mel! Can you hear me?" Hands cupped her head, supporting it—big, strong familiar hands, fingers extending expertly down the back of her neck. "Don't move, baby. You'll be all right."

"I *am* all right," she said. And then, "Ow!" because *all right* wasn't the same as *not battered*. It didn't stop her from trying to get up—though Jim did.

"No," he said, and he was using his paramedic voice. "You could have spinal injuries."

There was no fighting that voice, or those hands. She subsided, and she took careful inventory. Minor aches and pains everywhere, and an echoing impact along her left side—especially shoulder, elbow, and wrist. Her cheek, perhaps, but it felt more numb than anything, and it was hard to tell, still pressed to the floor. "I don't think so," she said. "I think I landed pretty much straight on. Did you see me? Did you see what happened?"

"I saw you," he said drily, a tone that couldn't hide the anxiety in his voice. "But I have no idea what happened."

"I mean, I didn't trip . . . did I? I just fell. And you know, this face-on-the-floor thing is getting old."

"You just fell," he agreed, and added more darkly, "Like a rock. Does this hurt?" He pressed at the base of her skull, following the length of her neck to her shoulders. "Anything there, even the slightest bit?"

"No, not even the slightest bit." She bit back impatience.

He sighed. "You'll tell me . . . ?"

"I swear. You know, if you weren't here, I'd have climbed to my feet already."

"I know," he said, his voice still dark, still holding the fear of the moment. His hands changed from restraining to supporting, from capturing to caressing.

She took it as permission to move and pushed herself off the floor, but not without a gasp of pain. "Okay, *that* hurt," she said, cradling her wrist to her body.

"Could be broken," he said, but this time he didn't go all paramedic on her, didn't take the injured limb and poke and prod. This time he just drew her into his lap and kissed the top of her head, then held her apart just far enough to examine her face. "Definitely gonna have a good bruise there," he said, and barely brushed the high point of her cheekbone. "What *did* happen? They usually know better than this."

Annoyance swept over her. "They do, don't they?" She raised her voice, just in case anyone was listening. "They usually realize that if they break me, I won't *be able to help them.*" She shook her head, and offered no resistance as he drew her in close, rocking her slightly—comforting himself, she realized, as much as her. "The barbershoppers . . . their crash. They must have gone through a guardrail, over an embankment. After what happened to Eileen, I really wanted to see what I could figure out about the spirit who affected her . . . who affected me. But I may need to deal with these guys first."

"This weekend?" he said. "That getaway drive you were talking about? The two of us, a nice little B and B?"

She gave a short laugh, but pressed a hand to her ribs. "Ow. Yes, except . . . New England in the late spring, just a few days' notice? It could be more of a sleeping-in-the-car thing."

"Hey, I'm always up for camping." He gave her a careful squeeze. A teasing embrace. He knew well enough her reaction.

Didn't mean she could hold it back, or the grump that came with it. "*You* are," she said. "Me, not so much. Even when I haven't just tried to fly down the stairs."

"Hmm," he said, so thoughtful that she immediately became suspicious, and pulled back to look at him. Yep, that was definitely twinkle deep in those so-blue eyes. But he took one look at her own narrowed-down eyes and instantly gave it up. "Okay, okay. When you first started talking about going up there, I mentioned it at the station. I wanted to get a feel for the schedule, you know? Turns out one of the guys knows a guy on the job up there who—" He gave the slightest of eye rolls, and went for his back pocket, shifting them both carefully around in the process as he retrieved his wallet. Then he caged her in his arms again as he thumbed through it, finally pulling out an already-crumpled piece of paper. He showed it to her in triumph.

"It's a phone number," she said, keeping all inflection out of her voice. Maybe she *had* hit her head when she fell.

"Uh-huh. To a brand-new family inn. Just opened. Desperately trying to scare up bookings."

"Ooh!" She forgot herself—too much enthusiasm. "Ow! But ooh! My hero!"

"And don't you forget it. But first things first—we're headed over to the hospital. X-rays for that wrist of yours."

"No!" At the stunned expression on his face, she said, "I mean, okay, yes—but not until after we eat! There's no way I'm sitting around the ER for hours with my stomach grumbling, not when we have those incredible sandwiches sitting at the table next to that really great beer."

Understanding replaced his surprise. "No excuses after that?"

"No excuses," she promised. Because truth be told, while everything else just felt bruised and insulted, her wrist truly felt sorry for itself. But still Jim frowned, and she said, "What?"

He reached around her, fished a moment, and came up with what used to be her cell phone. "I guess Professor Payne won't be calling you back after all."

The sandwiches, as it turned out, were most excellent. Even a little cooler than they should have been, even a little more hurried than Melinda had planned for dinner to be. Why they had to hurry, she didn't know. They'd only ended up spending the rest of the evening in the ER at Mercy General.

"And to think it could have been longer, if not for professional courtesy," she told the fancy splint on her wrist. Not broken after all, but sprained enough to keep it throbbing; she'd come home with some mild pain medication and, her head reeling from the day, popped in the soft earbuds and an environmental sounds CD with distant thunderstorms to ward off any alluring lullabies.

Because after all, Eileen had died this day. A sturdy little girl with her copper-tinted freckles and curly hair and definite air of *I know what I want* about her. A healthy little girl who'd been exposed to the same music that ran so hauntingly through Melinda's thoughts, and who had then simply stopped living . . . to the point where her spirit hadn't even been present for her death.

Melinda hadn't even known it could happen.

Then again, she'd always trusted that the spirits who came to her for help wouldn't actually *hurt* her, either. Wouldn't set up her up for a dangerous fall down their long staircase.

Things were different here in Grandview. The spirits had become more intrusive, more insistent. Not to be taken for granted.

She'd been glad when Jim had wrapped an arm around her from behind, pulling her in to spoon close—earbuds and all. It hadn't been a night to be alone.

The morning, on the other hand . . .

Between customers, she'd called the phone number on Jim's crumpled piece of paper, and gotten a proprietor so startled to be on the receiving end of a customer that she could only hope they were truly ready for occupancy, after all. The sound of hammering in the background didn't offer reason for confidence, but that didn't keep her from pulling up the archived news article on the barbershoppers' deaths and making some careful notes—their names, the name of the show: Barbershop Review, The Old & The New—and from hunting up information on the show itself and their obituaries. Their next of kin, the show manager . . . she had plenty of people to talk to. She hunted up a few cozy-looking restaurants while she was at it, and discovered a delightfully kitschy tourist trap of cave and cavern tour not far off their route home. *Too perfect.*

And then she was no longer alone. Gentle, harmonious tones filled the shop. "*Let me call you 'sweetheart,' I'm in love with you . . .*"

"Oh, right," she said. "*Now* you try to make nice. Well, I'm busy. See?" She pointed at the laptop. "I'm getting ready to go figure out what happened with you all. And unless you start talking to me, that's all I can do from here."

"*Let me hear you whisper that you love me too. . . .*"

"Not so much right now." She held up her wrist—gingerly, for in spite of a couple of ibuprofen, it throbbed good and hard this morning. Big mistake, trying to move stock around. The brace protected it, but only so much.

Their voices grew mournful. They appeared in the middle of the store, right in front of the double doors. Puppy-dog-sad eyes, hats held in beseeching attitude at their chests, their stripes vivid and their whites crisp. Even the mustache on the bass seemed to droop. "*Keep the love-light glowing in your eyes so true. Let me call you 'sweetheart,' I'm in love with you.*"

"Actions speak louder than words," she told them crisply. "Although if you'd just *talk* to me—"

Quite suddenly, the door swung open behind them; Melinda got only a glimpse of movement before Delia walked right through the quartet, vertical red stripes clashing with her pretty plum surplice top with bold white horizontal shoulder patterns. The quartet stopped singing, mouths open in astonishment; they looked down at themselves, eyes wide. Delia swung around, her pleasant smile faltering, her arching brows raised in reaction.

The men backed away, hasty and appalled, and, with a brief, uncertain flicker, disappeared. *Prudish*, Melinda would have called them.

*Prudish* hadn't been what happened on those stairs yesterday. That had been dark and distant and uncaring of the consequences . . . or possibly without any understanding of what those consequences might be. That happened, sometimes, with a spirit who had been disassociated from life long enough.

Worth pondering.

But not now, with Delia twisting back around, the confusion so clear on her face. "Do you have the air-conditioning on . . . ?" But she trailed off, because although the day was pleasant, it wasn't nearly that warm, and the AC was quite clearly not turned on.

For a moment, Melinda thought about telling her the truth. *You just walked through a patch of ghosts who were serenading me.*

A very short moment.

And then she shook it off, smiled, and said, "It'll warm up in here once the sun shifts over a little more—but I can turn the heat on if you want? It *was* pretty cool last night."

Delia shook her head, and if she tried to hide her thoughts—the inner war of, *Should I ask? Or should I be happy with not really knowing?*—she wasn't terribly successful. In the end she put her pleasant smile back in place and said, "It'll be fine. I should have known to wear a sweater." And then her eyes widened all over again, and she rushed to the counter. "What *happened*? Your wrist! And are those bruises on your face?"

"Darn, I thought I had gotten those covered." Because of course she had a big purple and blue blotch over her cheek, and under that eye, too. "I took a tumble last night, that's all. Nothing broken. Just banged up."

Delia pointed mutely at the wrist in its brace.

"Sprained," Melinda said. "Not even a bad one. Seriously. It was just one of those things."

"*One of those things* the way you have them, or the way anyone else has them?"

Melinda just gave her a look from beneath her lashes and closed her laptop.

"Okay, that one wasn't fair," Delia admitted, because of course she didn't really want the answer . . . sometimes she just couldn't keep herself from asking. Definitely in conflict over the whole ghost thing, but it was something she'd have to work out for herself. "But seriously, are you okay?"

"I'm sore, but I'll be fine. But you know . . . Jim and I had been talking about going upstate, and I've decided I really don't feel up to working this weekend. We've found a place to stay, and I'm going to close the shop this weekend."

"You don't think I can handle a weekend?" But Delia quickly shook her head. "No, no, I didn't mean to say it like that. I'm just all off kilter right now."

"Hey," Melinda said, and smiled, waiting until Delia took a breath and really looked at her. "It's okay. *I'm* okay. And of course I think you can handle weekend traffic. I just also happen to think you've been doing more than your fair share lately, and I *know* you're going to be doing most of the carrying and moving and unpacking over the next couple of days, too. I think we can both use the break. Call it vacation days with pay."

"Yeah?" A slow smile lit her friend's face. "You know, there's this movie I've wanted to catch with Ned . . . one he'll actually go see with his mom."

"There you are," Melinda said promptly. "We all win."

"But a spring antiquing weekend . . . are you sure?"

"Trust me. By the time you're done with my left hand's share of things around here, you'll be ready for the break."

Delia laughed. "You're the boss. Let me put my stuff away, and we'll get started."

"Good. Because you should *see* what's been piling up here this morning so far. And I was thinking about moving that pier glass over here, at least until I get the bathtub ornaments replaced. The old stuffed animals and dolls in the tub are cute, but not quite the same effect. Plus if we move one of those old wind chimes so it reflects in the pier-glass mirror . . ."

"Okay, okay, I get the idea! You've been sitting here all morning plotting and planning, and now you can't wait. I'll be right out!" Delia laughed again, and headed into the back room.

Melinda would have rubbed her hands together if the brace—or her wrist—had allowed. Delia wasn't far off, at that. Among other things, Melinda was perfectly ready for a few hours of completely normal, store-oriented activity. She slipped her laptop behind the counter and stood, stretching. A loose, long-sleeved tunic top for her today, gently shirred along the bodice and tied with a sweet little ribbon in front, and soft old jeans—both in consideration for her bruises. If Delia had been concerned for the half-hidden bruise on her face, she'd go nuts over the ugly purple blooms everywhere else.

She headed for the pier glass, pondering the logistics of both moving it and securing it in a new spot without a wall against which to lean it; two coat racks ought to do it, and some discreet twine. . . .

When the door opened, she didn't immediately recognize Hayley. The young woman dressed more casually than when she'd been on duty with Eileen Starcroft—jeans, a bright spring top, a saucy matching headband holding back her explosion of loose, crimped curls. But her hesitant look was the same, and sorrow sat behind her black-brown eyes.

"Hayley!" Melinda said. "How are you?"

Hayley lifted a shoulder, offered a smile. It wasn't convincing. In fact, the corner of her mouth trembled briefly, but then she managed a genuine smile in return—although she didn't quite answer the question. "I'm glad you're here," she said. "I wanted to thank you. You tried so hard. . . . I think you almost got through to him."

"Travis Starcroft," Melinda said.

Hayley nodded. "It's not that he doesn't love her," she said, and then bit her lip. "I mean, didn't."

"Oh, I expect *doesn't* is probably the case," Melinda said. She gentled her voice. "That's how it is for you, isn't it?"

Hayley looked away. She started to speak, blinked rapidly, and turned away. From there, she said, "It doesn't seem fair, you know. I lost Eileen . . . and now I've lost the family I've been part of for three years. The job seems like the least of it."

Of course she'd been let go. No more child to watch. "He didn't waste any time, did he?" Melinda observed, but her words were without bite.

"He—" Hayley started something defensive, something she couldn't quite finish. Instead, she said, "You were so right. Maureen is devastated by how things were, that she wasn't nurturing Eileen when . . . when she passed. And Travis . . . he's still too busy trying to control everything. But . . ."

"Once he realizes he can't . . ." Melinda finished for her, and Hayley nodded. Melinda said, "And what about you?"

Hayley turned back to her; surprise blooming softly on her features. "You know . . . I had more time with her than either of them. In her life, and then . . . in the ER. I sang to her. I held her hand. I'm so very sad. . . . But I'm *okay*, if you know what I mean."

Melinda nodded, gave her a smile. "Yeah," she said. "I do."

Hayley took a breath. "And anyway, I didn't come to cry on your shoulder. I came to thank you. It was really kind of you to come by . . . to try to help. I think Maureen feels the same, she's just . . . conflicted."

"I understand," Melinda assured her.

Hayley gave her a curious look—a perceptive one. "You do, don't you?"

Melinda shrugged, a minimal gesture. "I think I mentioned I have some experience in dealing with this sort of thing." So matter-of-fact, it didn't invite questions. After so many years, she'd learned how to strike just that note.

Hayley frowned, her eyes narrowing, her gaze flicking to Melinda's wrist from her makeup-covered bruises. "What . . . are you all right?"

Melinda made a dismissive gesture. "Oh, I—" She looked over as Delia reentered the room. "Oh, Delia. You remember Hayley."

"I do," Delia said, compassion flooding her features. "And I'm so sorry for your loss. So sudden . . ." That she was thinking of Ned reflected clearly on her features; Melinda knew her friend too well miss it.

"I don't think we'll ever know—" Hayley started.

The shop door opened, and Rick Payne walked in, already talking. "Finally! Do you know how long I've been trying to reach you? *Again*. Not one phone call did you return—and since when do you not even pick up for my calls? Here I am skipping out between classes not once but twice." He didn't hesitate as Melinda turned away, reaching behind the counter for the phone she had yet to replace. "And I'm beginning to get the idea that you're avoiding me—that, you know, this thing we have going is a one-way street and, you know, I *did* find a connection between that lullaby and the girl in the coma. Well, not that lullaby specifically, but music in general, and not a coma specifically, but if you read it metaphorically and totally between the lines, and what the hell happened to your phone? Come to think of it, what happened to your wrist? And your *face*?"

Melinda turned to Delia, still dangling the broken phone in midair, as she had for been for the past several sentences. "You see?" she said. "Pretty much always like this."

Delia's eyebrows couldn't have gone much higher. "Uh-*huh*," she said.

"But smooth," Payne was quick to note. "Always smooth."

Not quite as smooth as he thought. For there was Hayley, her mouth dropped open slightly, her shock finally making way for words. "What *about* the little girl in the coma?"

Payne looked at her, startled to discover she was even there—and then back to Melinda, his expression full of *wha—?* But she didn't really have to explain. Not when Hayley took a step closer and said, "What *about* Eileen?"

The *wha—* turned to deer-in-the-headlights. Melinda almost felt sorry for him.

Almost.

"This is Hayley," she told him. "Eileen's nanny. I'm very sorry to say that Eileen passed away yesterday afternoon."

"Nix on the smooth," Payne muttered, and very visibly pasted on what might be called company manners. "Rick Payne," he said. "Friend of Melinda's."

Hayley looked between the two of them, her body language grown mother-bear fierce. "And what about a lullaby? What about Eileen? What connection?"

"Wow," Delia said, so brightly. "That's either the best timing I've ever seen, or the worst. I'm going over to the Farmer's Market. Anyone need anything?"

Melinda shook her head ever so slightly, and Delia, no slouch on the exit line, had a five in her hand and was headed out the door by the time Melinda turned back to Hayley, and then to Payne—to exchange a minimalistic shrug—before she said, "When I said I had experience, Hayley . . . what I meant is that I've spent a lot of time helping people through their issues at passing."

Hayley frowned. "You mean, at their loved ones' passing."

"No, I mean that I communicate with—I see, hear, and feel—earthbound spirits. Those who have passed on, but who still have issues holding them back."

Hayley just crossed her arms and looked at Melinda, the frown verging on a scowl, the nanny comportment disappearing beneath the skeptical.

"I've been in communication with a number of coma patients," Melinda said. "Some of them before they passed, but mostly after. But I can tell you . . . they remember. They're aware. What we do in those circumstances really does make a difference." Except . . . *not necessarily for Eileen.* Because she wasn't sure Eileen had truly still been there.

Hayley's expression shifted; her eyes narrowed slightly. This was the moment when she'd say something sarcastic—when she'd make fun, or go scornful. And maybe she would have, if she hadn't been beside Melinda as Eileen died. "After she . . .

when it happened, you said her name. You think you were *talking* to her?"

Melinda ignored the implications behind her wording and shook her head, regretful. "I'm afraid not. I didn't see her. But I was looking for her." And for now, she hoped Hayley wouldn't pick up on the implications of *that*—that Eileen *should* have been there. That her absence was . . . wrong. Very wrong.

No worries. Hayley locked in on Payne. "And what do you have to do with it? What are you talking about, finding a connection between Eileen and some lullaby?"

Payne made a valiant try to break the line of conversation. "And hey, as long as we're asking questions, what *did* happen to your wrist, and face, and phone . . . ?"

"No," Hayley said, a touch of that mother-bear fierce in her voice again. "Not until I'm done with you."

Payne glanced around the shop. "What," he said in a stage whisper. "No convenient inconvenient distractions?"

Melinda lifted her hands, a gesture of helplessness. "I can't stage-manage these things, you know."

Hayley waited. Looking at Payne, looking at Melinda. And the truth was, Melinda didn't have to say anything more; Payne didn't have to say anything more. But Melinda's compassion was far from limited to the earthbound spirits she was so dedicated to helping. "Professor Payne teaches at Rockland U," she said. "I consult with him sometimes, when the messages and signs I get are garbled."

"Garbled? What do you mean? Either you claim you talk to them, or you don't." Desperation edged Hayley's voice; Melinda was familiar with that, too. The wanting to believe, the fear that it wasn't quite true.

"I *listen*," she said gently. "But earthbound spirits are sometimes confused. If the circumstances of their death were violent or confusing, or if they've been dormant awhile . . . then sometimes I just get snatches, or I get memories. Or it takes them a while to figure out how to communicate with me. That's what happened last night. One of the spirits I'm working with was involved in an accident with a terrifying fall, and that person"—*or all four of them*—"is still trying to figure out how to connect with me."

Payne frowned. "What, by sending you on a fall of your own?" When she nodded, his frown grew downright annoyed. "Since when? Isn't that like killing the goose that lays the golden egg?"

She made a face at him. "Because that's so how I like to think of myself. A goose, laying eggs. But you're right. They can be pretty wrapped up in themselves, and especially these past couple of years . . . they don't care so much if they upset or scare me. But hurt me?" She shook her head, left it at that.

"You really do believe it," Hayley said. "Both of you. You really think she does this thing." She took a step closer to Payne. *"What about Eileen's coma?"*

"Okay, you're scaring me," Payne said, glancing around—planning an escape route, Melinda decided.

She held her hand out, palm up, and wiggled the fingers. *Give,* the gesture said. Generally meant for money, but he still got the idea. He sighed, and said, "Okay, check it out. Pied piper."

"The guy with the flute?" she asked incredulously, quite certain they couldn't be talking about the same thing. "Payne, we've got a dead woman humming a lullaby here, not a living man paid to pipe away *rats."*

"The trick about these stories," he said, almost as if she hadn't spoken, "is teasing the kernel of truth away from the rest. Defining the important part, if you will." His fingers twitched, probably itching to close around chalk, or props, or at least pull a book off a shelf and flip through it so he had something to point at. "So, the pied piper of Hamelin. In 1284, a man named Bunting, after his, shall we say, idiosyncratic personal style, is paid to lure away the town's rats with his pipe music, which he does, neatly disposing of them in the Weser River—something the EPA would have a fit about today, mind you, but it seems to have worked for them. But the chintzy townsfolk decline to pay him, and he decides to make it in their best interest to do that thing. He lures away the children like little remote-controlled robots, packs them into a cave in the Koppenberg Mountain, and seals them in forever. Also not exactly standard procedure."

"He just knows all this stuff?" Hayley said skeptically, looking at Melinda once again as an alley.

"Just nod," Melinda said. "That way he gets to the good stuff faster."

"Hey!" Payne contrived to look wounded. "With me, it's all about the good stuff." It wasn't an expression he could hold on to, however, because he'd hit his stride, and now the words wouldn't wait for him. "Okay, but look. These things are always based on fact. There's some speculation that the whole piper thing came from that really regrettable children's crusade in 1212, although we're talking twenty thousand kids there as opposed to Bunting's relatively small one hundred twenty, and actually that whole thing's probably legend, too, but people believed it at the time due to some translation issues—"

"Right," Melinda said firmly. "But I'm guessing that *really* doesn't have anything to do with us right now."

"No," Payne said, although he seemed a little sad to admit it. "Probably not."

"So, then, you're thinking . . . ?"

"What if—" He looked around for something to use as a prop, gave up, and simply gestured wildly. "What if our friend Bunting is based on fact after all? Think of it. You're not the only one who can communicate with the dearly departed— not now, and certainly not through history. What if this thing happened, and someone needed to create a warning and didn't know how? Make up a story, that's what. Especially in those days. These days you'd just start an Internet rumor, slap 'Virus Warning' on it, and leave it to the good gullible people of the world to pass around."

Melinda tried to wrap her thoughts around his free-ranging associations. "So you think this isn't the first time?"

"Right!" He seemed particularly pleased that she'd gotten the point, although she was pretty sure he hadn't made one yet.

Nor was Hayley. "What are you *talking* about?"

"Our mystery piper," Payne said. "The lullaby Melinda mentioned to me. Now, I went out on a limb and assumed it was ghostly, because really, otherwise, why mention it to me at all? And your young friend."

"More than that," Melinda said. "I've heard it, too. The humming is just distracting, but the one time I heard her singing, it . . ." She looked away, hunting words, and finally shrugged. "It took me away. If Jim hadn't been right there . . ."

Payne breathed an impressed expletive, then gave himself a little shake. "That makes it personal," he said.

"There's more," she said. "I was there when Eileen passed." She looked at Hayley—at red-rimmed eyes watching her with acute interest, suspicion still lurking—and chose her words with care. "I didn't see her."

Payne rocked back slightly. "Ah," he said. "Sealed in the cave." And, possibly because he could see Hayley's building frown, her mouth closing in on words, he added, "Okay, more than ever, I need you to see my friend."

"What?" Melinda searched for a reference point, finally recalled that he'd been trying to reach her—not to tell her about his research breakthrough but to ask, again, that she meet with his friend about her undefined problem. "Why?"

"Because she's a teacher," Payne said. "A teacher of the little tykes' persuasion, in fact. And she's had some strange things going on in her classroom."

Hayley's hands fisted at her side. "You mean . . . it might not be just Eileen?"

It seemed like the perfect time for the shop phone to ring.

The perfect time for Jim to greet her, first with relief to hear her voice, and then with grim regret as he told her the news, picked up on his latest run, with word quickly spreading through the hospital . . . there was another young girl in an inexplicable coma.

# 7

"PLEASE," HAYLEY SAID, "please let me help, if I can. Who knows what this looks like better than I do? And I'm out of work, and I really don't want to be alone right now. . . ."

The mama bear had disappeared; in her place was a young woman, alone and grieving. Melinda felt a moment of what might have been panic; for all she did to help people, she rarely let them into her world so deeply. "Really, I work alone."

"It's true," Payne noted. "We talk about this stuff, and then she goes away and does something about it. It's not like I'm a sidekick or anything." He tilted his head at her. "Please tell me you didn't think I was a sidekick."

Hayley paid him little attention. "I can help," she insisted. "If this teacher friend of his is really seeing the same thing, that is. Introduce me to her. You can't stay there all day—and maybe I can't, either, but I can stay for a while. I can keep an eye on them. And I know what to do if I see that look. At least, I know what to *try*."

She was right about that. About all of it. And so she came.

"How much have you told your friend?" Melinda asked Payne as he came up to her Outlook in the Grandview Tiny Hearts Pre-K parking lot. It had made sense to drive their own vehicles, but together they took up a significant portion of the modest asphalt lot. The school itself was a short distance from town, set back from the road in a charming country atmosphere. A groomed woods surrounded the school lawn before giving way to fully wild nature, and if the building itself was unremarkable, the colorful touches more than made up for it. Giant wooden cutout flowers flanked the door, while grass and snails and butterflies lined the siding right to the edge of the picket-fenced porch; balloons rose toward the porch ceiling, and bright wind chimes hung at each corner.

Hayley slipped out the passenger side of Melinda's SUV and looked at it all with naked longing. "I was homeschooling Eileen," she said to no one in particular. "But oh, she would have loved this."

Too sentimental for Payne; he pretended not to hear at all, and answered Melinda's question. "Well, obviously she knows my specialty. And she came to *me*. She was spooked, let's say. She knows you have a certain connection with the supernatural, but I didn't give her any details. How about we don't set up expectations for either of you?"

"Works for me," Melinda said. After all, she already had a pretty good idea what to expect. Or she was afraid she did. She smoothed her tunic top, wished the day had brought a smarter outfit and fewer bruises, then decided it wouldn't really matter in the end and headed for the cheerful front porch.

The doorbell turned out to be unmistakable—surrounded by yellow wooden rays that turned it into a sun. But she had no opportunity to push it; as they mounted the porch, the door opened, and a trim woman beckoned them inside. Of Delia's age, Melinda thought, and probably with her own teenage children at home, but where Delia hadn't lost her quirky, freewheeling style, this woman had gone entirely to the practical side of the force—tidy polo shirt and dark khaki pants, jewelry minimal. But it was her expression that really caught Melinda's attention—the relief to see Payne, the underlying worry, the tension in her neck and shoulders, and the way her hand tightened on the doorknob before she released it when closing the door behind them, leaving them in a house-size hallway with construction-paper decorated walls, industrial carpeting, and bright recessed lighting.

"Thank you for coming," she said to Payne, and then shifted her gaze between Melinda and Hayley, her expression uncertain. In the background, several children laughed; a woman's amused voice rose over the sound to bring order again.

Payne said, "This is Melinda Gordon, the friend I mentioned to you. And this is . . ."

She could just hear him filling in his own blanks. *Someone who decided to come along for the ride; someone I don't know but who came anyway; a nanny who just lost her job because the kid died. No, thank you.* Quickly, as she held out her hand, she said, "This is Hayley. She has some professional experience with children, and I thought her perspective might be helpful."

The woman took her hand for a brief grip—no easy confidence there. "I'm Jeannette Limoux, and this is my school. I wish I could be more specific about what's happening here—"

"No, that's okay," Melinda said. "In fact, sometimes it's better if we can just . . ."

*Was that humming?*

"Melinda?" Not Payne, as she'd expected, but Hayley—the one who indeed recognized the look, the unnatural distraction. And Hayley wasn't taking any chances; she prodded Melinda on the shoulder, a good firm prod that just happened to miss the plentiful bruising along that side.

"Whoa," Melinda said, giving her a startled look. "You're a lot more . . . well, *feisty* than I first thought."

"Mr. Starcroft had expectations," Hayley said. "I met them so I could stay on with Eileen . . . maybe some of that even got to be habit. It was more than a job, you should know that."

"I'm sure *she* knew that," Melinda said.

"What, *what*?" Payne wore his best clueless-guy expression, although Jeannette . . .

Jeannette had gone grim. Jeannette had seen it, too. She said, "Tell me again what Melinda does?"

"For now, listening," Melinda answered for herself. "Is there a place we can watch the children without disturbing them?"

"We've got a small two-way." Jeannette indicated a room toward the end of the hall and led them in that direction. "The children are just finishing up their day. They've most recently had a rest time, a wake-up song-and-stretch activity, and now they're in closing circle before their parents come, doing their All About My Day exercise. They should be alert and participating, for the most part." They filed into the small room, and she turned to them with a finger to her lips, then made a face and whispered, "Sorry. Habit. But we do need to be quiet, or they'll hear us."

Melinda moved up to the mirror, leaving room for Hayley—not worrying so much about Payne. Of the three of them, he was the one who couldn't recognize the signs, or hear them. Not that he was about to be left out—he crowded close behind them, peering over their shoulders.

The children sat in a semicircle around a young woman who was sitting on the floor with them; all her attention was on the child who was speaking, with much lisp and excitement. "I had a Good-Morning Job today! I mistered the plants!"

"Transgender plants? These kids *do* need help," Payne murmured. Melinda gently elbowed him, without taking her eyes off the activity in the room. The prekindergarten children were four and five years old, and, aside from the teacher on the floor, they had two additional teachers sitting in chairs at strategic points outside the small semicircle—watching, touching a shoulder here, nodding encouragement there, and cheering as each child finished a recitation of his or her day. One of them wrote quick notes for each child—a report, Melinda supposed, that would go home with that child.

They all seemed perfectly normal. She exchanged a glance with Hayley, whose mouth had tightened but who barely glanced away to meet Melinda's gaze. Jeannette shook her head. "It doesn't always happen," she said, keeping her voice low. "Now is a frequent time for it, but . . . it doesn't always happen." She gave Melinda a frank look. "You must think I'm insane. Or imagining things."

No, she thought this was a place where people genuinely listened to children. But out loud . . .

"Actually," Melinda murmured, returning her

attention to the room, "I try not to judge. Given that I hear those words all too often myself . . ." And besides, she'd already heard . . .

*Humming.*

"Watch now," she whispered, barely putting sound to it.

Hayley gasped, and Jeannette pushed in closer. "Yes," she said. "That's the look. But it gets worse."

"They look stoned," Payne said, more fascinated than anything. The child in recitation still spoke, but her words grew halting in spite of encouragement by the central teacher. The other two teachers tensed in their chairs; one stopped writing. The other children . . .

"It's not what they're doing," Melinda said, realizing it, "so much as what they're *not*." Not fidgeting. Not squirming. Not watching one another, or looking at the teachers, or tugging at their clothes, or poking at the carpet, or . . .

None of those things. They sat quietly; they looked at nothing in particular. Melinda frowned; she dared to listen. Just barely, that humming. That familiar haunting tune . . . if she filled in the gaps with her own familiarity. She dared more—she closed her eyes, listened harder. Ohh, it was there, all right. Not directed at her—she didn't think it had ever been directed at her, and now, in the wake of examination, she felt downright excluded—but definitely there. She wasn't even sure it was directed at these particular children—it felt as if it were incidental somehow. In the background of something else.

"No," Payne said in fascinated disbelief. "Tell me they're not *humming*."

"I wish I could." Moving quickly, Jeannette led them out of the room and to the door of the classroom. She went into the room to stand beside the lead teacher; Melinda moved just inside the doorway. The children's disjointed humming caught only pieces of the tune, and she didn't even think before picking it up—before finding the tune and the words and singing them softly, as sweetly as they were meant to be sung. "*Sleep, my child, and peace attend thee, all through the night . . .*"

Hayley gasped, as much in horror as anything else—aside from Melinda, she was the only one there who understood the true ramifications of the song's presence. Payne merely gave her a surprised look, as if he hadn't known she could put two notes together—but the teachers, as Melinda's voice synchronized with the children, turned to her with a startled mix of relief and near accusation.

"What *is* that?" Jeannette asked. She kept her voice low, so as not to disturb the children, though she might well not have bothered.

"A lullaby," Melinda said, a bit distantly.

"*Hey.*" Hayley prodded her.

"Whoa. Right. Don't go there." She shook her head slightly, realized that the teachers were all looking at her—and that the children were all completely distracted and distant, much as she'd just been. Not like Eileen—not asleep, not worse. But bad enough. "Hayley, what were those songs? The ones Eileen liked?"

Hayley understood right away. "Something younger," she said decisively. "Something active. Something that will get through—" She stepped into the room, and Melinda marveled again at the difference in her when Travis Starcroft wasn't threatening her access to Eileen. "Quick," Hayley said to the other teachers. "The 'Head, Shoulders' song."

The three exchanged glances, uncertain—looking at the children with the doubt that meant they knew these youngsters weren't going to spring up to sing along. Melinda moved in by Hayley's side. "Just start it," she said. "We'll get them to join in."

As if any pre-K school ever existed that didn't know the 'Head, Shoulders' song. "Head, shoulders, knees, and toes," Jeannette sang in a strong voice, and the other three teachers got to their feet, joining in—moving among the children and nudging them to join in, too. Hayley and Melinda sang along, and Melinda gave Payne a meaningful look.

*Who, me?* he mimed, shaking his head, taking a chicken step back.

*You.* She pointed quite firmly, and beckoned him into the room, and her expression said the rest of it: *Your friend, your favor—you sing.*

He sang.

More or less.

Within moments the first child joined in, and soon enough they were all singing it, complete with gestures. And when the resounding little chorus stopped, the background lullaby had faded away.

"There," Melinda told Jeannette. "That's what you need to do, the moment you see them with that expression."

"Or hear that song," Hayley said, rather more grimly.

"Try going back to All About My Day," Jeannette told the teachers, who commenced rounding up the children and settling them down. She drew Melinda aside, bringing Hayley and Payne along. "But I don't understand," she said. "What on earth is going on? What's capturing them so?"

Melinda looked over at the group—a dozen or so children, all happily reporting about their day, including the exciting way they'd all suddenly been singing one of their activity songs in the middle of All About My Day. She smiled—relief to see such normality, but also just the pleasure at seeing happy kids emoting about themselves and their world. "Unfortunately, we're really not sure yet." She searched Jeannette's face for skepticism in waiting, for the signs that Jeannette was about to scorn or debunk Melinda's words . . . found nothing but genuine frustration. So she said, "Children often perceive things that adults no longer can. They have such open minds, such trust. Invisible friends aren't always just in the imagination. But this . . ." She shook her head. "This is different. This is more than just perceiving something. This humming is *involving* them."

"Like it *involves* you?" Hayley said drily.

"Yes, well . . ." Melinda shrugged. "I'm used to that. But *this* . . ." She indicated the children, shook her head again. "This is different. And you know these aren't the only children being affected."

"What're you going to do?" Payne asked. "Track down every pre-K and kindergarten in the area and give them counter-ghost lessons?"

"You know, I was really trying to avoid the *G*-word here." Melinda's exasperation momentarily got the better of her. "And you know what, if that's what we have to do . . . and first grade, too. Because Delia's son Ned is helping with that Teen Reader Leader program—"

"You're kidding," Payne said.

Confused and a little defensive on Ned's behalf, Melinda said, "Not in the least. Why wouldn't Ned be part of that program—?"

"What? No, no. What do I know from Ned? I

mean . . . *Teen Reader Leader*? Who thought that one up?"

"You are not helping," Melinda informed him, eyes narrowing.

"Don't worry," Jeannette said. "I know him well enough to ignore him. And I knew when I went to him that the *G*-word might come up. Just . . . do you really think it's that simple? Just get them in an action song the moment we see any signs of . . ."

"That they're being drawn in by that lullaby? Yes, I think it's really that simple. I've been managing for days with an iPod." Melinda smiled ruefully. "And truthfully, I don't think they're in any great danger, at least not as a group. I think individuals are being targeted, at least for now."

"But you don't know why," Hayley said.

"No. That's the problem." Melinda looked again at the children. "I don't know why."

"Then may I suggest," Payne said, in exactly the same tone as his smart-ass commentary, which is why the good stuff always came from the blue, "that you leave the other pre-Ks and kindergartens and first-graders on their own, and try to figure out the *why*. It's the only way you're going to stop it."

Melinda put her hands on her hips, hurt her wrist doing it, and ended up crossing her arms instead. "Okay," she said, and shook her head in bemusement. "Now *that's* helping."

\* \* \*

But first things first, which is how Melinda ended up back at the hospital, Hayley still at her side. Still resolutely at her side, in fact—in spite of the way her toasty complexion paled as the elevator door opened on the PICU floor, where the new coma patient now resided.

But when Melinda would have turned to her, interruption came in the familiar ghostly form of a scruffy young boy in his hospital gown, sitting cross-legged in the corner of the elevator and scowling at Melinda. Melinda stabbed at the Open button, startling Hayley out of her sad thoughts. "Did you have something to say to me?"

"*Yeah.*" His distinctly sour expression didn't waver. He looked sallow today, with none of the mischievous energy of his previous appearance; an IV line attached to his arm ran limply to a half-full bag on the floor. "*She's here.*" And away he went, clearly not in a social mood.

"Wait! *Who*—" But Melinda glanced outside the elevator to the staff, within very obvious eye and earshot, and stopped herself. The boy was gone, and she'd probably find out soon enough. Eileen, the lullaby spirit . . . she'd be ready.

"Who are you talking to?" Hayley asked as Melinda strode out onto the floor—with more authority than she felt, ignoring her sore body in favor of presenting the confidence that would discourage questions from those watching staffers.

Then again, to judge by the last time, the staffers were used to strange occurrences in that elevator.

"A little boy," Melinda said quietly. "I spoke to him last time. He's upset. He said she's here—but he didn't say who."

"Eileen?" The word was wistful.

Melinda cast her a quick glance. "You've stopped doubting."

That stopped Hayley short, if only for a moment. "I guess I have," she said. "I guess at first it was just desperation . . . I didn't dare not to go along with it. But you . . . you're just so casual about it all. You're not trying to prove anything to anyone."

"No," Melinda agreed. "I'm not." She took a deep breath. "But you should know—this isn't always easy. This is an emotional time for people. I might not be any more welcome than I was with Travis. *We* might not be any more welcome."

Hayley snorted quietly. "Can't be any worse."

*Ah, optimism.* But Melinda didn't respond out loud. For one thing, she'd spotted the room they wanted—down the hall, where the people who entered and exited still looked shell-shocked. For another . . . why not think positive? "Why don't you see if that little CD player is still available?"

And she'd see what she could do about introducing them. She headed down the hall with confident steps, having learned long ago that they took her where hesitation often failed. Learning to deal with ghosts, she often mused, had been the easy part. The part that came more or less naturally. Learning to deal with the living, on the other hand . . .

The room held another little girl—one not yet as deeply affected as Eileen had been. Although various machines cluttered the room, and an IV line snaked to the girl's arm, she was not on a respirator; and her features, though slack, still held the plump firmness of her age. Five, maybe six . . . just like Eileen.

Unlike Eileen's, this little girl's skin was a lovely deep brown; her hair was drawn back in a multitude of little braids with colorful elastic bands securing them. A pinkish abrasion marred her forehead; plump, childish lips parted slightly in repose. Melinda found herself filled with sorrow at the sight of this innocent life so stricken—and then determination, that she would not end up like Eileen.

The three adults in the room hadn't noticed her yet. Two women—they looked to be sisters—and a man, murmuring to one other, sitting close. Their lightweight coats were flung over the end of the long hospital bed where the girl's feet didn't begin to reach; all three were dressed smartly, in office wear. They'd been called in from work, then; the girl had probably been in a class much like the one she and Hayley had just left.

She shifted slightly, just enough to draw their notice. "Hi," she said. "I don't mean to interrupt. My name is Melinda. I'm here with a friend . . . we're hoping we might be of some help to you." She glanced over her shoulder; no sign of Hayley yet. "You may have heard that there was another little girl here earlier in the week—"

"That's *all* we've heard," the man said. A tall, lean man with a receding hairline and a carefully styled tight beard and mustache, he had a wary, distrustful look. A man who didn't trust the doctors to help his little girl, she thought, as opposed to any specific reaction to her.

"I'm Rhonda; this is my sister Alice, and her husband, Ted. And they think they're being quiet about it," she said. "They think we're not listening. But oh, we hear them—that little girl who died, and no one knows why."

"Just like no one knows why my Saiyesha just . . . fell asleep," Alice added. The girl's mother, then.

Melinda might not know why, not yet . . . but she knew *how.* And she knew what worked for her, what had just worked for a whole classroom full of kids. Although as with Eileen, there was no sign of this little girl's spirit in the room—no attempt to communicate with Melinda, as had a number of coma patients in the past.

"How is it you think you can help?" Ted asked.

"We have reason to believe—my friend and I—that music can be helpful. There are some CDs here in the hospital—Hayley is looking for them now—but maybe Saiyesha has some favorites you could bring in."

"They said we should talk to her," Rhonda said, and the other two nodded. All in all, a different feel than had been in Eileen's tense little sickroom. This was a family pulling together, not falling apart.

"Or sing to her," Melinda suggested. "If that's something you did together."

"I'm happy to do it," Alice said. "I don't even need you to tell me that. But why is it you think—"

From the hall behind Melinda, a muffled noise of surprise—and a man's voice. "What are you doing here?"

Melinda whirled, surprised to find Travis Starcroft standing there—his arms full of a lovely flower arrangement completely at odds with his confrontational body language. She was just as surprised to see Hayley's confident posture subtly give way as she exited the activities room, the colorful CD player clutched at her midriff. "Excuse me," she told the family, and headed into the breach—but as much as she bristled on Hayley's behalf, she knew it wasn't in their best interest to get loud here in PICU. "Mr. Starcroft," she said, "what beautiful flowers—for the staff here? It's a lovely gesture."

"And *you*!" he said, as if were an accusation all on its own.

"Yes." Quiet but firm. "Hayley, let's—"

"What are you doing here? Haven't you done enough already?" He was angry, and grieving . . . and he wasn't going to let it go. Already he had the attention of one of the male nurses, who came toward them with quick, meaningful strides.

"I'm afraid we don't have to explain ourselves to you," Melinda told him, words firm but voice still quiet—it took a moment before he really heard her, before his eyes widened. By then she'd looped her arm through Hayley's. "Let's go, Hayley."

Hayley hesitated, still intimidated. When she moved, she stumbled slightly, and Melinda steadied her as the nurse drew closer. She said to Travis Starcroft, "Here's someone to take those flowers. I'm sure everyone here will appreciate the gesture." Not his idea, she'd guess. Unless it wasn't from his heart . . . unless it was the kind of gift meant to point out his generosity under duress. Under her breath, she said, "Hayley, let's *go*," and they finally headed back down the hall toward Saiyesha's room. "Are you all right?"

Hayley glanced back, and Melinda followed her gaze. Starcroft still stared after them, a hard look. One that meant he could still cause trouble. PICU was not likely to allow disruption on their floor, not with stressed families in the various rooms and critically ill children throughout. "I just didn't expect to see him."

"He has no authority over you now," Melinda reminded her. "There's nothing he can take away from you. And don't you ever forget—you had something he needed, too. You had something he needed badly, and he knows it."

Hayley nodded, but looked no less troubled. "That's why he resents me so much," she said. "And why he fired me so fast. I think Maureen would have been glad if I'd stayed on long enough to help . . . well, for a little while. Through the funeral. Through the packing and sorting."

"Please tell me you're going to the funeral," Melinda said, pausing far enough from Saiyesha's room that their conversation wouldn't be disturbing. "Please tell me you won't let him keep you away."

Hayley didn't respond. Worse, she didn't look at Melinda.

"Hayley, you can't let him—"

"*Sleep, my child, and peace attend thee, all through the night . . .*"

Melinda stopped short. Not just the humming, but the singing—singing she'd heard only once before, and at that in her sleep. She steeled herself against it, but something must have shown on her face. Hayley turned to her, concern in her eyes. "Melinda?"

Melinda gave her a little push toward Saiyesha's room. "Introduce yourself. Play the music. Do it now, Hayley!"

"But what about you—" For clearly Hayley saw the pull it had on her, even if she couldn't hear what was happening.

"I'm okay," Melinda said. For now, it was truth. For now, she was alert and awake and fighting the pull. "But I need to work on this ghost—this is as close as I've come to her—" She didn't soften her words, or waste time sidestepping the blunt truth of it. Another little push and she moved away, trying to keep the whole big picture in mind as she ducked into the empty room beside Saiyesha's. Travis Starcroft, still down the hall, still potentially ready to make trouble. Saiyesha, needing their help more than ever, but her family still unaware of the nature of the problem. Hayley, rattled by Starcroft's presence and behavior and now on her own, clutching that poignantly bright CD player as if it was all she had for courage.

And here Melinda was, inside a darkened room, blinds drawn, lights off, bed made . . . the whole thing looking particularly abandoned. The song's phrases beat against her mind, striking hard; she dug in her metaphorical feet and pulled herself together for a rousing if silent chorus of "Rock the Roll" and then, to her relief, the mellow four-part harmony of "Beautiful Dreamer" floated through the background. Not an intrusive presence, but a welcome reminder.

Melinda took a deep breath and said, "I need to talk to you. I know you're here. I can hear you. I don't know if you realize what you're doing to that little girl, but you have to stop. Whatever's driving you, whatever you need . . . just talk to me. I can help you."

The singing faltered; a cold breeze blew through Melinda's bones, one that tasted of darkness and bitter disappointment. A familiar feeling, one she'd briefly felt in her own home, when she'd felt this spirit's attention glance her way and then unexpectedly dismiss her.

*Not this time.* Not if she had anything to say about it.

"That's a start," Melinda said. Not an encouraging start, but . . . it was *interaction.* The spirit had at least finally deigned to notice her again. "I know you haven't been looking for me. I'm not sure what you're actually looking for, but I'd be glad to help you."

The breeze faded. She had the impression she'd gained a brief spotlight of attention . . . and then lost it again. *Not this time!* "Listen to me!" she said fiercely. "What you're doing is *not okay.* A little girl *died* yesterday. I can't believe that's what you mean to do. I don't feel that in you. Not with your beautiful song." And she didn't. For Melinda had encountered evil; she had especially encountered evil in the past two years. This spirit was *doing* harm, but that didn't mean she meant to.

Then again, given the single-minded nature of many spirits, it also didn't mean that she cared.

"You may not think I matter to you," Melinda told that wisp of a remaining presence, "but you're hurting people. And *I'm going to stop you.*"

The room quite suddenly disappeared from around her. She lurched to find her balance in the darkness—no floor, no walls, no ceiling—nothing but vertigo in the dark. She went down to one knee, bracing herself on her uninjured wrist, and closed her eyes, hunting a more familiar darkness. But this wasn't her reality; closing it out wasn't an option. "Come on, then," she muttered. "Talk to me! Because this isn't going to stop me, and you can't do it forever!"

Still no floor, still no walls—but not far from her, a white glow of a woman's silhouette, reminding Melinda of a paper cutout. The cold breeze turned into reality, shivering down her arms and tangling in her hair. The woman said nothing; she wavered in her own gusting bitterness, and she thrust denial at Melinda as if it was a shield.

Melinda opened her mouth and discovered that in this reality, she no longer had words. Her hand went to her throat; she directed her most focused thoughts at the spirit. *I mean it. You're hurting people. Do you even realize it? Do you know that you're leaving death in your wake?* She thought of Eileen, picturing her in the park—her spunky attitude, her lively nature. And then she pictured her as she'd last seen her.

The bitter breeze turned harsh with denial—and confusion, and then a swift, cool breath washed those images away, watercolor paints spreading into nothingness between them. Dismissed as meaningless, as insignificant.

*No. I don't believe it.* There was love in this spirit's song—there was longing. Anyone who could experience such longing wouldn't consider loss insignificant. She tried again, picturing little Saiyesha so still in the room beside this one, her parents and aunt looking down on her, the machines beeping all around her.

Anger lashed back at her; the breeze lashed back at her, whipping to a sudden wind and staggering her even in her crouched position. She raised a hand to shield her eyes; she tried to cry out a protest. The words lodged in her throat, a great big choking physical presence. She coughed on them, bent double, going down to both knees in the merciless, battering wind. Sound joined wind, words and notes so distorted she could barely recognize the familiar lullaby, and still she fought for breath—

*"Beautiful dreamer, wake unto me!"* Full-bore,

full-throated, four-part harmony, male voices strong and beautifully blended. They shattered the darkness; they turned the wind inside out. Melinda fell from one reality to another, faced with diffuse daylight that suddenly seemed bright, a hard linoleum floor, the sharp scent of hospital air. . . . She pushed to her feet.

A woman in colorful scrubs—a dancing crayon print—pushed through the half-open door. "What are you— Are you all right?"

Melinda took her first deep breath in what seemed like forever, and swiped at her watering eyes. "I'm sorry," she said. "I just needed a moment. I hope that's okay."

"There's a family lounge just down the hall," the woman said, not without sympathy. "You really shouldn't be in here."

"I'm sorry. I know. I just . . . got taken by surprise, if you know what I mean." *And I'm really pretty sure that you don't.*

"Take a moment if you need it," the woman said. "But try to use the lounge in the future, okay?"

Melinda nodded mutely, and if it looked like she couldn't quite manage her voice at that moment, it wasn't far from the truth. Words still seemed stuck in her throat; the spirit's bitterness seemed stuck in her throat, too, a sharp poignancy still squeezing her body. But when the crayon-festooned woman left—carefully leaving the door open a foot that said, *You can have a little privacy here, but don't get too comfortable*—it was to the barbershoppers that Melinda turned her immediate attention. "You guys," she said, keeping her voice low. "I just don't get you. Saving my butt one moment, putting me through the infinite falling nightmare the next. I know there are four of you, but could you maybe decide on one approach so I have a clue what to expect?" Silence greeted her. She bent to dust off her knees and added, "And thank you. I appreciate the help."

As if right on cue, noise erupted from next door. "You don't actually think she's doing you any *good*, do you?" In the background, Melinda heard a brightly sung version of "B-I-N-G-O," but Hayley's voice faded out, as did the sound of several people clapping gently along.

Whoa. Good-bye frying pan, hello fire. Melinda scrambled to the door and into the hallway, and found Travis Starcroft all but blocking Saiyesha's door.

"You don't look like a doctor," Saiyesha's aunt Rhonda was observing.

"He's not," Melinda said. "He's someone who's not very happy with Hayley. It's a personal thing."

"Is that what you call it?" Starcroft snorted. "Just because my daughter was in her care when she got sick? Or because she was pulling this same absurd play-music-to-make-everything-all-right spiel when Eileen died?"

Saiyesha's mother gasped.

Melinda lowered her voice, a respectful gesture. "No one said it would make everything all right. We hoped it would help, and you still don't know that it didn't—or that it wouldn't have made more difference if you'd done it all along."

Saiyesha's father came to the doorway, indicating the hall—tall, imposing . . . a quiet lion, inspiring the first flash of doubt on Starcroft's face. Melinda moved right out of the way, meeting Hayley's eyes with a little shake of her head—a stay-where-you-are signal. This man, she thought, wouldn't let his own issues interfere with what might possibly help his daughter.

"Listen," Ted said, moving in close to Starcroft. "I get what you've lost. But you won't talk like this in front of my little girl." He sent an encouraging smile in to his wife and her sister; the women fussed with a loose band in Saiyesha's hair. "Maybe this will help, maybe it won't. But it's *doing* something, man, and it's going to help *us*. Already I've seen my wife smile. That's worth something, too. Why would you even think of interfering with that?"

Melinda crossed her arms, lifted an eyebrow at Starcroft. *Go ahead. Explain your way out of that one.*

Starcroft pointed a finger at her. "She's not official. She's no one. It's not right, that she should—"

"Give people hope?" Melinda said. "Volunteer knowledge I think will help? Knowledge that can't possibly *harm*?"

"It's a scam of some sort," Starcroft said, working up to righteous anger. "It's got to be. Eileen died before you could get around to asking us for whatever it is you want, that's all; but you're getting to these people early. You're just here to prey on them."

Saiyesha's father shifted a wary look her way. No man wanted to be made a fool when his family was vulnerable.

Melinda held up both hands. "Nope," she said. "In fact, I've done what I came to do, and I'll leave you and your family to your privacy. Just . . . don't give up on her, that's all I can say. Keep that music playing. It could be more important than you know. And if you have any questions, if you need anything, please don't hesitate to give me a call. I'm at SAME AS IT NEVER WAS antiques in the square."

"I don't know what to say." Ted shifted uncertainly—ready to be back in the room with his family, after a hard look at Starcroft. "Except thank you, and we appreciate your good thoughts."

"I hope it'll be okay if I stop by later, to see how your daughter is doing," Melinda said. "I know it might seem unusual, but as I said . . . this is close to something I'm dealing with, too. I'll try not to intrude."

Starcroft snorted. "You see? She's not done here after all."

Ted turned his hard look back on Starcroft. "You," he said, "need to talk to someone. Your pastor, your shrink. But not here outside my daughter's room." And to Melinda, he said, "We'll see." And he left them both to return to the room, where he quite deliberately turned the music up a notch, kissed his wife on the cheek, and bent to wrap his hands around Saiyesha's torso through the sheets, tickling her gently.

Hayley took the cue beautifully, murmured farewells that could be seen but not heard over the music, and joined Melinda in the hallway—albeit not without a wary look at Starcroft.

*Ignore him.* Definitely the best policy. The man couldn't control someone who wouldn't engage with him. She headed back down the hall for the elevator, passing bright rainbow murals with pots of gold and butterflies and random flowers and grinning frogs. "Thanks for your help," she told Hayley, though it took determination to pretend Starcroft hadn't followed them. "I needed to have a discussion with someone. Well, I *tried* to have a discussion with her."

"You mean—?" Hayley's eyes widened, and the impact of Melinda's unspoken words genuinely drew her attention from Starcroft for the moment.

Melinda nodded. "One and the same. I didn't learn much, though. She's bitter about something, and she's definitely searching for something. She doesn't have a very good sense of her self . . . she's not good at communicating." She shook her head, stabbing at the elevator button even as they reached the door. "I just don't know what she's looking for . . . I have no idea why she's doing what she's doing." She shifted as they waited for the elevator, putting her back to Starcroft. He hovered, a little too closely for politeness, but she'd expected that. "Hayley," she said, "I don't really think this is relevant, but . . . have the Starcrofts lost anyone recently? A family member, a close friend? Someone either of them works with, or even a friend of Eileen's?"

"How shameless *are* you?" Starcroft burst out, overriding anything Hayley would have said. She cast him a frightened look and closed her mouth.

"Not as much as some," Melinda said coolly. "I also wasn't talking to you. Hayley?" *Come on, Hayley, answer. Don't give this man the power over you.*

Mute, Hayley shook her head. She finally managed, "Not that I can think of."

"You need to stop this," Starcroft said, moving around so he could look at both of them—still too close. Melinda caught the eye of a staffer hovering not far off, a mature woman with a slight frown and a very clear awareness that this man was pushing boundaries; she was already exchanging glances with another scrub-dressed young woman making notations in a chart at the floor station. Best not to escalate this—although if it weren't for the entire floor's awareness of his loss, he might already be facing several implacable nurses. He showed no awareness of the potential, however. "You need to leave my family alone."

"Mr. Starcroft, you're the one following *us*," Melinda pointed out. The elevator finally arrived; she held back a step so Hayley could scoot on board, and then entered the car. Starcroft would have entered on her heels, but the elevator doors slammed abruptly shut in a fashion no elevator door was ever engineered to do, startling him into a shout as he jumped back. She thought his toe might have been pinched.

At least, she hoped so. But she bit her lip on a smile as she turned to the elevator-riding boy. "You really should be more careful," she told her new friend. "But thank you."

# 8

"Is this guy gonna be a problem?"

Chilly spring night air surrounded Melinda
on the porch swing, but so did Jim's arms.

She didn't want to say it, but lying wasn't something they did to each other. And the moment she
started was the moment he would no longer be
able to trust her with the intensity of what she did,
and how it had come to intrude upon their lives.
So she answered honestly. "I don't know."

Jim tensed, of course. He stopped breathing for a
moment, although he probably didn't know it. She
quickly added, "He's grieving. He's a controlling
man, and with Eileen's death his life is out of control
in the worst possible way. Plus, I think he was spending a lot of that controlling energy on Hayley—and
she's gone, now, too. For years she's lived with them,
and now she's staying with a friend. Looking for
work, looking for a new place to live."

"Mel, I know you're trying to help, but . . ." He shook his head; the motion tickled the back of her neck, and she snuggled more firmly against him. "Don't get caught between those two. It doesn't have anything to do with your ghost."

"We don't know that." But the words were automatic, because as much as she spent her time helping the dead, she was herself very much alive . . . and very much appreciative of good friends and good people.

"Mel," he said.

Their words sat in the darkness for a moment. No porch light tonight, just the delight of bright stars visible unimpeded by big-city lights, spring peeper frogs warming up in soggy ditches by the road, and a screech owl off in the neighborhood trees wondering if it was all alone. Then he tightened his arms around her. "Do you know how very obvious your stubbornness is?"

"Every bit as obvious as it was before you married me," she said promptly—a challenge. *You knew what you were getting into, mister.* But almost instantly she regretted the words, the tone. "I'm sorry. I just really don't know where I am with this one. I'm frustrated."

"You sure you don't want to stay here this weekend?"

"What?" A little jolt of disappointment rocked her. "Don't you want to go?"

He laughed. "Are you kidding? A weekend up-state with my girl? I just thought you might want to look into the Starcroft . . . maybe find out more about this other little girl's family."

She relaxed, if only a little. "I do need to find out more. But the Starcrofts . . . that's a kid-gloves-only situation, and, according to Hayley, they haven't lost anyone recently. If there's someone further back than that, I'll need to do some digging. And Saiyesha's family . . ." She shook her head. "Travis Starcroft pretty much put an end to any questions I might ask them, at least for now. My best bet is to start with some online archives, and I can do that on the road."

"Mm," he said. "The best of both worlds."

"I'm sorry," she said ruefully, another apology in a matter of moments. "As getaways go, I guess it'll be more multitasking than vacationlike. But I'm sure we can find an opportunity for French toast. I bet we can even find an opportunity for whipped cream."

He moved his mouth close enough to her ear so his breath tickled. "With or without the French toast?"

She giggled at that, and rubbed her arms—carefully, around the bruises—at the goose bumps he raised. It seemed to satisfy him; he relaxed back into the porch bench, smoothing her hair from behind until she leaned into his hand and wished she were cat enough to purr. He sounded more relaxed, too, as he said, "It'll be good, I guess, to clear some of this up—to pin down just what this ghost wants from these people."

"I'm not sure she wants anything," Melinda heard herself say. She heard how strange that sounded and quickly added, "I mean, I'm not sure this is about *them*. I think maybe they're as incidental as I am."

"What do you mean?" He didn't like categorizing her as *incidental*, that was clear enough. "Eileen Starcroft is dead, Mel—that's hardly incidental. And what happened with you at the park the other day . . . don't even tell me—"

"I didn't say it wasn't *important*," she told him. "And it's just a feeling, but . . . she's made no attempt to interact directly with either family, just like she's never come directly to me. And seriously, I don't think she was very happy to realize I was trying to grab her attention today. She sure doesn't want my help."

"I guess it doesn't really make any sense to assume she's attached to any particular kid, when so many of them have been affected in one way or another."

"Now you're thinking like me," Melinda said with satisfaction. "That's all we really know for sure—she's got some sort of interest in kids. Pre-K, kindergarten . . . young first-graders like the ones

Ned is helping. Possibly little girls, but we don't even know that for sure. It could just be that Eileen and Saiyesha happened to be vulnerable to her. There certainly isn't any blood relation between those two."

"So she's not talking to you, and she's not related to the two girls who got sick, and she's spread her attention over the entire county of kids. Not much to go on. You got a plan?"

"The plan," she said firmly—perhaps more firmly than necessary, as the lullaby drifted through the background of her thoughts and she resisted it, grounding in the here and now of the porch and in the song of the peeper frogs—"is to go upstate for the weekend. Because I've done what I can for Saiyesha, and I'll do background work on the road, and I think Rick Payne will keep chewing on the big picture now that he's seen the spooky, zombie preschoolers. And meanwhile I've got this quartet of ghosts getting impatient with me." She held up her braced wrist. "*They* quite obviously want my help. They just don't seem to be able to break from their sheet music to give me a clue."

"Then we'll go find one," Jim said promptly. "And at least I'll have you to myself while we're driving."

Famous last words. Really, he should have known better. Because even with the laptop tucked away, with the mysterious pied-piper-ghost effect fading as they put miles between the packed-up Outlook and Grandview, with Melinda tucked in behind the passenger's-side seat belt while Jim himself pulled driver duty by dint of winding roads and two working wrists . . .

Even then, she got that look.

Not the blank, terrifying look from the park. But there, in the middle of pondering what light romantic comedies might be on the B&B cable offerings, came that certain *listening* face. The pondering face.

Light romantic comedies . . . not really Jim's thing. But if it meant snuggling up in the privacy of a cozy getaway room, he'd definitely make it his thing. At least for this weekend. And so he said, "What about *Shakespeare in Love*? I bet we could rent it. Watch it right on your laptop, even."

"Ooh, that would require some close quarters." She said it in her suddenly thoughtful voice, the perky one that always made him half suspect that she would then suggest they plot to take over the word while they were at it.

After all, she'd already accomplished so many other unlikely things. What was one little old world takeover in the light of the apparent conspiracies going on beyond the dark side, the strange events tangled around first Romano and then Gabriel, and the deft way she'd handled all the backlash in between? Spirits gone angry, spirits fighting the lure of the Dark Side, spirits playing with powers they shouldn't have. Spirits doing stupid things, like pitching Melinda down a flight of stairs.

*She could have broken her neck.*

But she hadn't. And she had that look on her face, staring out at the winding road to their small-town destination. Something on her mind . . . an idea about to come through that would resolve some big piece of this.

Well, even if he didn't quite have her all to himself, he still had her to watch. Take over the world, indeed. Pinky and the Brain had nothing on Melinda. So it didn't particularly take him by surprise when she pointed out a little state road that peeled away from their highway route and said, "Would you take that road?"

There wasn't enough time to question it and still make the turn, so he concentrated on safe navigation first, and then, as he straightened out the wheel, asked, "Why, exactly? Or did you plan to take the whole weekend just to get there?"

"Can't do that," she told him, straight-faced. "I guaranteed the reservations for tonight."

"Okay, then. Give."

"It's my BGPS system." She held that straight face for only a moment longer, and then it broke into a big grin, because she could see him just biting his tongue on that whole BGPS thing. "Barbershop GPS. I think they're playing hot and cold with me."

"You're kidding," he said. "We're navigating by the you're-getting-warmer system?"

She threw her arms open to an invisible audience and burst into song. "Won't you come home, Bill Bailey?" And then paused, her head tilted slightly. "You know, that's really quite a bawdy little song, if you actually listen to it."

"No kidding," he said, quite possibly a bit flatly.

"Oh, don't feel left out," she said, affectionately chiding—which she instantly made up for by putting her hand on his leg. "You know you don't really want this stuff going on in your head."

"You're so right about *that*," he said, not as under his breath as he'd meant it to be. But a moment later he shrugged. "Well, we're good on gas, and we've got plenty of road food."

"We'll watch *Shakespeare in Love* tomorrow night," she promised, and patted his leg. "And did you happen to pay any attention to just what I packed?"

That got his attention—her tone of voice more than the words. "I know it was heavy," he said, speaking as the person who'd carried the suitcase downstairs and tossed it into the back of the SUV.

"Well, I wanted to have choices," she said, sounding very wise at that. Wise and wicked. And the look she gave him from beneath those long lashes—also wicked.

He briefly clenched his jaw. "This is *not* the way to keep me casual about any extended side trips. And looking satisfied—that's not going to make it any better."

"It makes it better for me," she noted, and her smile also looked satisfied.

Probably fortunate that they came to a T-intersection that demanded attention. "Ask your BGPS which direction. Given that I have all the incentive in the world to head for the four-lane and a nice quick trip—"

Her smile faded into concentration; she briefly bit her lip. "Unfortunately, they want something to react— Oh, wait, I know. Tip the wheels right, then left."

At least there was no one behind them. Jim did as instructed. "Just so you know, barbershop guys, I'm humoring you here. Speaking man to man . . . this would be a really good time for you to take a break."

"Turn right," Melinda said. And, so innocently, "I don't think they're listening to you."

Jim grumbled something deliberately obscure, because he knew it would make her laugh, and it did. And he sighed to himself, and tucked away all his impulses to pull the SUV over to the side of the road and behave like a fifteen-year-old, and followed her directions as the roads grew narrower and higher and twistier, well into the Adirondacks. Grudgingly as it was, he had to say, "Okay, this *is* a prettier drive than going straight up Route 87 and cutting over."

"Isn't it, though?" The happiness in her voice warmed him—and the relaxation there. Here, she wasn't on guard against the lullaby music, that which had dogged her dreams for so many recent nights. Even if she'd found the iPod—and packed it, just in case—he couldn't imagine that quality sleep came with music pounding in her ears—for soothing music didn't counter the lullaby factor. It had to be rousing. He'd found her listening to *Phantom of the Opera* for starters . . . and then, a long-time favorite, *My Fair Lady*. Albums that had enough energy to counteract the lullaby, but not so much that she'd never sleep past them at all.

Thinking of it, he'd wandered away from the nature of their travel here—the swoopy roads, the narrow lanes, the guardrails set right up against the asphalt with no longer any room for a shoulder. It came as a surprise when Melinda frowned and said, "I think they want you to slow down. Either that or their batteries are running down."

"Okay, *that* I would like to hear," he admitted, doing as instructed.

She wrinkled her nose. "Not so much," she told him. "At this point they're pretty loud—and they're enthusiastic enough so they're not really hanging together any longer. It's getting a little chaotic, not so easy to follow."

"And just exactly what is it you think they're doing?'

She glanced at him in surprise as they slowly took a corner. "I'm pretty sure they're taking me to where it happened. To where they died."

"Mel . . . it's a stretch of road."

"I know that. You know that. But to them it's a very meaningful place. They may hope that I'll discover something here. They may find it acts as a catalyst, where they can finally communicate with me in something other than songs. Though 'By the Light of the Silvery Moon' is seriously romantic. I think I'm going to have to go download-hunting when this is all over." She hesitated, covered her smile with her hand, and then explained out of the corner of her mouth, "They're pretty smug about that."

"They can afford to be." They, after all, were the ones calling the shots. "Are we still crawling along at this pace? Because if anyone comes around that curve—"

To his astonishment, Melinda interrupted with a short shriek, scrunching down in her seat with her hands over her ears. With his own hands full of driving, all he could do was reach over to grip her shoulder. "Mel!"

It was short-lived, whatever it was. She emerged

from her protective position—warily, her eyes opening into a cautious squint. Upon finding them right where she'd left them—if somewhat farther down the road—she straightened and said, "That was *really* unpleasant. You sure hit a nerve."

"I didn't know they were paying any attention to me," he admitted. They sure hadn't heeded his little man-to-man plea. "What happened?"

"I'm not even sure—except it was really loud and not a single note was in tune with any other note." She gave an exaggerated shudder. "Just be grateful you couldn't hear it."

"Always," he murmured. "Are they still here? Or are we on our own?"

"On our own for the moment," she admitted. "If you're worried about our speed, you might as well take it up a little. That could be it for the day, for all I know." She reached for the seat side pocket and pulled out their map. "Might as well see if I can find us." She sat back and looked around. "Wow. I can't say as I'm sorry they're taking a break. I was so busy listening to them, I didn't even see this place. How gorgeous!"

"You know, we should come up here more often," he said. Plenty of lakes for fishing, plenty of grandeur for the eyes, trails for hiking . . . even this drive was a feast, taking them through the worn, age-old mountains covered with green leaves and dramatic gray granite outcrops, with enough little roadside waterfalls to keep him on the lookout for more. Sparse traffic left the narrow road free of distractions, other than the need to navigate the sharply winding asphalt and avoid scraping the bumper on the guardrail when things got really tight around the outside curves where the road fell away. He glanced at her and clarified, "I mean, come back for some real camping, not just our little trek to the forest outside Grandview."

"It's pretty there," she protested. "It's close."

"You mean it's close enough to escape home if the nights get too cold."

"No, that's not what I meant at all." She gave him a haughty look. "That's what *you're* for."

"Okay," he said. "Good answer."

"I meant it's close enough to escape home if you don't catch fish for dinner, or if I have a sudden need to tend antiques."

He spared the road his attention long enough to give her a glance and a promise. "I'll convert you one of these days."

But he'd lost her attention again, and she leaned forward against the seat belt. "Hey, look at this."

Back to the journey, then, where he found them coming up on a scenic overlook, an unusual bit of width at the road's shoulder, where the land jutted out to offer an extensive view of jumbled green mountains and the deep mysterious crevices where lakes and waterways gleamed. And he knew the look on her face, so he slowed even before she said, "Here . . . there's something here."

He might have asked her about their barbershop guides, had he not seen the tortured twist of the guardrail at the far end of the overlook area—it caught his eye, held it. He'd responded to far too many accident scenes not to recognize the mayhem wreaked upon stolid metal by a hurtling vehicle. But he didn't begin to anticipate Melinda's reaction as he pulled off the road.

The moment the right front tire left asphalt for gravel, she gasped—a terrified noise, and when he looked her way, he found that familiar expression—the one that meant she was somewhere else, maybe even some*when* else, reacting to someone else's distorted memory. He'd been there . . . once. When Eva Turner had reached out to him after her death, remembering his kindness when they were both but teens. She hadn't quite known how to communicate with him, and he sure as hell hadn't known how to hear what she was saying, and the insertion of someone else's memories into his own stream of thought had purely blown him away.

Melinda had grown up with such things. Melinda—beautiful, headstrong woman now absolutely grown—left herself constantly open to such things. And so he wasn't surprised by the gasp, or by the fear behind it, although he didn't think she was responding to cacophonic music this time.

But it took him entirely by surprise when the gasp led to a shriek led to a full-throated scream led to scrabbling at her seat belt. "Get me out, get-meout, *getmeout*!"

"Mel!" he said, his gaze darting between the rearview and the overlook, riding the tricky balance between pulling off road with enough speed to avoid getting hit from behind and not so much speed he couldn't get stopped in time at all. Except by then she'd freed herself from her seat belt with those fumbling hands, hands so frantic they acted as though they'd never even touched a seat belt before this moment—and she'd started in on the door. "Mel, no! Mel, you can't—"

She could. Even as he aimed the Outlook for the best possible path and slammed his foot on the brake, even as he abandoned the wheel to dive sideways for her, she'd somehow blindly—still shrieking mindless phrases—managed the damned door. He flung himself across an empty seat, his fingers barely whispering against the thin cotton weave of her spring top even as his foot remained jammed on the brake. The Outlook rocked to a jarring stop and bounced back slightly; the remaining guardrail groaned.

And Melinda was gone.

# 9

Trapped. Trapped in *the car and careening straight for the guardrail. Adult voices shouted at one another; alcohol made the air sting. She had to get out before the car went over, because it was going over, it was, and no one was doing a single thing to stop it and Mommy, Mommy! Mommy I need you! but not in words, because who had words? And so she did her best to escape that rolling death trap of metal and rubber, scrabbling in every way to find freedom but instead falling, falling, falling—*

Fetching up against something hard with such a thump all the air whooped from her lungs.

"Mel! Don't move, Melinda! Don't— God, don't move!"

She ought to be able to make sense of this, but she just couldn't. Not with the ground tilting beneath her and cold metal at her back and the fight to get air. Instinctively, she reached for less precarious ground, her fingers digging into dirt; air whooped on its way back into her lungs, and fireworks sparked against grayed-out vision.

"Don't move!" Jim said, closer now—and it was the panicked note in his voice that finally got through to her. *Jim Clancy doesn't panic.*

Normally, neither did she. But this wasn't a ghost-given vision, and it wasn't a dream. This was real. As real as falling down a flight of stairs. The fireworks died from her vision, and now she didn't dare open her eyes. "Jim?"

"I'm right here, Mel." Loose dirt trickled down over her hands; his voice didn't seem far, if strangely flat. "Don't move. Don't open your eyes. Just think about it, and tell me—are you hurt? Does anything hurt?"

She didn't move. She didn't open her eyes. She dug her fingers a little harder into the moist, mossy north-side soil, and she thought about it. "Nothing that wasn't already hurt. Bruises. But I don't under—" And then she shrieked again, for strong hands snatched her up, making no bones about it, one on her upper arm, one deftly snagging her jeans waistband, both jerking her several feet so she arced up through open air and then—she opened her eyes just in time to see—bringing her down right on top of Jim. Flat on his back, he instantly released her, but only so he could wrap his arms around her and hold her tight, so tightly she could barely take advantage of that precious, hard-won breath of hers. "Jim," she said, with barely enough breath, "what—"

He silenced her with a fierce kiss, his hands planted on either side of her head—a plundering, romance-book kind of kiss. By then neither of them was truly breathing, and if Melinda hadn't been so completely baffled, so entirely confused . . .

Not to mention extremely aware of their very public roadside display . . .

She rested her forearms over his upper chest, smoothed a smudge of dirt away with the hand that wasn't in a brace, and said, "What *happened*? What did you just—?"

A car pulled up on the other side of the SUV; a window rolled down. A man's voice said, "You folks okay?" and said it with the kind of tone that left all sorts of other things unspoken. Things like, You folks know you're in full view of the road?

Melinda rolled aside; Jim rolled to his feet. "We're good," he said, moving to the front fender of the Outlook so the vehicle wasn't blocking their exchange. "We were admiring the view . . . and my wife slipped, there, where the guardrail is down."

*I did what?* For the first time, as she climbed to her feet, Melinda looked over to the side, where the earth fell away and the guardrail folded back. She bit back her gasp as she quite suddenly realized . . .

She'd been over that edge.

She eased closer, found the scuff of her body's imprint in the dirt against the guardrail, well past where it twisted away down the steep drop . . . and just happened to be close enough to the ground to catch her up. No wonder she hadn't been able to make sense of the world; no wonder it had all seemed atilt.

*Because it was.*

She looked herself over, found her long sleeves torn but her skin remarkably whole; her jeans had a single rip strategically placed over one butt cheek. Great. Well, at least she had that nice heavy suitcase full of choices.

*I did this.* Fingering a tear in her sleeve, she forced herself to put all the pieces together. She'd been stuck in ghost-vision, and she'd panicked her way out of the vehicle—the *moving* vehicle—and rolled right over the edge of this. She shuddered. *No way around it. The edge of this cliff.* "Not smart," she muttered to the barbershop guys. "Who's going to help you if you keep throwing me down stairs and out of moving cars and over the side of a mountain? I get it, okay? It was a terrible, terrible thing. But you're not helping me to help you. I still don't know what's holding you back. Frankly, I still don't even have a clue."

Resounding silence. If they were here, they weren't admitting it. "You guys," she muttered.

"The Jekyll-and-Hyde ghost quartet."

From behind her, the conversation became louder. "Yep," the man's voice said, "this is the place, all right." She turned to join them, double-checking her shirt—no tears where she *really* didn't want there to be tears—and brushing off some remaining dirt. "You were really lucky," the man told her, admonishment in his words. *Stupid tourist, what were you thinking?*

"I really was," she agreed readily. "Did I hear you say this is where that terrible accident happened?"

"Near a month ago," he agreed—an older man, with an older-model little pickup. Flannel shirt, khaki trousers, multipocketed vest—he could have stepped out of an AARP outdoor-activity brochure. "I'm surprised you folks heard about it, though."

"It came to our attention," Jim said drily. He picked something out of Melinda's hair—she didn't even want to know what—and his gaze lingered on her just enough to let her know the charade of this conversation, of making light of what had just happened, was killing him, and that he truly just wanted to scoop her back up and hold her and hold her and . . .

She certainly knew the feeling. There, behind the front end of the Outback, she took his hand and twined her fingers in his; he gave a grateful squeeze of response. She said, "They were a barber-shop quartet, right? Four of them?"

"In the van, sure," the man said. He reset his hat—a definite fishing look to that hat, just as his small pickup had several rod cases secured in the back. Retired to fishing, if Melinda had to guess. He said, "I don't know who all was in the car. They weren't from around here, that's all we heard."

"There was a car?"

The man gave them a skeptical look. "Whatever came to your attention wasn't all of it, ayah? It was a head-on in the fog." But he grew more thoughtful. "Truth is, they didn't make such a big deal of that. Not sure just why. Ongoing investigation, no doubt. But people died that night, that's for sure."

"Probably no way to keep quiet the loss of an entire quartet on the way to a performance," Melinda said.

"Probably," Jim added under his breath, "pretty easy to keep people focused on that part of things, once the inevitable happened and it got out."

"It doesn't make much sense." Melinda wrapped her hands around her torso against the sudden chill that came over her. Was it her imagination, or was there fog wreathing up around her feet? "What could they have to hide?" She looked over at the man; he'd leaned on the truck hood for the duration. "Did they say who was at fault?" None of the scant articles she'd found had pinpointed even that much detail, but she wasn't about to let him know she'd done that much looking. It invited question.

"Nope." The man looked at her with some curiosity anyway. "You got an interest?"

"I've been listening to a lot of barbershop music lately," Melinda said, far more truthfully than she would have preferred. "The whole thing just seems to have struck a—"

"No, no, no," Jim said, already groaning.

"Chord," Melinda finished. And then, contrite, "Sorry. Dark humor." Ghost whisperer humor. The kind that got her past moments when she realized the current spirits hunting help had also very nearly killed her.

"You're gonna pay for that one," he told her, an undertone their Good Samaritan—or perhaps just a nosy Samaritan, given the apparent circumstances when he'd pulled up—couldn't have heard.

But the nosy Samaritan wasn't paying any attention. His neck had gone ruddy red, his expression stiff. "Y'know, you really want to be careful with what you say hereabouts. You never know who you're talking to. And this has been real hard on ol' Dick's wife—they were on the phone when it happened."

"You knew them," Melinda said, taken aback by the wealth of information she'd just been given, as well as the inadvertent effect she'd had on this man. "I'm sorry . . . I didn't realize."

"Lotta people around here knew them. It's a small kind of place. Dick was the bass, as it happens. Good man. They were all good men, all too young."

Melinda found herself momentarily lost in her mind's eye. "Dick . . . the bass . . . the mustache?"

Jim gave her the slightest nudge. Too late, of course.

The man's eyes narrowed. "Are you newspaper folks?"

Melinda laughed, and gestured at herself—at the two of them. "Do we *look* like we're from a newspaper?"

"Just because you're dumb enough to walk over a cliff doesn't mean you don't dig dirt on people for a living." Definitely not friendly any longer.

"Okay, point there," Melinda had to admit. "But I swear to you . . . we're not here to dig up dirt. We really are just a married couple here to follow up on some personal matters and spend a romantic weekend at the High Peaks Lodge in Otigwa. And boy, I sure hope they have a hot tub, because after that, I'm gonna need one."

"It's a small kind of place," the man repeated. "No one's going to like it if you cause trouble."

Melinda put up her hands, a no-way gesture. "Last thing on my mind, trust me." Even if she knew all too well that *causing trouble* was a not infrequent side effect of helping the spirits who had come to her.

"Uh-huh," the man said. He nodded at the edge

of the overlook, where the guardrail twisted away. "Watch your step, then." And briskly returned to his truck and threw it into reverse, the little engine whining in protest at the speed.

Melinda looked out over the dramatic mountainous vista—full of life, full of green and running water and living things—and blinked watering eyes against the incongruous juxtaposition of all that had happened in the past few moments. Jim slung his arm around her shoulder and they stood in silence a moment, long enough for those moments to sink in, until Melinda was ready to take a deep breath and move on. Then he gave her shoulders a squeeze and said, "Seriously. You okay? We weren't moving very fast, but you still just bailed from a moving car."

"Seriously," she said, "I am. And surprisingly. These guys . . . they protect me from the influence of the pied-piper ghost, and then the next moment they're so . . . *careless* with me."

"*Let me call you 'sweetheart.'* . . ."

She turned, pouncing on them, finding them out near the road with no concern for the sparse traffic passing by. "No!" she said. "You can't! Not right now! Not until you start explaining. What is it you need from me? Why did you bring me here? What were you thinking, to put me in that kind of danger?"

Hands to their hearts, they pleaded with her

through their music; she crossed her arms and drew her line in the spiritual sand, glaring at them. With performance-worthy expressions of woe, they flickered away.

*Oh, good job. That really accomplished a lot, didn't it?*

Jim rested his hand at the back of her neck. "Mel . . . I thought you told me that earthbound spirits don't always have a sense of those things. That they're too self-oriented to realize what effect they're having on you—or if they do, to care about it."

She wanted to stamp her foot. Dammit, she *did*, right there in the dirt and gravel. "They don't, not always," she said, her voice tight and frustrated. "But these guys . . . these guys *do*. These guys have a very good sense of themselves, of who they were when they were alive—they seldom even manifest with their injuries. They show an excellent awareness of what's going on around them—at times I'd say they've even been mischievous. The only off-kilter thing about them is that they've never spoken. It's only the music—it's always all four of them, singing together."

"That and tripping you down stairs and sticking you into ghost-vision situations that send you over the edge."

"Yeah," Melinda said, giving the overlook a dark glance. "Right over the edge."

# 10

HIGH PEAKS HAD no hot tub. . . . Melinda settled for a thorough massage by the world's best husband, after a shower to get rid of the last of the overlook's dirt. The shirt went into the wastebasket . . . not salvageable. She'd find a way to save the jeans. And tomorrow, she'd look up Dick the bass with the mustache guy's wife. But for now, she was ensconced in this delightful little log cabin with all the charm of the backwoods and all the luxury of hot running water and modern fixtures, not to mention a sinfully comfortable bed. "Have I mentioned lately," she murmured into the pillow, totally surrendering to the strong, capable hands currently working up and down her back, "about your being the world's best husband?"

"Three times in the past ten minutes," Jim said. "But it works for me. Have I mentioned what a coincidence it is that you brought this lotion thing?"

"Don't be silly," she told the pillow. "I *always* have lotion."

His hands left her back for a moment while he reached over her. "'Vanilla and lavender luxury massage bar,'" he read. "'Soft and sensuous.'"

"So I think ahead. So shoot me."

"You must be kidding. Just don't blame me if I get caught sniffing your neck in public."

"You haven't done my neck yet," she pointed out.

He set the box aside, rubbed his hands together to warm them. "That," he said, "is not going to be a problem."

Dick Berg's house wasn't hard to find, just at the edge of the small Adirondack town—a sweet little ranch in a quiet neighborhood, with plenty of attention given to flower beds and the mature trees shading the yard. The garage stood separate from the house, though at one point an enclosed breezeway had been constructed between them; now it was covered in years of ivy growth, and made a column of green between the two structures.

Melinda stood at the curb beside the Outlook while Jim came up beside her, and contemplated her best approach. *Careful,* she thought. *Tread lightly.* And then, "Are you sniffing my neck in public?"

"Mm," he said. "Oh yeah."

"Behave yourself," she said. But she didn't mean it, and she was smiling as she led the way up the cracking, moss-edged sidewalk to the front door. Here, the house lost its cheerful air; here at the door, a black ribbon hung beside the happy little painted sign: DOREEN & DICK BERG. Melinda hesitated—but only until she heard faint humming in the background—not the pied-piper lullaby, which she seemed to have left behind in the Grandview area, but a four-part harmony—gentle, sad. Wistful, even. *Were you* all *married?* she wondered. Would she need to go to all four wives before she could understand this?

And would the community even let her? Because for sure she'd get in only two visits before the others knew she was coming, if that.

*So do this right. Do this so they* want *you to talk to them, if that's what it takes.*

The door opened before her. She could see the mustached bass with this woman—a short, healthily plump woman with shoulder-length dark hair and bangs. A claw clip drew the hair from the sides of her head and attached it haphazardly at her crown; she wore little makeup, and otherwise presented herself in the classic dressed-down, outdoorsy look of the area—docksiders and blue cotton slacks and a pretty flowered thermal shirt under a stylish vest with fancy quilting. Probably in her mid-forties, she looked fresh and attractive . . . or she would have, had her face not been drawn and her eyes so shadowed with grief. She took one look at them and said, "I'm sorry, I'm happy with my own religion," and started to close the door. She might have done it, too, if Melinda hadn't burst into laughter—that surprised her, and she stopped long enough to take a second look at them.

"I'm sorry, too" Melinda said. "I didn't mean to laugh. But"—she spread her empty hands—"no handouts here."

Behind her, Jim sounded apologetic. "Nothing here," he said.

Startled into bluntness, the woman said, "Then who are you?"

"Actually," Melinda said, "I'm an acquaintance of Dick's. My name is Melinda." And then, because things could go so quickly wrong here and she'd had women make the wrong assumption before, she quickly added, "And this is my husband, Jim."

"You . . . both knew my Dickie?" She didn't quite believe it.

Melinda couldn't blame her. Looking at the charming, well-loved house, looking at the personable, well-loved woman . . . the couple probably hadn't had a lot of secrets from each other. "Not Jim," she said. "Just me. And . . . I find that I have some questions about what happened to him. I was hoping you could help me."

The barbershop quartet popped up right behind the woman—*right* behind her, arrayed around her as if offering a private concert for five. "*Hello, my baby,*" they sang, bawdy and raucous, but gently . . . softly. Crooning the words. "*Hello, my honey . . .*"

The woman stiffened slightly; her eyes widened. Then, quite firmly, she stepped outside and closed the door behind her, as if she could leave whatever effect they'd had on her inside the house behind her. They took no notice of the door, of course; they followed her right through it, all their attention on her—humming, earnest. They thought she could help, all right. Doreen's closed expression made it clear she didn't feel the same. "We shared most of our friends, Melinda. It's a small town. You might have noticed."

"I did, in fact," Melinda said, somewhat ruefully. Otigwa was a gentle, pleasant town—but smaller than Grandview, and clearly everybody knew everybody else. Not to mention what they were doing, who they knew, and probably where you were likely to find them at any given time. "Truth is, I know Dick from the road. From his performances. All of the quartet, really."

"You're telling me you're a fan," the woman said flatly.

"He sings the classics," Melinda said easily. And then, on impulse, she echoed the song the quartet was singing—the same inflections, the same atypical crooning for that piece. Gently. And as she sang, the woman gasped. Her eyes filled with tears, and she abruptly turned away. The quartet hastily backed up so as not to overlap her; they stopped singing and appeared to be holding their breath. Old habits . . .

"Stop," Doreen said, her voice muffled. "Please."

Melinda let her voice trail away. "Doreen . . ."

Doreen whirled back around, anger closing down her features—and just enough wonder to keep her in the conversation. "That's how Dickie used to sing that song to me. No one else sings it like that—they all sing it the same way that cartoon frog does. All energy, all cocky. Only Dickie could turn it into a love song. How—" Her voice broke; her anger turned to pleading. "How could you even know? That was *my* song. Only for *me*—"

"It's still only for you," Melinda told her gently. "I only know because I've heard him singing it for you." She hadn't known, going in, if she'd tell this woman about the quartet, about their lingering spirits. She always had to feel her way, to see if those left behind were receptive, if they were ready. Even so, she could never be sure. It was always a leap of faith.

It was only fair, she supposed, given the leap of faith she was asking in return.

And now Doreen just stared at her. She'd taken a step back; she'd cycled quickly through relief and straight on into wary. "What do you mean?"

"Doreen . . . I can hear him singing it for you right now."

"Oh!" Doreen's hands closed into tense, reactive fists; her mouth flattened. "Oh, how cruel you are! I can't even imagine what you're thinking, coming to my home to say such things!"

"I'm thinking that I can help," Melinda responded quickly. Quickly, because now was the moment she either moved fast or lost so much ground it could take days, even weeks, to regain it—and she didn't have that kind of time. Not if the quartet was willing to fling her down stairs and over cliffs and who knew what else. Not when she had the pied-piper ghost to deal with while she was at it. "I'm thinking that you must have loved him very much, and it's clear to me that he loved you. And I know that sounds crazy, but I've come all the way from Grandview to try to help him and his friends, because I *can* hear them, and I can see them, too."

Doreen looked straight up at Jim. "You really should keep her at home. And get her some help while you're at it."

Jim laughed, short but heartfelt. "I count myself lucky to be here with her." His hand squeezed her shoulder.

"I have a gift," Melinda told her. "Sometimes, when people die, they aren't ready to move on to the Light. There's something left undone in their lives, or some message they need to give to those they've left behind. I call them earthbound spirits, and they come to me for help. Except this time it's all four of them—the quartet. And in order to help them, I need to get a better idea of what happened that night."

"If you're on such good speaking terms, why don't you just ask them?" Doreen snapped.

Melinda laughed in quick surprise. "Oh," she said, "I *like* you." And as Doreen blinked in surprise, knocked off balance from her skeptical resentment, Melinda hit her casual stride. "Unfortunately, it doesn't always work that way. Spirits are affected by the circumstances of their death—how long it's been, how sudden it was, how prepared they were—that sort of thing. In this case, the quartet really seems to be bound together; they aren't coming to me as individuals. And they've never been able to do anything but sing to me—songs from their repertoire, I'm guessing."

"Such as . . . ?" Doreen said, eyes narrowed. The look didn't suit her face; it was a face that wanted to smile, to open the door to her home and welcome visitors to refreshments and a seat on the back patio to watch the birds flit across the lawn and the deer nibble at the edges of the lawn.

Melinda smiled. "According to what I've heard, they were really drawn to the classics—late last century, early this century. 'Hello, My Baby,' of course, but also 'Daisy Bell' and 'Beautiful Dreamer' and 'Let Me Call You Sweetheart'. . . is that enough, or should I go on?"

Doreen crossed her arms, the picture of an unconvinced woman—but a woman who also wanted to believe.

"Doreen, I'm not here to cause you trouble, or to hurt you. Your husband and his friends are stuck here, and they can't tell me why. Helping me to help them might give you some peace about his passing."

"Nothing will make me feel better about losing him," Doreen said, lashing out—offended and stricken both.

Melinda didn't need Jim's reassuring touch at the back of her neck, much as she appreciated it. She'd been through this too many times before; she knew it wasn't about her. "You might be surprised," she said gently. "And even if that's true . . . don't you want *him* to find peace?"

Doreen huffed out air in offense. "And if you're just full of baloney?" she said. "If this is some strange deluded game you're playing?"

Melinda shrugged. "Then I can hardly cause them harm, can I?"

Quite abruptly—quite unexpectedly—Doreen

shifted her attention to Jim. "And what about you?"

What she loved about Jim most was that although she had no idea what he'd say, she also had no concern for it. She knew it would be honest and still kind; she knew it would be supportive. So it didn't surprise her when he said, "I'm afraid this isn't my thing. I can't tell you too much about it."

"You really count yourself lucky to be here? You should be ashamed, enabling this craziness. Of standing there behind her while she comes to me when it's already so hard—" Her voice choked off; she couldn't continue.

"Ah," he said, understanding gentling his tone. The quartet crowded around Doreen, full of curiosity; Doreen shivered and buffed her arms. No doubt she thought the shade was chill on this spring day. "The thing is, Doreen—I hope it's okay if I call you Doreen—I see what this does to her. I see what she goes through to help these spirits— and to help the people who love them. So yeah, I'm standing here behind her. And if you can just open your mind a little bit—if you can just believe in the possibility that she's seen what she says she's seen—then you might be surprised at how lucky you count yourself that she's here, too."

*Ooh, baby,* Melinda thought. *You can sniff my neck anytime.*

"Just . . . pretend," Doreen said slowly.

Ah-ha, the first hopeful sign. The quartet crowded back around her, eager and encouraging. "*Daisy, Daisy, give me your answer, do!*" And of course Doreen shivered, anxiety mixing with her already churning emotions; she didn't have the means to interpret what she felt, other than to be overwhelmed by it—and she was only one short step from fleeing the whole thing.

"Guys," Melinda said sternly, "you really aren't helping. Give her some space. All of you."

Abashed, they backed away—but they still looked like kids at Christmas, barely containing themselves.

"I'm serious," she told them. "I can't figure what's going on if you don't give me the chance. And we won't even talk about that thing with the overlook."

"Oh my—" Doreen cut herself off, closed her eyes, gathered herself. "You're talking to them."

"Yes. They're here. They're really eager for me to understand what's holding them back . . . to help them. I wish I knew why they can't just tell me what they need . . . or at least *try*."

Doreen laughed shortly, and harshly. And this time she did say, "Let's go around back." And though she didn't offer them anything to drink, she seated them at comfortable patio furniture in the sun, and she said, "You have to understand my amusement, dark as it is, at the notion that those four could tell you anything as a group. Because while they made beautiful music together—the most incredible harmony—" She stopped herself, and looked more closely at Melinda, who was slipping out of her sweater to enjoy the sun on her shoulders, twitching the straps of her sundress—all big splashy red flowers on a field of white—into place. "But then, if you've heard them, you already know that."

"I'm no expert when it comes to barbershop music," Melinda said, struggling a little to get the sweater over her brace. "I had to look up the songs they've been singing before I knew they were all basically turn of the century. But they certainly sound wonderful to me."

"That's the ironic part. For all their harmony, once you got them together to discuss anything else, there was no chance that all four would agree on any one thing." Doreen frowned at her. "You've certainly taken a beating lately."

Melinda glanced down at her bruised arm, suddenly remembering why she'd worn that baby-fine sweater in the first place. "Spirits can be confused," she said, as obliquely as possible. Doreen certainly wasn't ready to hear that her *confused* husband and his cohorts had not only hurt her, they'd seriously endangered her. "Sometimes their first efforts to communicate don't turn out well." She rested the sweater back over her shoulders. "Can you tell me what you know about that night?"

"You really think it's important?" Doreen asked, looking doubtful again.

"I do." Stay firm, stay confident. "They worked pretty hard to take me to the spot where it happened."

"Just pretend," Doreen repeated slowly . . . but she seemed to be saying it to herself. Convincing herself. The quartet had relocated with them and now slowly closed in around her, eager for her words. Melinda gave them a warning glance, and if they couldn't bring themselves to back off, they at least stopped advancing—and she thought again how Jekyll and Hyde they were. How responsive, and then how invasive.

Doreen closed her eyes. She said, "They were arguing, as usual. About nothing of any great consequence, also as usual. But it had gotten really out of hand. They were on the way to the performance; they were dressed and ready. And it was one of those foggy nights, and I said to Dick, 'Behave yourself, all of you, because Craig needs to pay attention to the road.' And they didn't, and look what . . . look what happened. . . ." She shifted, digging into her front pocket for a tissue.

Behind her, Dick scowled; he punched the tall man in the arm, who gestured and in turn shoved the balding man, and soon enough they were tight-lipped and red-faced and their background humming had gone completely dissonant. "Gentlemen!" Melinda frowned at them. "Have a little respect, will you?"

"Don't even tell me." Startled from her search for a tissue, Doreen looked up at her. "They're acting like little boys, aren't they?"

"Like bad little boys at that," Melinda said. "Poking, pushing—I think it's just as well that they can't talk to one another right now." Even at that, she winced at the clash of their music—and she didn't fail to notice that as they broke off their squabbling in sudden consternation, their injuries reappeared. Fog twined around Melinda's feet; the odors from the accident—the burned flesh, the acrid rubber and insulation and what would have been toxic gases had they actually been real—those things stung her nose and eyes, biting at her concentration as well. "Please," she said, barely restraining herself from waving away the smoke that Doreen wouldn't be able to see, "what else do you know about what happened? You said they were arguing . . . how. . . ?" Because they were on the phone, that's how—the man at the overlook had said that much. But Melinda knew better than to scare her off by dropping that little nugget—that they'd already talked to someone else about Dick's accident. That they'd talked about Doreen, too.

"Can you believe it?" Doreen sighed. "I was talking to Dickie on the phone. They were arguing about some detail in the program, something they'd already hashed out half a dozen times. Craig was driving because he had the van, and they had some stage props to lug along. Dickie wanted my opinion about something—you know, I'm not even sure now what it was. Should they enter small to tall or tall to small? What had they done last time, I think, was the question." At Melinda's expression, she said, "No, seriously."

A glance at the quartet confirmed it. Abashed, as if they couldn't quite believe it now.

"And I said it again, *behave yourselves,* because the fog—and that *road* . . . but they just got louder and then Jay must have seen the car, because he shouted something, and Dickie swore and then he started to say that he loved me, and then all I could hear was this horrible crashing and screaming and crunching. And then it was quiet." Doreen said it all very quickly, as if it was the only way to get it out at all, but there were tears streaming down her cheeks. Behind her, the quartet had gone gruesome with their injuries, wreathing Melinda in the aftermath of fog and odor.

She coughed, and couldn't help but wave at the smoke—but only an absent gesture, as she took in the entirety of what Doreen had experienced, exchanging a glance with Jim to see if he'd understood the same thing, and seeing her own horror reflected in his striking blue eyes. "You *heard* the accident?"

"His cell stayed connected," Doreen said, glancing at them as she seemed to realize her own tears. She went hunting for the tissue again. "There, that's what I know. I don't see how it possibly helps anything."

"You'd be surprised," Melinda said, slowly gathering her thoughts, glancing at the barbershoppers. They watched her keenly—dripping blood, their burns smoking, their bones exposed. They watched her with hope. "I know they were arguing—that they weren't in a good place with one another even as they died together. I know that their argument might have played a part in the accident. But I also know that the other car . . ." She glanced at Jim. He was the one who responded to accident scenes; he was the one who saw these things as a matter of course.

And he nodded. "It sounds like the other car was in their lane," he said. "Whether it was just stopped there or whether it was coming at them. It took them totally by surprise."

"The police haven't said a lot about it," Doreen said. "But they told me it wasn't the guys' fault. I don't know about that. Maybe if they hadn't been all caught up in that silly argument, Craig might have been able to handle it all so they didn't die, even if the other people *were* at fault."

"Or maybe not," Melinda said, looking at the quartet . . . searching them for reactions. Because she might understand a little better what had happened that night, but she still didn't know what was holding them back.

"What about the other people?" Jim said. "Did the police ever say anything about them to you?"

Doreen sighed. If she still harbored disbelief, she was doing a pretty good job of pretending. "Not much. They cleaned the accident site up pretty quickly, and there's been little in the news—I certainly don't have any inside information. I asked about them—asked if there were people who needed support, you know—our church would have reached out to them, found a way to put up family if necessary. And they really just put me off. Nicely, but that's what it was. And otherwise, they really don't know exactly what happened. Just an accident in the fog that sent both cars over the edge."

Melinda glanced at Jim; his frown told her that he wasn't buying it—but that he kept quiet told her his disbelief didn't lie in Doreen. The woman had nothing to gain, as long as she was talking to them, by playing cat and mouse with the truth.

"Can you do it?" Doreen asked suddenly. "Can you help Dick find peace? And his friends?"

"I get the feeling that with these guys, it's pretty much a package deal. And I'm not sure what's going on just yet . . . but I'll keep working at it."

"But *can* you."

Okay, if she was still pretending, she was doing a darned fine job. "Let's just say I don't have a long line of disgruntled spirits still trailing me around," Melinda told her. "And I have no intention of giving up on your husband and his friends."

In the background, the quartet broke into triumphal humming, and Melinda couldn't help laughing. "I'm sorry, I'm sorry," she said helplessly at Doreen's startled look, gesturing at the four even though no one else would see them. "It's like having my own personal background sound track."

Doreen shook her head. "That's possibly the most convincing thing you've said yet. I'll be darned if they didn't used to do that sort of thing to us wives all the time." She hesitated. "Jay wasn't married, but . . . what do I tell the others? About what you've said to me?"

"Whatever you're comfortable sharing." Melinda couldn't bring herself to say it out loud, that whatever held these four men back didn't have to do with family. Doreen had been important because of the information she'd had, but Dick didn't appear to have any significant matters to resolve with her.

No, it was about the guys. Somehow. And she had more pieces, but they still didn't quite go together.

She'd figure it out.

Somehow.

\* \* \*

Although first, they needed to eat dinner.

"Yum," Melinda said, savoring one last bite of the brownie sundae she'd shared with Jim. Ooey gooey fudge, chewy brownie with tons of nuts, smooth French vanilla ice cream. "Let's have another."

"Don't even tell me you have room for another bite." Jim had given up ten minutes earlier, in the wake of his giant slab o' steak.

"There's a reason I had that seasoned chicken salad," she said, quite smug. "Planning ahead. But no," she then had to admit, "I have no room for even one more bite. I just thought . . . we could look at it for a while." She picked up the bill that had discreetly appeared at the edge of the table, reluctantly putting the spoon aside to deal with money matters. "Well . . . maybe tomorrow. Maybe one for the road. After we've walked this one off. Though I swear, if you see any big potholes, keep me away from them! There's no telling what these guys will throw me down next."

Jim cleared his throat. "Yeah," he said. "About that . . ."

She looked up from her wallet. "About potholes?"

"About the accident, actually. Mel, I know this is small town—hell, Grandview is small town. But when people die and there's a question about road safety or equipment failure or cause, there're accident investigators all over it. Whatever they told Dick's wife, the cops here know what happened at that scene. Skid-mark angles, skid distance—unless there's something really hinky involved, an experienced eye can read the scene pretty clearly."

"Hinky," she said.

"Hinky," he repeated firmly. "That's official rescue jargon, and I'm standing by it. The point is—"

She got the point. "Why wouldn't they tell her?"

He shook his head. "Because there's something else they don't know, maybe. Something else they're still looking into, so they're playing the whole thing close to the vest."

"If that's part of what's holding them back, it's not going to be easy to sort it out." She poofed out a resigned breath. "It would be *so* much easier if they'd talk to me. Because right now I'm really thinking their sticking point has to do with the circumstances of their death, but what they need for resolution . . ." She shook her head, tucked money away in the leather bill wallet of the cozy little restaurant, and stood. "I don't know . . . I may need to come back here, but at this point I think I'm at a dead end."

He gave her a wary eye as he stood.

"Oh, don't look at me that way. You know perfectly well I'd go talk to the police if I thought it would get me anywhere. But right now the vibes seem pretty locked down on this one, don't you think? I mean, maybe later, but . . ."

"Yeah," he said. "I know." Getting involved with the police wasn't ever first on her list—not with the risk of exposure it entailed.

"So that leaves the evening to . . . well, to *us*," she said, and headed out through the restaurant, flashing him a teasing look. "Gosh darn it. *Bo*-ring."

"I," he told her, weaving through tables behind her and pretty much as close as he could get, "am gonna make you so very sorry you said that."

Melinda laughed, skipping on out of the restaurant in front of him and down the rustic steps, heading out to the roadside path that led back to their lodging. But her smaller size and nimbleness in the tight quarters of the restaurant made way to his longer legs on the path, and her dress sandals, flats for walking or no, were no match for his sensible guy shoes. He readily caught up to her, grabbing her up by the waist to swing around on the path with great triumph as if that wasn't just what she'd had in mind in the first place. It all dissolved into a great deal of giggling and stumbling and taking turns pulling each other along the path, paying no attention to the late-Saturday-afternoon traffic along Otigwa's single incoming road.

At least, not until one of those cars pulled onto the shoulder slightly ahead of them, light bars and paint job declaring official nature and intent. And if the lights weren't flashing, the deputy who disembarked looked serious enough to make up for it.

Melinda's silliness evaporated; Jim put out a hand to steady her as they both abruptly came to a halt, laughter fading. The deputy left his car and crossed the uphill strip of ground cover between the road and the footpath, and Melinda decided that if he didn't know what poison ivy looked like, she wasn't going to be the one to point it out. Or maybe he just thought it wouldn't dare affect him. He had that look about him. Confident, fit, wearing the uniform well.

"Evening," Jim said to the man, the question in his voice.

*I'm making assumptions. It's not always about me.* In fact—"This *is* a public path, isn't it?" Melinda looked back to where they'd started, as if they might have missed a sign. But the High Peaks manager had directed them here, so surely—

"No problem, ma'am," the deputy said. "Everyone hikes this path. I just happened to spot you here—you do stand out some." Then, as if realizing that might not sound quite appropriate, he nodded at her braced wrist. "Between that and the two of you, I mean."

"I'm sorry . . . I don't really understand." Though she was afraid she very much did.

The deputy rested his thumbs on his belt buckle, an assured stance. "You've been asking questions about a recent accident."

Doreen wouldn't have said anything . . . not unless she'd had a complete change of heart since earlier that afternoon. But the fisherman from the previous afternoon . . .

Jim must have come to the same conclusion. "We were at the overlook," he said. "We did talk to someone there, but only because he stopped to ask us questions."

*Ooh, once again my hero.*

"You were looking the place over, I understand," the man said. He was old enough to be seasoned—to be good. Laid back and confident, not the least thrown off by Jim's response, and not bothering to dispute it. "Looking over the actual accident scene, as well."

Melinda didn't have to feign astonishment. "You mean over the *edge?*"

"My wife *fell,*" Jim said. "It scared the hell out of both of us. If that fellow had come along a few moments earlier, he would have known that. Excuse me for saying so, Officer, but it sounds as if someone's trying to make trouble for us."

"I'm not sure I understand the problem,"

Melinda added. "It was a conversation at a public scenic overlook."

"Mm," the man said, unaffected. "It all seems a little more deliberate when you add in your visit to Dick Berg's widow, doesn't it?"

Well, darn.

Jim's slight shift in weight wasn't a necessary warning. She knew when it was time to say nothing. No one would care about the overlook if there wasn't an ongoing investigation into the accident; no one would care about a visit to Doreen Berg. Just as the scant details of the newspaper accident report had implied, there were definitely things going unsaid here in the Adirondacks.

So she said nothing, and she waited. Quiet, calm . . . interested. Waiting for whatever else the deputy might say.

When he did speak, it was to change tracks entirely. "You staying here long?"

"Another night," Melinda said. "Our romantic getaway, believe it or not."

"You might do better to keep your curiosity to yourself," he said. "Otherwise, enjoy your stay here."

"Oddly," Melinda muttered as he left through the same poison ivy through which he'd come, "not as welcoming as we thought it'd be."

Her phone rang, startling her—she slapped her purse and then quickly fumbled in it, not missing the fact that Jim had put himself between her and the departing deputy. Not a whole lot more privacy, but every little bit . . . she finally retrieved the phone, frowned at the unfamiliar number, and flipped the phone open. "Hello?"

"Melinda? This is Hayley. I'm so sorry to bother you on your vacation—" Right. Such as it was. Falling over cliffs, upsetting widows, getting the warning eye from the local law, not to mention the we'll-be-watching-you vibes.

Well. There *had* been the fudge brownie sundae.

Not that Hayley needed to know about any of that. "Don't worry about it, Hayley," she said, catching Jim's eye and watching him react to Hayley's name. "What's up?"

"I just really thought you'd want to know . . . there's another one."

"There's— What? Another what?" But she was very much afraid she knew.

Hayley hesitated, made a false start sound in her throat, and then burst out with it. "Another child in a coma! Another little girl! I was here in PICU with Saiyesha—I was covering for her family, so they could go get a *real* meal, and they never want to leave her alone—and they just now brought her in."

Another little girl. Melinda closed her eyes, battling the hard despair in her throat. And then she said, as evenly as she could, "Did you see her? Does she have anything in common with Eileen and Saiyesha?" Not that the other two had much in common to start with. Age range. Being little girls in the first place.

"Age," Hayley said, sounding strained. "But she doesn't resemble either of the other two. And the family—they're lucky if they have health insurance. They look like they're going through a really rough patch. But oh, they love her to pieces, you can just see it—"

"Go to them," Melinda said.

"Without you?" Hayley's startlement came through the connection clearly enough, chasing away the grief of her fresh memories. "Oh, I couldn't—"

"Of course you can." No nonsense—no room for it. "I'm here; you're there. And you know what needs to be done; you're already doing it. You know what to say; you've already said it. What do the doctors think about Saiyesha?"

Hayley hesitated; her voice lowered, grew muffled—as if she was cupping her hand around the phone. "They won't talk to me, of course, but just from what I'm hearing between her mom and dad—compared to what I heard about Eileen— she's doing better than Eileen did. I mean, she's in the coma, but she doesn't seem to be losing ground as fast as Eileen. Maybe even holding her own."

"Wonderful! And *you're* doing that, Hayley. You can make the difference for this new little girl, too."

And still Hayley hesitated. One moment confident, the next a wreck . . . Melinda wanted to shove Travis Starcroft's face in what he'd done to this bright young woman. "You never mind *him*," she said, and she didn't have to say who she meant. "You never mind what he's said to you." Sudden inspiration struck. "Has he been in touch since I left?"

Hayley didn't respond. It was enough.

"Hayley, you can do this. That little girl is depending on you—*I'm* depending on you. I'll be back tomorrow, and I'll do what I can—but you don't need me. Not for this." No—what she needed was to grab this ghost's attention again, to figure out just what was going on. To put a *stop* to it.

Before any more children died.

And when she'd wrestled reluctant agreement from Hayley, when she'd flipped the phone closed, when Jim had taken her into his arms in full view of the passing cars, pressing his cheek to the top of her head and stroking her back in full understanding of what that phone call had meant . . .

"I thought it was the right thing to come here," she said, her voice so choked it barely came out at all. "I thought I needed to get the barbershoppers off my back so I wouldn't end up at the bottom of our stairs again."

"You did what you thought was best," Jim told her. "And for the record, I thought it was best, too. You can't help anyone if some confused quartet is flinging you around."

"I really can't," she agreed, in a watery sort of way. "But . . . now there's another little girl in the hospital. And now we're suddenly on that deputy's watch list."

For though he hadn't bothered to ask their names or their contact information, she had no illusions—their destination on this path would be obvious enough. It would be as easy as walking into the lodge and asking.

If he wanted to find her, he'd find her.

If he wanted to follow her to Grandview, he'd do that, too.

# 11

Delia was all bangles. She'd come into the store looking much the better for the weekend off, relaxed and refreshed and humming to herself.

Not, Melinda was relieved to hear, the "All Through the Night" lullaby. Or even "It's a Small World After All." Just something pretty and light, and it went perfectly with her pale green keyhole-gathered top and the rows of delicate silver bracelets on her wrist, and the spiral earrings with little jade drops sprinkling down. She'd drawn her hair back with soft twists, applied makeup with a light touch, and all in all fit right into the spring day.

"Wow," Melinda said when she walked in the door. "I wish I was you right now."

"As if I believe that," Delia said, but of course she looked pleased. And then she took a closer look at Melinda as she secured her purse behind the counter. "Hey, that drive upstate was supposed to be a *getaway*. Romantic, even. Don't tell me you two have forgotten how to do fun and romantic already?"

"Not a bit," Melinda said promptly, but she glanced down at herself. "Too bad it's not Halloween. I could draw on a few slashing pirate scars and be done with it."

"Another couple of days and those bruises will hardly show." Delia crossed her arms, eyes narrowing critically. "Although I swear there weren't as many when you left here on Friday."

"You're not supposed to be able to tell!" Melinda had gone for a gauzy lace shirt over a flirty camisole, long-sleeved and still cool enough to look seasonal, all over a swirly skirt with tiny eyelet flowers that should have been distracting enough in its own right. Not a day for moving furniture or cleaning up dusty treasures.

"I'm a mother," Delia said drily. "Not to be fooled."

"There, see? We all have our own superpowers." Melinda's airy pronouncement would have come off with more flair had she not fumbled the pen cup with her braced hand and sent pens and pencils everywhere, but it was probably better that way; Delia burst out laughing and bent to pick them up—though her laughter didn't distract her.

"What did happen?" she asked. "More of the same?"

"I'm afraid so," Melinda admitted, deciding to leave out the part about stumbling into an ongoing investigation, and gaining more attention than she'd wanted on that front. "I'm calling them my Jekyll-and-Hyde barbershoppers. One moment so sweet, trying so hard . . . and the next, they put the whammy on me and try to dump me off some precipitous edge. That's official ghost talk, by the way. *Whammy.*"

Delia raised an eyebrow. "If you're not careful, you'll start to sound like your professor friend."

"Hey!" But, crouching with pens in hand and reaching for one just barely within reach, Melinda couldn't help but have second thoughts. "I really should go talk to him—see if he has any insight on these guys. Ghosts in batches . . . I'm not used to that." *Or to a lot of the things happening around Grandview lately.*

"Oh, hey," Delia said, standing to dump pens back into the cup, her expression growing more than serious. "Did you hear that there's another little girl in the hospital? It's hit the news, now— three of them is enough to get attention. Apparently they're calling in the Centers for Disease Control."

It hit her hard for some reason—crouching there, her hand closing around that last pen, her mind instantly going to the scene at the hospital that morning: early visiting hours, and her first encounter with the most recently affected family. As Hayley had said, they looked worn and weathered. They didn't spend money on vending and coffee machines, but had a thermos and some homemade trail mix there in the room. She'd decided on the spot to drop off fresh fruit from the square market the next time she visited—or to see if Hayley could do it. For although Hayley hadn't been there—on her way to a job interview instead—she'd left definite signs of her presence, and she'd obviously prepared the family for Melinda's visit.

The lullaby had surrounded her, had hummed through the hallways as if the entire ward had been dipped in melody . . . but the spirit had not responded to her entreaties.

And Saiyesha, she thought, had a gray tinge to her pretty chocolate skin that hadn't been there the last time.

"Melinda?"

Melinda made a wry face and stood, dropping the pens into place. "Sorry, I was just . . . I mean, yes, I know. I was there this morning. The CDC isn't going to do them any good, I can tell you that much. I just wish I could get this woman to talk to me."

"You mean . . ." Delia hesitated in an obvious search for words that didn't include the term *ghost*. "The one who sings."

"The ghost who's doing all this, yes. And I still

have no idea why. If Payne's pied-piper theory is anywhere near close, she's still got to have a *reason*. The original pied piper got stiffed, but—"

"Oh, no," Delia said, without really thinking about it. "This is a *mother*. She's not killing children out of spite."

"I— What?" Not that Melinda disagreed so much as she was taken aback by who was saying it.

Delia waved a generic gesture, flustered. "I mean, come on. The song you sang? This . . . *spirit* wandering around, having an effect on children and on little girls? It's a mother, you can bet on that. And she had a little girl, too."

*Ohh-kay. Go with the flow.* "And she's doing this *why*? It's hardly motherly instinct to put little girls in the hospital, especially if she's identifying with them somehow. Or to kill them—Eileen's funeral is tomorrow."

But Delia was not to be budged. "Maybe from her perspective, that's not what she's doing."

"Well, *huh*," Melinda said, brows raising as she rocked back on her metaphorical heels. "From the mouths of babes." And then, quickly, "Oh—I mean, no offense. In the earthbound spirit sense, I meant. I mean, half the time you can't even talk about it, but that . . . that was pretty insightful."

"It comes and goes," Delia admitted. "It's like I get used to the idea, but then it's quiet for a while and I have to start all over again, you know?"

"Kinda not," Melinda admitted back. "It's been part of my life for so long, it's hard to imagine not *knowing*. But it means a lot to me to be able to talk about it with you." And then, because she also knew better than to get too direct about such things for too long, she brushed her hands free of imagined pen and pencil dust and stepped over to the clothing rack. "Now . . . let's play with clothes, shall we? I'm thinking that it won't take much to give this area an entirely different look—maybe put a few pieces in that wardrobe and leave it open, change out the dress on the dummy—"

"Oh!" Delia raised her hand. "Dibs on the dummy dress-up!" But she stopped, looked at the hand, looked at Melinda. "I did not just say that."

"Oh, you totally did," Melinda said, and laughed. "But I won't tell. Let's see what we can do with this place."

Delia emerged from the back of the store with a dress that had just come back with repairs—"Could this be more perfect?"—and set to work with the mannequin, clothing it in a sparkling peacock-design flapper dress. Shades of teal, gray, purple, black, and gold radiated in peacock feathers from a side-waist circle of sequins, covering the entire expanse of the dress. Heavy, swingy material . . . show-off material. Melinda hung a flapper head-dress with a peacock feather off the corner of the nearby open wardrobe door, and they highlighted carefully chosen spring clothing—big-buttoned Jackie-style coats in yellow; bright, modest sundresses from the fifties, a cluster of little girls' shoes hanging like fruit waiting to be plucked . . .

By the time they stepped back to admire their work, Melinda's stomach had gone growly and the shadows out in the square had shifted significantly. A stylish older woman wearing the yellow Jackie coat appeared long enough to stroke the real thing and give an approving nod. "*Nice job*," she said, looking at that whole corner of the store. "*Excellent taste, young lady.*"

"Thanks!" Melinda said, and then winced, giving a sideways glance at Delia.

"Never mind," Delia said. "As long as it was complimentary."

"She likes our taste." And Melinda turned to their new companion—not a solid ghost at that, but a wispy spirit whose edges trailed gently behind her—to ask if she could help, but the ghost anticipated her and shook her head.

"*You're up to your elbows, my dear. And there's nothing that ails me that a little courage won't set straight. In fact, seeing that coat . . . seeing it right out there in the open like that . . . I do believe I . . .*" But if there was a second part to that sentence, Melinda didn't hear it—suspected, in fact, that she would never hear it. Preoccupied, decisive in quietly classy fashion, the woman faded away. Gone,

Melinda thought, to do what she needed to do after all these years.

Sometimes it didn't take much.

"What?" Delia said, a stage-whisper kind of mutter. "What's that all about?"

"Actually, I don't think we're ever going to know." Melinda shrugged. "It can be like that sometimes. But hey, our first critic likes us. And here comes our second!" She nodded at Ned as he pulled the door open and ambled through—Village Java cups in hand. "Hey, Ned, what do you think?"

Ned hesitated, looking at Melinda, looking over at Delia . . . taking in their pleased expectation. A faint deer-in-the-headlights expression crossed his face. "About what?"

Delia motioned toward their redecorated corner with both hands, a *ta-da!* gesture if there ever was one.

"Um," Ned said.

Melinda had mercy on him; she swooped in, rescued the cups, and said, not so under her breath, "The clothes. We rearranged the clothing display."

Comprehension lit his features. "Oh, cool dresses," he said. "I mean . . . really cool. They look nice."

"That is so lame," Delia told him. "But for bringing coffee, you can have it. This time."

"And green tea for Melinda."

"And did you notice how I kind of had to reach *up* to get them?" Melinda said, sniffing each lidded cup in turn and handing the coffee over to Delia.

"My kid is *tall*," Delia agreed, switched over into proud-mom mode—but not one to be fooled. "But my kid is also not quite *this* thoughtful. 'Fess up. Did you bomb a pop quiz, or what?"

"Ooh," Melinda said. "She sees right through you. But thanks for the tea. It's perfect."

Ned scowled. "I did great on the pop quiz."

"But. . . ?"

He glanced from Delia to Melinda, who shrugged, and back to Delia again. "I quit the reader program."

"That's right!" Delia looked at her watch. "You should still be there! Ned, you loved that program!"

Another scowl. "That was before the kids got all spooky."

Melinda winced. She'd seen it, and she knew what was going on. Hard to imagine it from Ned's point of view, but . . . spooky just about covered it. "I might be able to help with that," she told him, "if you'd like to stick with it."

"But it's that teacher!" he burst out, and then made a face at his feet.

Delia had slipped totally into mom mode. "Did she say something to you? Because I'll talk to her if—"

"No, Mom, no," Ned said hastily, a clear note of panic there. "Don't talk to her. It's not about me. I'm fine. I just don't want to deal with her. Why would she want to be a teacher in the first place, if she doesn't even believe in the kids?"

*Believe in the*— Melinda had it. "Ah," she said, hating that she understood so readily. "They started talking about the music." They were slightly older than the pre-K kids Payne's friend was dealing with. More likely to talk about what they were experiencing.

"Yeah," he said, shooting her a grateful look. "And she told them not to make up stuff like that! As if she has a better explanation for what's going on with them." The gratitude shifted to startled realization. "You *know* what's going on with them?"

Melinda put her hand out, waggled it back and forth. "So-so."

Ned shot his mother a look, hesitated, and visibly decided against asking—later, Melinda knew. "Anyway, it just made me mad. Why would the kids make it up? And why would they all make it up at once? If they say they can hear this woman humming—"

"You're right." Melinda fought against the swell of protectiveness she felt for these children—the empathetic frustration. "They *can* hear her. And they deserve a little benefit of the doubt."

"Right!" Ned said. "I figure, when a little kid

tells you something like that, you should listen. It doesn't matter if you can't see it or hear it . . . it's important to them, right? It doesn't even matter if it's really real, not in the end."

"Oooh," Melinda said. "You'd better watch out, Ned Banks. I'm going to hug you!"

"Ah, you made him blush," Delia said. "Ned, I'm really proud of you."

He gave her the world's wariest look. "Because I . . . quit?"

"Because you care so much. But you know what?"

He shook his head, wary expression still in place.

"I would be even more proud of you if you went back there and told them you'd acted hastily, and you'd rethought it, and you hope they'll take you back."

"But, that teacher—"

"Exactly," Melinda said. "If you're not there, who's going to listen to the kids?"

"I—" Ned made a face, scruffed his hand through dark blond hair. "I didn't think of it that way. I just didn't want to be part of what she was doing."

"I don't think you have to be," Delia said. "That doesn't mean disrespecting her in her own class, or openly disagreeing with her. But you can still listen. Show those kids that not everyone is like that teacher."

"She's just scared," Melinda added. "But you can make the difference for the kids while she deals with it."

"Me, huh?" Ned said, thinking about it. He nodded to himself. "Okay, then. I can do that. Teen Reader Leader. That's me. Guess that was worth the price of tea and coffee." And with that, he headed for the door—but not without throwing over his shoulder, "Cool dresses, though."

"Nice try!" Delia called after him. And Melinda grinned, but her thoughts were already far away. Their brief visitor had said it quite succinctly—*"up to your elbows, my dear"*—Melinda could only hope that the pied-piper ghost showed up at Eileen's funeral tomorrow—that she could begin to get an understanding of what drove the spirit to steal away little girls' souls.

Before the rest of Grandview's children fell under her spell.

"I'm not sure I should be here." Hayley touched the French twist of her tightly contained hair, checking—again—for escaping hair. With her makeup minimized and her café-au-lait complexion muted beside her black dress, she looked small and uncertain. The sun went behind a cloud, instantly chilling the day and making Melinda glad for the vintage capelet she wore over her own crisp black dress.

Funerals, as it happened, were no stranger to her. Nor were the emotional conflicts that often came with them.

"How will you feel," she asked simply, "ten years from now?"

"If I don't stay, you mean?" Even Hayley's voice sounded diminished. Not from grief or loss, but from her concerns about the man who hadn't yet noticed their presence. "Terrible. But if I stay and cause trouble—"

Melinda cast her a wry look. "If there's trouble," she said, "I'm pretty sure you won't be the one causing it."

"I don't want to make this any harder for Maureen," Hayley said, and her voice finally firmed up.

"I know." Melinda sent an inner frown at Travis Starcroft. "But we'll give them a respectful distance. And the truth is, I can really use the help right now."

"In case . . . *she* shows up?"

"Exactly." And although Melinda hadn't mentioned it to Hayley, she hoped, too, that she might see Eileen. Just a glimpse . . . even in passing. Because she hadn't seen Eileen's ghost pass from her body at the time of her death, and she hadn't seen her since . . . and she didn't have a good feeling about it. The little girl's spirit could be trapped somewhere. . . . Until she got a better understanding of what drove the pied-piper spirit, she'd have no idea. She only knew that the girl's spirit had been missing in death.

Nor had she seen any sign of Saiyesha's spirit in her coma, or even the new little girl's spirit.

Melinda shivered again, shaken by a new awareness of the stakes surrounding this woman's ghost. *Are you here?* she thought, more of a calling-out than a question. While Hayley's attention was drawn back to the funeral and the diminutive coffin at the center of it, Melinda searched the grounds—the older section with its mature trees and impressive headstones, the newer grounds with more compact sites and still-shiny stones.

"*You looking for anything in particular?*"

The voice came from behind her, startling her; Hayley followed her sudden glance behind and gave her a questioning look.

"Be right back," Melinda told her, whispering in deference to the funeral in progress, even if they *were* far enough away so it didn't matter. And to the ghost who sat so casually on the headstone not far back, she said, "That's really rude, you know. Unless it's yours."

"*What? Oh, sorry.*" The man was string-bean lanky, dressed in cargo shorts and a lightweight, long-sleeve shirt, a plain billed cap on his head and binoculars around his neck. "*I've been here long enough so— Well, I've been here a long time. You get used to things.*"

"What are *you* looking for?" Melinda asked him, giving the binoculars a pointed glance, and then casting a look back over her shoulder at the funeral.

"*I— What? You think I'm just being nosy? Now that would be rude. Warblers, young lady, warblers! Don't you know this is the best place for them?*"

"Is that what you were doing when you died?"

"*Yes,*" he said, and smiled. "'*What a shame,*' *they said at my funeral. I don't know why. What better way to go? Heart attack out among the peaceful trees. But I really did want to see the Townsend's warbler, and you know, I still do. So don't talk to me about the Light, or worry that I'll get caught up in this other nonsense, this Dark Side business. I know what I want, and I'll go when I get it. But you, my dear . . . you're not here looking for birds.*"

Melinda gave a mental blink. Ohh-*kay*, then, this was one all-together ghost. "I'm looking for a little girl. This is her funeral, in fact. I'm worried about the state of her spirit."

He frowned, making his thin face look even longer. "*Is the Dark Side going after them so young, then?*"

She shook her head. "This is something different, I think. I'm also looking for a woman . . . she doesn't really come through clearly. She sings and hums to herself all the time—a lullaby. I think she's had an effect on this little girl, and I need to talk to her."

"*Now that, I'd remember. And I'd help you if I could. I mean, sure, I know why I'm hanging around, but that's my choice, and I'll be all right. But a little kid? No one should interfere with that.*"

Just as with the young man at the hospital. Whoever this pied piper was, she wasn't mingling with the locals.

"*Oh, hey, gotta go!*" The man reached for his binoculars, squinting off into the older section of the cemetery. "*Maybe this is it!*" And he disappeared, although she saw him pop back up among the distant tombstones, focusing his binoculars up into the trees.

"I guess that's really what you call a life list," she murmured, but she didn't watch him long. He was right—he knew what he needed, and he was going for it, and he didn't need her help to get it. Especially since she wouldn't know a Townsend's warbler if it landed on her hand.

Hayley made a strangled noise; Melinda turned back to her and followed her attention to the funeral, which was breaking up—and to Maureen Starcroft, who had quite clearly spotted Hayley. Both of them had, in fact. They exchanged a few emphatic words, and to Melinda's surprise, Maureen was the one who firmly shook her head, who put her fingers to her husband's mouth in a quiet but decisive gesture, and who turned to walk in their direction. She'd lost weight; she looked wan and frail . . . but her steps were firm.

"It's okay," Melinda murmured in reminder. "You were part of Eileen's family, too."

"Hayley," Maureen said as she reached them, and then hesitated there, as if she didn't really know what to say. Hayley took a half step forward, and Maureen blurted, "Thank you for coming, Hayley. I know it couldn't have been easy. I know Travis has been unpleasant. I hope . . . I hope things haven't been too hard for you."

"I had to come," Hayley said. "I just had to." And then she was crying, and Maureen was crying, and they clung briefly to each other while Melinda stood quietly, as unobtrusive as possible.

But soon enough they were talking again, and soon enough Maureen said, "I'm so glad you're trying to help those other families. Travis told me, of course. I don't think he expected my reaction." She saw the unspoken question in Hayley's expression and said, "I told him he needed to get help. That this loss would destroy him if he didn't. That it would destroy *us*."

"Do you think he will?" Melinda asked. She didn't bother trying to hide how strongly she agreed with Maureen's assessment.

Maureen shook her head. "I really don't know.

He still thinks he can *just be strong*. He has no idea he's *just being strong* all over everyone else."

"And you?" Melinda said quietly.

Maureen looked straight at her. "He's my husband. We've lost our child. He needs my support."

"Oh, Maureen," Hayley said. "Take care of *yourself*, too."

"I'm stronger than I look," Maureen said. Melinda could only hope so. Maureen's hands trembled constantly; so did her chin. Her face had no color; her eyes lit only intermittently with life. Even her hair—curly, like Eileen's—tumbled lankly around her shoulders. But what she said next surprised Melinda, and left her with an unexpected opening. "If there's any way I could help spare those other families what we're going through—"

"Maybe there is." Melinda said it quickly, not about to let opportunity get away. "I'm trying to reach someone I think can make a difference . . . and I'm running into some roadblocks. It's possible you might be able to help."

Maureen looked startled. "Really?"

Hayley looked just as startled. "Melinda, are you sure—"

"I'm sure," Melinda said. Give Delia the credit for that one, with her motherly instinct . . . a mother-to-mother appeal might be just the thing to reach a pied piper who didn't want anything to do with Melinda. "I've got to get back to the store, but I've got Delia covering tomorrow morning, too. . . . If we could meet at the hospital . . ."

"Tomorrow morning," Maureen said, and glanced back at her impatient husband. "Travis will be at work. I . . . I hate to go back to that place. But maybe it's something I need to do."

"If you mean it about helping to spare the other families," Melinda agreed. And then, when Maureen nodded, already growing used to the idea, Hayley turned on her—no doubt with words of dismay, with protest about springing the whole ghost thing on Maureen, the whole lullaby thing. Melinda cut her off with a short shake of her head. "We're running out of time, Hayley. You saw those girls. You know it, too. *We're running out of time.*"

And so were those girls.

# 12

MELINDA'S NOT GOING *to like this*.
Aw, hell, *Jim* didn't like it.

He pulled his truck into the driveway past her SUV, snugging it up close to the garage—and then just sat there a moment. There was no good way to break this news so it wouldn't be upsetting—or angering. Or more likely, both. So . . . before dinner? Not so good for the appetite. After? Melinda was just a little too good at spotting when he wasn't talking about something.

*Face it. No-win situation.*

A light tapping on the driver's-side window jumped him right out of his skin, and there she was, with just a little bit of grin at his reaction. "You coming in, or should I get creative with place settings out here?"

He hit the seat-belt release. "Much as I'd like to see that, I'll be coming in."

But by the time he gathered up his jacket and lunch bucket and exited the truck, she stood back with a slight frown on her face, arms crossed. Her toe tapped twice, then stilled. "Okay, mister. Talk to me. What's going on?"

*Aaaand, so much for* after *dinner.* "Have I ever mentioned," he said, "how damned cute you are in that dress, whatever it is?" Nothing but truth, that filmy thing with its layers and flounce. The sleeves ended just before her elbows and showed the remnants of last week's adventures with stairs and overlooks, but even those were fading.

"This old thing?" Melinda said. "And I mean that literally, of course. What we have here is a Victorian tea dress shortened after skirt damage, beautifully fashioned with layers of ecru cotton tulle. The floral sprig tulle top layer has panels of lace inserts and embroidered flowers, and the flounced hem border and bodice capelet are made from rows of decorative lace. *Like you care!*"

"Bare feet," Jim said, honest if desperate. "Cute toenails."

"OPI Melon of Troy," Melinda said sweetly. "Now talk."

Jim gave it up with a gesture of defeat. "Talked to some cop buddies today. Looks like our friends upstate actually checked on us."

Just the incredulous expression he'd expected, sweetly tilted almond eyes gone wide and angry, chin gone don't-tread-on-me—and the worry betrayed by the corners of her mouth. "They *what*? Don't they have anything else to do?"

"That's pretty much what I asked," Jim admitted. "Truth is, I got the impression my cop buddies were a little baffled, too. Hey—" This last because he'd seen the telltale glint of tears and knew them for what they were: frustration and helplessness. "Look, Mel, I don't think there's anything to worry about. The guys wouldn't have come to me if there was—they'd have kept it to themselves and looked into it. But you're still working on these barbershoppers, right?"

She nodded, lips tight. He reached out to cup her jaw, to run his thumb along the side of her mouth. "I just thought you needed to know. In case you need to decide about going up there again."

"Okay," she said, and nodded, chin still defiant as she processed the situation. "I hope I don't have to. But I will, if that's what it takes."

"I know." And he did, dammit. He knew she'd do whatever it took, because she always did. "It just seems like the rules are changing, y'know? You'd have time to figure this one out without thinking about going back there, if these guys weren't going into Hyde mode and dumping you down stairs. I mean, I haven't been in on this thing for very long, not compared to what you've done, but still. It didn't used to be like this."

"No," she agreed quietly, and some of the defiance made way for that little bit of truth. "Until we moved into this place, they'd never even come inside my home before. Now we deal with that all the time."

"Now *these* guys have thrown you down the stairs." He couldn't keep the anger from creeping into his own voice, as he spoke to the surrounding space in general, well used to the notion that there were spirits around whom he couldn't see. "A little more respect would be nice!"

"It's not like that," she said.

"I know, I know. They're too caught up in their own thing to understand what they're doing to you. And that was fine, when they didn't use to be able to— Mel!"

Because there she went again. Her gaze went blank, just an instant of warning; her head tipped back as her eyes rolled up. He dropped his jacket and the lunch bucket and swooped in to hook an arm around her waist just in time—down she went, bent back over his arm in an extreme dip. "All righty, then," he muttered, and scooped up under her knees, swinging her into his arms to tackle the porch steps, the doorknob, and the front door. "The question is, the couch or the floor?" Because the couch would be so much more comfortable . . .

But she couldn't fall off the floor.

* * *

*"No, no, no! I won't go!"* She fought the hands pushing her at the open car door—harsh hands, but hands that were careful to avoid bruising. Those hands knew tricks, though—fingers snarled at her hair, clenching . . . twisting. She wailed at the pain of it; the fingers eased just enough to silence her. "I hate him, I hate him!"

"Bob Gleason does a lot for us!" said the woman who should have been seeing to her welfare. "And it's no big deal—a freakin' couple hours of time, nothing more. Pictures, that's all. Big money. You owe it to us, Angie. You think that monthly check covers your expenses? That pretty dress we got you? Those school supplies? Don't make me laugh!"

*"Soft the drowsy hours are creeping, hill and vale in slumber sleeping . . ."* The words enfolded her, surrounded her, and before she knew it, she was in the car, she was buckled in, and they were driving, engulfed in fog and speeding blindly over familiar roads, and the fog took on a sharp-edged neon gray, bleeding the color from everything it touched and taking it into itself—spring green leaves and brown bark and caution-yellow road signs, all taken into the fog, all possessed by it. She looked down; tendrils of fog had made their way into the car, wrapping around her thin wrists and ankles like manacles. The fog went flesh-colored, the pale,

fair color of her very own flesh; it chilled her skin and twined around her throat in a thin but infinite scarf, and where it touched her deep brown hair, it darkened; it crept up each strand, sucking away color and sinking toward her scalp, and it was the very same way she felt when that photographer watched her take her clothes off and suddenly she couldn't *stand* it—

She shrieked and screamed and fought, flinging away fog like broken streamers of manacles. She grabbed at the wheel. "I won't go! I *won't*!"

Curses flew; they turned to bubbles of black fog splashing against the inside of the windshield; the car moved in abrupt slow motion. She had time to see the gap in the fog outside as it revealed the overlook, as it revealed their path across traffic straight for the guardrail. Time to see the maroon van come out of nowhere in the other lane, the stark horror on the startled driver's face laid clear through its sweeping windshield, the passenger freezing at the inevitability before them, a cell phone plastered to his ear. The absurdity of their red-striped jackets and their boater hats.

And in that instant, she felt only relief. *She wasn't going.*

And then came the fear, as the other driver cranked aside the wheel, desperate to avoid a head-on collision, and yet too little, too late; fenders clipped and crunched, and now both vehicles hurtled toward the guardrail and she scrabbled at her seat belt and she screamed and screamed and screamed—

The change in her breathing should have warned him. It had been uneven all along, while her hands twitched and her eyes moved under her lids as though she was dreaming. He could see it all clearly enough, holding her as he sat on the couch, her legs curled up against the cushions and her shoulders nestled into the crook of his arm.

He knew better than to believe she dreamed. But even when her breathing hitched, when she stiffened, he wasn't expecting the explosion into full-shriek battle mode—arms flailing, legs pushing against the end of the couch. She caught him a whopper on the side of the face before he captured her arms and still she fought him, and all the while he crooned her name. "Mel, Mel, Mel, honey—"

Just as suddenly, she froze, and he knew he had her back. Cautiously, she opened her eyes—she looked at her arms in midflail, at her legs shoving couch pillows onto the floor. "Oh," she said. "Wow." And then, as he released her, she looked at his face, and winced. "Please don't tell me I just did that."

"I'm thinking maybe I should have picked the floor instead of the couch," Jim told her, his hand going to the sting on his cheek; it came away smeared faintly with blood. "It's nothing."

"It's *not* nothing, it's—" She touched his face, mortified.

"Hey," he said, and squeezed her shoulders. "Where did you go?"

Her eyes widened; she pushed up from his arms and up from the couch altogether, suddenly brimming over with words and energy and gestures. "The barbershoppers!" she said. "It's not them! I mean, it *is* them but it's also someone else, someone from the other car."

"Wait," he said. "I don't understand. The guys . . . they're not the ones pulling the rug out from under you?"

"No! That's just it! That's why it seems so Jekyll and Hyde. I've been dealing with the same event, but for two different ghosts. Okay, for five different ghosts, but four of them were in the van, and then there's this girl in the car—"

It seemed about time to put his hands on his head to keep it from spinning. He couldn't imagine what it was like to be in Melinda's mind—although things seemed pretty clear to her right now. "Okay, so it's the girl who's been messing with you, and the guys have just been singing to you—they never dumped you down the stairs after all. Guess I owe them an apology, then."

A wry smile lifted one corner of her mouth. "I'm sure they'll understand. And get this—this is why the cops have been so antsy. The woman she was

with—not her mother, but some sort of guardian,
I'm thinking her foster mother—was taking her
somewhere for a photo session. My bet is the cops
are still looking for the photographer."

He shook his head. "Should I be following
this?"

All traces of that smile vanished, went grim.
"She dreaded it, Jim. She's the one who *caused*
the accident. I don't think she really knew what
she was doing—that she'd thought through what
would come of it—but she definitely did it. Her
thoughts, what she just shared with me . . ." She
clasped her arms around her torso, hugged herself. "Child porn. I think those pictures were child
porn."

"Whoa." He blew air through his lips, pulled
his hands down his face—thinking, thinking.
Thinking, *Damn, no wonder all the secrecy*, and
*Damn, they're not going to let up, either*. Mrs. and
Mrs. Perfect Small-Town Couple—à la Jim Clancy
and Melinda Gordon—were every bit as likely to
be running a porn site from their own server in
the basement as the obvious slimeball hanging out
near the school yards.

But Mel was thinking of something else entirely.
"It's no wonder she's been so difficult. When you
add the sudden, violent way she died to the horrors
she lived with . . . she's in no condition to communicate clearly. She's just stuck in that same moment

of terror, over and over and over. And the really sad thing is that for an instant, for just an instant, she saw the accident as a relief. A way out of what her life had become."

"Did they mistreat her as well?"

"Physical abuse?" Melinda shook her head. "I didn't get that impression. They—and I do think it was a couple—weren't exactly nurturing, but if she was bringing in money with her body . . ."

"Ah," he said, hating himself even for being able to voice the words. "Right. Don't damage the product."

"But this doesn't tell me how to help her," Melinda said—and then she stopped the whole conversation short by freezing in midstep, poised with her head lifted to the air. "Oh, no!" She dashed into the kitchen.

Only then did Jim notice a distinct aroma in the air, and the little dining table in the kitchen—the cozy nook table—was covered in heavy crockery dishes, not to mention the candles, the wineglasses . . . "Lasagna?" he asked, a little too much hope in his voice.

She gave him a knowing look as she pulled the oven door open and grabbed pot holders. "Secret-recipe lasagna, at that."

"Cottage cheese," he said, all knowing.

She briefly pouted. "That's not fair."

"Hey," he said. "Just because I'm a gourmet

at heart doesn't mean I can't figure out cottage cheese."

"Well, figure out *this*," she said, somewhat more smugly than made him comfortable as she set the glass casserole dish on the stovetop. Those words were about to lead to a scheme or a plan or a grand caper, he would bet on it. "I know who they were going to meet for those photos, and I bet the cops don't. I bet if the cops *did*, they wouldn't be poking around the local police to see what they can see, making us show up on all sorts of undesirable Persons of Interest lists that mean we won't even be able to fly anymore."

"Yeah," Jim said, sarcasm gently lurking. "Because that would mean your imagination isn't getting way out of hand here."

"I'm not the thing getting out of hand there," she said pointedly. She leaned over the bubbling pasta, cheese, and sauce, inhaling. "But the point is, I have the name."

He pulled the plates over, ready for serving. Big generous hunks of servings, if he had anything to say about it. "So you're going to call them?"

"Heavens, no. You think I didn't learn my lesson with the TSA?" She'd tried to warn them of the status of Flight 395, and then of course when the plane crashed, they'd come to her for answers. "I'll do it the old tried-and-true way. I'll find a public phone and I'll cleverly disguise my voice.

Or, oh!" She pointed at him in sudden revelation. "Even better, I'll have Rick Payne do it. He'll talk circles around them and they still won't know what he's saying, except for the part he wants them to know."

"You really think that's such a good idea?"

She waved away his concern. "Oh, I know he's a little intense sometimes, a little world-revolves-around-me, but he's too excited by seeing his studies come to life to do anything to jeopardize that."

Jim grunted, very guy. "As long as you put it in that world-revolves-around-him framework, I guess there's some comfort in that."

"The thing is," she said thoughtfully, sticking a finger smudged with sauce into her mouth for a quick cleanup, "that helps *us,* but I'm not sure how it helps Angie. That's her name, *Angie.* And I'm not sure it helps the quartet at all." She served up a whopping helping of lasagna for him. At about that point reality came crashing around him, and all he could do was stare, shaking his head ever so slightly. She stopped, poised with the spatula. "What?"

"Just . . . *this.*" He gestured at the cozy little table, the lasagna. "One minute you're stuck in someone else's memories—a *dead* someone else's memories—and the next we're sitting down to dinner. And I did mention that you look amazing, right?"

"You did. But you can say it as many times as you like." She gave him a look from beneath her lashes.

"Mel—"

"Hey." She served herself a portion half the size of his and took it to the table, sweeping her skirts aside to sit. "As for the rest of it . . . same old, same old, right?"

He sat across from her, grumbling under his breath. Words he was better off if she didn't hear. And a little louder, "Three ghosts at a time, all of them as intense as these three are?" Angie, the pied piper, and the barbershop set. "When children's lives depend on figuring out who the pied-piper ghost is and what she needs, and this Angie ghost dumps you down stairs to get your attention? No. Not same old, same old."

She shrugged, but her voice seemed smaller. "No. Maybe not. But I need you with me on this one. I can't manage, not if it feels like three ghosts and you, too."

"No," he said instantly. "Mel, no. That's not what I meant."

She took a deep breath, clearly putting herself in a different headspace. "Nooo?" she said, with just enough tease at the edge of her voice to warn him. Or entice him—he wasn't sure which. He wasn't, he was sure, supposed to know which. And he probably wasn't supposed to notice the grape she'd plucked from the bunch at the side of the table, big plump and juicy purple. Dessert, probably, mixed in with some whipped cream and yogurt concoction with chocolate sprinkles. If he was sure of anything in this continuing surreality, it was that there'd be chocolate sprinkles.

"Aw, come on," he said, letting just a little bit of his rising desperation sneak through as he put down his fork; he'd made pretty quick headway on that lasagna in spite of the circumstances. "It's not even three ghosts at the same time, it's *six*, and four of them are guys in suits serenading you at every opportunity."

"Ah-*ha*!" She flipped the grape at him. He was fast, but not quite fast enough; the grape boinked off his shoulder and splooged to a safe landing in his lasagna. "You're jealous," she said, quite smugly. "You're jealous of the dead barbershoppers."

"I am *not*." One had to take a stand. "Not jealous, exactl— Hey!" Another grape pinged off his chest. He caught this one on the rebound, popping it into his mouth and hoping he wouldn't suck up too much lint in the process.

"Jealous," she said firmly, and she had another grape ready.

"*Not*," he said, equally firmly—and then, as her fingers drew back in firing position, a hasty "*Left out*, maybe."

"Hey, there's enough of me to go around." She

left her half-eaten lasagna to walk around the table and around to the back of his chair, and he had to admit to qualms. That grape could end up anywhere.

But no, she pressed her cheek up against his on one side and wrapped her arm around his neck so the grape appeared before his mouth on the other side, and she said, "Finish your dinner, and I'll prove it to you with dessert."

His brains abandoned him. "I thought we were having grapes for dessert. With something. Grapes with something."

"We are," she said, and reached over him to snag the entire bunch of grapes. "Grapes, with . . . something. See you when you're done with that dinner." And she sauntered for the stairs, grapes dangling over her shoulder. He never would have believed it.

He still didn't believe it.

But he shoveled down that last bite of lasagna, he did a quick food-on-the-chin check, and he headed for the stairs.

And he locked the front door on the way by.

Melinda plucked a nightgown from the dresser drawer, choosing one by feel in the darkness and slipping it over her head, sleeveless lightweight cotton slipping down to her knees and swirling there. She found the thick bathrobe at the end of the bed and pulled it on, padding downstairs as silently as possible and—*mission successful*—without waking Jim.

But it wasn't so easy to sleep with a war going on in her head. The pied piper, as loud as Melinda had heard her yet—frenetic, almost, and no longer just humming her song and not quite singing it, either.

More like wailing it.

And the barbershop quartet had taken up the challenge, singing in full-voiced opposition; Melinda hadn't even had a chance to don her waiting iPod as she tucked up under the covers with Jim. And while he'd fallen asleep quickly enough once they'd relaxed into snuggling phase, Melinda spent a lengthy time staring at the ceiling with a cacophony inside her head.

Eventually, the contrast of his peaceful sleep— of their peaceful, private bedroom—with the very busy Grand Central Station effect in her mind grew too great to bear. And thus her clandestine exit.

Once downstairs, she poured herself a short glass of the wine they hadn't quite gotten to over dinner and pondered the house. Not the living room, she decided; conversation could wake Jim. And too cold, still, to take up residence on the front porch. And she definitely wasn't doing kitchen duty at this time of night, even if dinner and dirty dinner dishes sat out in all their glory, and the lasagna pan would have to be soaked for three days before she even tried to wash it. So into the den she went, where the TV stared blankly at her, a square dark spot in the darkened room.

The pied-piper ghost wailed in the distance of her mind, distorting the beautiful melody, distorting her hauntingly lovely voice. "I can hear you," Melinda said. "Can't you come and talk to me? Won't you let me *try* to help you?" *You know,* before *you drive me insane?*

The barbershoppers pitched in, appearing before the television within a tight spotlight of their own making. "*By the light,*" they sang, ever so sweetly, "*of the silvery moon . . .*"

"How about you four?" she asked. "Can't you even give me a clue what you need before you can go to the Light? A hint?"

"*I want to spoon . . .*"

"Great." She slumped back in the den sofa and pressed the heel of one hand to her brow. *Ow, ow, ow. Head so very full of noise.* "Angie," she said. "I know you're here somewhere. I think you've always been here when the guys are around . . . I just think your life—and your death—were so very intense that you don't really know how to talk to me. Can you give it a try, now? Can you tell me what you need from me? I promise you, I'll make sure the police get the name of the man who was taking those pictures." On second thought, she quickly set the wineglass on the coffee table. Just in case.

But aside from a faint, odd *tap, tap, tap,* Angie remained tucked away . . . perhaps exhausted by her efforts earlier in the evening, perhaps not self-aware enough to know what she needed in the first place, never mind how to ask for it. Melinda pondered how she might learn more about the girl without exposing herself to the police.

Well, perhaps once she had Payne phone in that tip—once the cops broke the case—maybe there'd be some public information then. And maybe Angie would back off on her Flying Wallendas routine now that Melinda had recognized her presence. Jekyll-and-Hyde barbershoppers, indeed. *What was I even thinking?*

After another cautious moment, with the quartet still crooning in the background—practically sparkling with their stage presence and their attempt to connect with her as performers to audience if not as ghosts to ghost whisperer—Melinda picked up the wineglass, sipping the warming liquid. She also picked up the television remote. "Sorry, guys," she said. "But I really need a break."

She could have sworn they looked disappointed as the volume clashed with their music; they stopped singing as one, and disappeared. "I *know* you're trying to help," she said. "And you *are* helping. But variety is a good thing, you know?"

So was silence, but she didn't look likely to achieve that this evening. Nor, possibly, sleep.

She'd been hoping for a late-night show or post-news B movie, but newscasters were still talking, and a glance at the DVD player clock showed her that it was indeed still early enough for the evening news.

Well. Dinner hadn't lasted very long at that.

She flicked between channels until she settled on her favorite station, the lone station directly out of Grandview, where the broadcasters were earnest but unpolished. "Breaking news," the young woman anchor said, looking oh so serious. "Earlier today, we mentioned the unusual coincidence of the three young girls hospitalized with mysterious comas in the past weeks, the first of whom passed away last week. While doctors have no explanation, they have not considered it a communicable disease. That assumption comes into question this evening, as *five* additional children have been admitted to Mercy General under the same conditions. All five, as it happens, are also little girls, but they otherwise appear to have little or nothing in common. A CDC team is expected to arrive tomorrow. Until then—and possibly until further notice—the pediatrics intensive care unit is under quarantine, and all other cases are being diverted to Bayview."

"No!" Melinda said, pure reflex. The wineglass

dipped in her hand; she set it aside, her mind completely locked in on what she'd seen. No wonder the pied piper had sounded so wound up this evening. She *was* wound up . . . and she was acting on it. She'd gone berserker, whatever she was trying to do—and now Melinda's time had run out. Her time to figure out what this spirit wanted, what she needed . . . how she could be handled. How Melinda could even get her attention.

How she could even get into the PICU to meet Maureen, where she'd hoped to bring the two together, mother to mother—because the PICU, near her victims, was where Melinda had at least once been able to connect directly with the woman's spirit.

Maybe it didn't have to be the PICU. Maybe it could be anywhere in the hospital. Maybe the spirit had been there not because of the children, with whom she seemed to have little other connection, but because she'd died there somewhere.

"I'll figure it out," she said to the talking heads on the television, two of whom had gone on to make happy chat about the spring sports season. Basketball and their first downs. Who cared, anyway? Besides Ned, of course. "I'll search that whole hospital if I have to." But whether she'd have Maureen's patience that long was another thing altogether.

"Are you listening to me?" she said, raising her

voice. "I know what you're doing, and I'm going to stop you. I've got someone you'll want to talk to—"

*Whoa.* The faltering wail told her she'd been heard.

"Unless you want to talk right now," she said evenly, happy enough to switch tracks. To end this thing if possible. "I don't think you wanted to believe me in the hospital, that children are being hurt. But it's true. Whatever you're doing, it needs to stop."

The cold, bitter breeze stirred her hair; anger wrapped around her. Offended denial. But no true communication, no true connection. Just the distant awareness of a powerful spirit with more than the usual effect on the mortal world. Melinda sought more . . . went back to what had gotten that first hint of awareness. "I don't know what you need, but you'd better listen up, because *I know about you and I'm going to stop you.*"

Oh yeah. That did it. That darkened the nighttime walls to utter stark blackness; that snatched the feel of the couch out from beneath her. Her sense of the world disappeared—no trees stirring in the breeze beneath the moonlight, casting shifting shadows across the window; no talking news heads muttering from the television. And just as in the hospital, even her voice disappeared, leaving her in the spirit's world and at the mercy of that beguiling, battering song. She searched the blankness for any sign of the brilliant silhouette that had manifested beside Saiyesha's room and found herself still alone. *Show yourself!* she shouted silently. *Come and face me, instead of running away from what you're doing!*

The song shattered but never faltered, turning into a chord of fury that scraped against her mind. She struggled to keep her thoughts coherent, and realized suddenly that if she faltered, if she lost herself to the dissonance of this voice gone wild, she would be just as ruined as if Jim had never been able to bring her back in the park.

But she couldn't hear the barbershoppers, not here. And her own voice was just as silent. Only the pied piper's voice held sway, shards of glass cutting her thoughts to pieces until she snatched only at fragments. The will to survive . . . the frustration that had driven her to challenge this ghost in the middle of the night . . . *Jim. The store. Delia and Ned. Jim and Jim and* Jim—

No voice, no music. Nothing to counter the once-musical attack, the nonverbal shriek of denial and fury and possessiveness, the obvious intent to destroy her annoying presence. To make her *go away.*

*Go away go away goaway . . .*

*Jim and the store and Delia and Grandma. I'm not done yet and—*

*Go away!* She shouted it at the spirit's dismissive cruelty, denying her own dissolution. In that instant, she felt a hint of hesitation—realized she'd made a shield with that purity of want, a bare instant of silence in the scraping noise around her. An instant in which she gathered herself, knowing herself again, and wrenched herself out of the connection she'd invited.

"Another beautiful spring day in the downstate area, if you happen to be headed that way," the television murmured. The tree shadows shifted slightly over the window; the moon glinted off glass. The soft couch cushions pillowed her head and face; she found herself in a fetal curl, gasping as if she'd just run a marathon . . . shuddering as if someone had thrown a bucket of cold water over her at the finish line. Gradually, her breathing slowed. The television segued to the late night talk shows she'd been expecting in the first place. Her thoughts pulled from pure visceral reaction back into ordered thought.

*Damned stupid,* said the thought. *Damned lucky.* A regular chant, tied in with her breathing. *Damnedstupid,* breath in; *damnedlucky,* breath out.

But no. Luck hadn't gotten her out of that situation. *She* had. She'd created a weakness by creating a silence, and that silence had given her room to retreat. *Retreat.* Right. Tonight, just a fancy word for *run like hell.*

But only so she could come back another day. The *next* day, in fact. She only hoped that having Maureen by her side—the mother of the child the spirit was in such denial over harming—Melinda would have some hold over the pied piper, some sway. A handhold on the situation that would allow her to figure out what the woman wanted, and why—and what could be done to help her. Who she was, as well.

Really hard to get identity clues from a spirit who never showed her face, never spoke her name, never did anything other than sing a lullaby in a voice so beautiful—so throbbing with expression and love—that it made you want to cry.

A thought tickled at the edges of her mind then, and she grasped at it . . . and lost it. "Sorry," she said, talking out loud to herself most earnestly. "Too tired for that. I'll try again in the morning." She fumbled at the down comforter slung over the back of the couch, pulling it over herself in a haphazard motion, and snuggled into place just exactly where she'd found herself. The pied piper remained silent . . . busy elsewhere, or simply shocked back into her own private place by Melinda's successful escape. So she let the cadence of the late-night host doing his intro schtick fill the gaps in her thoughts, aware that for the first night in uncountable nights the pied piper herself had retreated to silence—and for however long that lasted, Melinda could sleep in safety.

But not in ease. Not when the silence revealed new sounds, until now buried in the layers of noise—the pied piper and the noise that Melinda created around herself to cover the lure of it.

Someone in the distant elsewhere, with *tap, tap, tap* in the background, a little girl cried.

# 13

"No, no, nonono," Rick Payne said, with feeling if not variety. "You are *not* calling me this early."

"But, in fact, I am," Melinda told him. "And you picked up the phone, so here we are."

"Oh, God, you're one of those wide-awake people in the morning." He hesitated. "Is this even morning? Doesn't this still count as the middle of the night?"

*Depends on whether or not you actually spent the night sleeping.* Not that she hadn't tried. She'd need her wits today, and her resources.

And so would those children.

"I need a favor," she said. Quietly, because it *was* still early, and although Jim would be up any time now, he wasn't up *yet*. She'd already snuck around in the kitchen to deal with the remnants of their meal, glad she'd packed the leftovers into the fridge after serving the night before. She'd been into the bedroom, too, swiping a breezy tunic from the closet—long, filmy sleeves and deep sweetheart neckline, the perfect frame for the necklace she'd also quietly swiped, all of which went with the crisp white pants, the dangly earrings . . .

It felt important to look nice today. To look confident and casual and *I can do this* and *I belong here.*

"I figured that," Payne grumbled, interrupting thoughts that threatened to spin off into the morning before her. But his voice had acquired that edge of interest, the one he was never able to hide. "And what's this about, then? Carrying messages for one of your supplicants? Deciphering inscrutable clues?"

"We already tried that," she reminded him.

"And hey, I did good!"

"Actually, you did." *Pied piper* suited the woman's spirit well enough—enough so Melinda now thought of her that way. Stealing children as with the original, maybe not. Stealing their souls? Definitely. And who knew, maybe Payne was right. Maybe that's all the original had done, too. And Melinda wasn't a target at all, just collateral damage, thanks to her gift, her ability to listen so deeply. "It just didn't get us any closer to figuring out this spirit. Or to stopping her."

"That's your job."

Okay, definitely awake now. "Nobody likes a smarty-pants," she told him.

"So true," he mourned. "So very true." Not that it had any real effect on him. "So, then, Melinda Gordon, what am I doing—or not doing—for you today?"

"I need you to call the police." She tucked the phone under her ear, transferring items to a tidier purse for the day.

"Okay, you got me." Not that it took him back, because when did anything ever interfere with his flow of words, even when she'd jump-started his day with a wake-up call? "*That,* I wasn't expecting. Is there a beginning to this story?"

"Not so much. I just need you to call in an anonymous tip that the child-porn photographer the Otigwa Lake police are looking for is named Bob Gleason."

"No," he said, fascinated and horrified at the same time. "You're not going to do this to me! You're not going to say just that much without telling me the whole thing. Or without at least dropping clues. Big fat clues."

"Sadly for you, I am." But she hesitated. "Will you do it?"

"You're kidding, right? I mean, sure, I'm self-centered, and yes, the world definitely revolves around me, but help get Bob the Perv Gleason off the street? Because I'm assuming you have an impeccable source here, and Bob the Perv is totally without question truly Bob the Perv—"

"Impeccable," Melinda said. She slid her feet into blue leather sandals with sparkly details, tightening the straps one-handed.

"And you're not calling in this tip because. . . ?"

"Are you sure you're not mainlining caffeine?" She'd thought at least to find him a little less insatiable than usual at this hour . . . because in this case, one question would only lead to another.

"If I am, that's my little secret."

*Ha.* "Well, we all have those," she said. "Make the call, Rick."

"Damn," he said, good-naturedly enough at that. "But you owe me."

"I'll bring you noodles," she told him. And as she moved the phone away from her ear she heard his voice, distant and tinny. "Oh, hey! There's this great little Thai place on the other end of the Square, have you ever—"

Later.

She thought the singing had diminished during the night, that she now faced the grim task of cleaning up after what the distraught spirit had already wrought—of facing her off long enough to free the children already entrapped and to discover what the woman needed to cross over. And she thought that with Maureen's help, she might have a chance.

So she'd gone back upstairs just as Jim's alarm sounded off, kissed him awake, and headed out to Mercy General.

But as soon as she left the house, she realized the woman's quiet had been an illusion. She had not stopped her rampage; she hadn't even dialed it back.

She'd simply withdrawn herself from Melinda's home.

So now Melinda sat in the Outlook on a beautiful spring morning with robins singing their few garbled notes and cardinals chirping a harder call and something altogether unknown serenading from high up in the trees, and she pressed the heels of her hands against the sting of tears.

*This has gone so, so wrong.* Instead of connecting with this ghost—a woman who had never looked for her in the first place—Melinda had tangled with her, succumbed to her, struck back at her to escape—and ended up with more distance between them than when she'd started. Instead of working toward resolution and understanding, she was as baffled about the ghost's needs and motivations as before she'd realized there was a ghost involved at all. Instead of protecting the children at risk, she'd watched one die and others take ill—now so many that the CDC was involved, for as little good as they'd do.

*Rick will call in the tip about Bob Gleason,* she reminded herself.

Except it didn't really seem to be what Angie needed—or if it was, Melinda had no indication of it. And that left her with five ghosts from a single accident, none of whom had managed to convey how she might help them cross over.

*If there's a better way to get nowhere fast, Melinda Gordon, I don't know what it is.* Sitting here shedding tears wasn't going to solve a thing. Feeling a helpless failure . . . just a good way to get more of the same.

"You have a plan," she told herself. "And since when has being in over your head been a reason not to try?"

Besides, she ought to be used to it by now. Grandview certainly had a way of stretching her out.

She wiped a careful finger beneath each eye and turned the key in the ignition.

"*We'll be just as happy as can be,*" crooned the quartet in the background . . . softly. Considerately. And with just a hint of question. "*Honey, keep a-buzzin', please . . .*"

"You guys," Melinda said, more affectionately than she'd expected. "Such flirts. Don't worry, I'm not giving up on you. And you just *might* think about doing more than singing at me, okay? I have a pretty good idea what happened at that accident—" She backed down the driveway, swung the familiar angle out into the street, shifted into drive, and, taking a deep breath, put it all together. "I know you were on your way to a performance, and you were all dressed and ready to go. I know you had Craig's van because you were carrying props. And I know that you'd planned everything out, and that there was somehow a new disagreement about it, but that that wasn't anything new. But it was foggy and you should have all been paying more attention to the road, even if it wasn't your fault that Angie had finally had enough of what her foster mother was doing. She fought back and sent their car out in front of yours, and that sent you both over the edge of that overlook . . . and so you never made it that performance after all."

"*Hello, my baby——!*"

Melinda squinted into her rearview mirror, looking at the snug lineup of barbershop singers emoting in her backseat. "You're kidding," she said.

"*Hello, my darlin'!*"

"You're *not* kidding," she murmured, looking at their earnest faces, their dramatic flourishes cramped by the close quarters. The man in the right-most seat flung his hat wide, without regard to the fact that it passed right outside the vehicle. She winced as it passed through a cyclist's back, closed her fingers around the wheel . . . drove resolutely on. "Okay," she said. "You argued when you should have been paying attention to the road, and because of that you never made it to the performance—and you were *really* ready for that performance—"

"*Hello, my ragtime gal!*"

She shook her head, a wondering gesture. "That's why you argued, wasn't it? That was part of your pattern, the way you built yourselves up. Maybe you didn't even know it . . . you just did it. And this time it went . . . wow." She couldn't help but shake her head. "It went pretty wrong for you this time. The arguing got out of hand . . . and it didn't give you an edge. It killed you." Not Angie and the foster mother . . . they'd been heading for that overlook no matter what. But the quartet in their van? "And now you're all messed up about it. You played a little too hard and mean, and this time someone really got hurt. *All* of you got hurt."

The balding man withdrew his hat to his chest, no longer full of vigor and drama. He was, if she read him correctly, sulking. The others settled, too, looking down at the hats they all held, and as Melinda drew closer to the hospital, their humming changed tunes, and into a new song altogether. Something both somber and hopeful at the same time. "*I'll leave them each a song, to sing the whole day long, as toward the end they plod . . .*"

She shook her head again. "That's just too easy." A quick turn, and the hospital was nearly within sight. "And honestly, I'm just not sure what I can *do* for you. But you know what? We're going to have to figure it out another time." For their singing had done its job—had kept her head free and clear, driving safely in toward the confrontation she both feared and hoped for.

*Just because you made it out of her world in one piece last night doesn't mean you can do it again.*

*"I'll leave the moon above to those in love, when I leave the world behind . . ."*

"Yeah, I get it," she said, just a tad impatiently. "But it's going to have to be another time. You guys strike me as having it pretty much together, if you don't count the whole stuck-in-song situation. Tell me that you really think I should walk away from these little girls—that you think they'll be okay if I get around to them later."

It silenced them. Mouths open on notes that never emerged, faces abashed . . . it silenced them.

"You're important, too," Melinda said. "I'll figure out what you need. I'll find a way to make it happen. I promise. It's what I do. You know that, or you wouldn't have come to me."

They glanced at one another then—silent, clearly frustrated by their inability to converse. And amid shrugs and nods and generalized agreement, they disappeared.

*Down to one thing at a time, then.* More or less. With the barbershop music gone, the pied piper's song swelled around her, immediately crawling through her thoughts . . . slowing them, making them distant. Not a beautiful song any longer, but a voice split into different pieces that scraped against each other in a harsh dissonance. She flipped on the radio and didn't care about the station or the song; the hospital wasn't far now. A glance at her watch showed that Jim would be up and showered and already dressed, probably grabbing a day-old sticky bun on his way out the door, and figured she'd be just on time to meet Maureen. She'd meant to be there early, to assess the situation and take a few deep breaths—but she hadn't counted on self-pep-talk time in the driveway.

A quick, efficient drive, an unusually empty visitor's lot . . . Melinda grabbed her bag, checked her bouncy ponytail for sticky-outies that would show better in this daylight than in the downstairs bathroom, and headed briskly for the main hospital entrance—only to pull up way short and do an abrupt U-turn, putting her back to things best left unseen. "Oh, for heaven's sake," she said. "That hospital gown doesn't have to get caught in the breeze unless you *want* it to."

"*Hey, if it was up to me, I'd be wearing black biking leathers.*" But the young man grinned; she could hear it in his voice. He'd been at the bus stop bench the last time she'd seen him; they weren't far from that bench now. "I *don't make the rules.*"

"But you sure do have fun with them," Melinda

muttered. Then, louder, over her shoulder, "Scott, right?"

Without warning, he was right there in front of her, but his gown hung still and modest, and he'd even faded himself somewhat. That got her attention. "What is it? Because I have to tell you, I'm really in the middle of something—"

"*Don't I know it*," he told her.

Melinda turned to him with her full attention. "Do you know something about it? Do you hear?"

"*Hey, everyone hears her now. She's got no boundaries—and she doesn't respect anyone else's turf, if you get my drift. It's all about her. Things are all messed up around here. What if I miss—*" He scowled, cutting himself off. "*Okay, and those kids. It's not right, not any of it.*"

"No, it's not." Melinda couldn't help the tightening of her mouth—thinking of Eileen and her missing spirit. Of all the children since affected. "But that's why I'm here."

"*Yeah, so that's the thing. You might want to head around the back side. You know, the emergency entrance. Kind of cruise in with the next scoop 'n' run, you know?*"

She turned a frown on him, amused in spite of herself. "You were one of those scoop 'n' runs, once."

"*Don't I know it. So who has a better right to be*

*disrespectful about the whole thing? Especially since I was more of a scoop 'n' pour."*

She kept her jaw from dropping, but it was a close thing. "You did *not* just say that."

*"Could be worse,"* he said. *"Seriously. Do you know how much time I've had to think of ways to entertain myself?"*

She held up her hands in surrender. "You totally win. It could be worse. But why go around back?"

He snorted. *"Thanks to her, this place is a madhouse. No one's going in the front—unless you're an emergency or a girl kid in a coma, you're going to Bayview today. No visitors for anyone who's already in there, either."*

"You're kidding! The CDC?"

*"You got it."*

"But it's not catching! They can't just shut down the whole hospital—"

He snorted. *"I peeked. You know it's not catching, and I know it's not catching, but these people? They don't have a clue."* He shifted uneasily, looking over his shoulder. *"Listen, I don't like to be away from . . . I mean, I gotta go."*

"Wait!" She said it just quickly enough, catching him just in time—he disappeared for an instant, then returned, wobbling a little at the speed of his own response. "What's her name, Scott? How long have you been waiting?"

He gave her a wry little smile. *"So clever, you.*

*Linda Allaire, that's her name. And I haven't the faintest idea. Minutes, maybe. Forever, maybe.*" And he disappeared.

"So clever, *you*," Melinda murmured after him. Not a caught-napping kind of guy. She'd bet there was some sort of miscommunication between him and his Linda . . . something she could clear up for him.

Later. For now she went to the front entrance of the hospital, heading out with confident strides—but without any intention of actually reaching for the door. "I know," she said to the officer stationed at the front, as he stepped forward to warn her off. "But I was supposed to meet someone here, and I don't think she does." And so she waited, humming to herself to offset the discordant sound of the pied-piper ghost, and glad enough when she saw Maureen coming with Hayley at her side. "Here," she said, well aware they could be overheard. "We can't go in to visit today, so let's just walk together."

"But—" Hayley looked at the front door, a flash of stubborn on her features. As much as Melinda rejoiced to see it—to see that spirit asserting itself—now was definitely *not* the time.

"We don't have any choice," she said, keeping her voice light. "We'll try again tomorrow." She took Hayley's arm as if it was all no big deal anyway and led her toward the tree-lined sidewalk.

"That's it?" Hayley said. "You're just giving up? Have you even *seen* the news—"

"Of course I'm not giving up," Melinda said, her voice low. "But we're not getting in that way. We're going to have to find another way."

"Oh, I don't know," Maureen said, a woman without any of Hayley's conviction. Then again, Melinda couldn't blame her. She had no way to understand the stakes—or how she might possibly be the one to make the difference.

"Maureen," she said, "I need you to trust me—go with me on this, if you still want to help the children here, and not just the ones Hayley has visited. *All* the little girls who have come here in a coma since Eileen passed away."

"I don't understand," Maureen said. Fragile, pale . . . what determination she'd shown at the funeral was wilting fast.

"I know you don't. I know this is confusing, and it's hard . . . but it'll be easier once we're inside." *I hope.* Because unlike was often the case, Melinda couldn't appeal to Maureen's need to connect with her loved one—not with Eileen's continued absence. Instead, she would be asking the bereaved woman to speak to the ghost of another mother— one Melinda knew nothing about, except that she needed something and needed it badly, and she was wreaking death and destruction in her search for whatever it was.

*Little girls.*

Except she was still looking . . . so not just any little girls, but a very particular little girl. She'd looked at Melinda—examined her from within—and instantly rejected her. Not even close.

But with Maureen . . . Melinda felt hope for the first time—strong, lively hope. All she needed was to get the ghost's attention long enough to learn a name, a location . . . to find the girl for this ghost. *To stop the search.*

"Please," she said to Maureen. "I need your help so badly. These children need your help."

But Maureen . . . she hesitated.

"It's Travis," Hayley said sagely. "He found out you were coming, didn't he?"

Maureen looked down at her hands, where her fingers twined together, white knuckles and stark, tense tendons against fragile bones. "He loves me. He doesn't want me upset. And he's right. Being here is upsetting."

Hayley opened her mouth to say something full of scowl, something angry; Melinda cut her off with a sharp shake of her head. Criticizing Travis Starcroft would only trigger Maureen to defend him. Instead, she said, "I'm sure it is. But if you can help me—if you can help these children—how will you feel then?"

Maureen looked away. "If the hospital is closed, I think I'd better—"

"Imagine it," Melinda persisted. "Close your eyes and imagine it. What would it be like, to know you've made a difference? To watch little girls walk out of this hospital and know you helped to make it happen?"

Clearly stung, Maureen said, "That's not fair. You don't know I can really do anything. You haven't even been clear on what you think I *can* do."

*No kidding.* And not yet, either. Not until it was a little bit harder to turn back. "I know you can do what any of us ever do—I know you can *try*—I know this is your chance to be heard in a way that you may never get again. To express what having Eileen in your life meant to you."

Maureen gasped lightly; she half turned away, and Melinda thought maybe she'd pushed too hard at that. She touched Maureen's arm. "Just give yourself that," she said. "A moment to imagine making a difference, in Eileen's name." More than she could ever imagine at this moment, if it came to that. Reaching out to the ghost who'd taken her daughter from her . . . mother to mother. Because if Delia was right, if from this spirit's perspective she wasn't, in fact, taking these young lives, then who better than a grieving mother to make the pied piper see differently?

She certainly wasn't interested in talking to Melinda.

Maureen hesitated, there at the side of the hospital with the gorgeous landscaping all around them and the incongruous sense of urgency twined with the pied piper spirit's fractured song . . . but Melinda finally acceded. Maureen closed her eyes; her lashes fluttered, as if she had to fight herself to keep them that way. And then her face relaxed; a rueful little smile found the corners of her mouth. "To know I helped make it happen . . ." she repeated, and took a deep, long breath. She looked at Melinda and said, "It would mean everything."

"Then trust me," Melinda said. "Help me." She gestured at the hospital. "We'll go in through the emergency entrance, and we'll see how things are set up. And you know what? If we get turned back, we get turned back. I'll handle it, okay?" Easy enough to say—she didn't intend to get turned back. And she intended to take every advantage of her connections to avoid it.

Hospitals, above all places, were full of ghosts.

# 14

THEY WERE THREE women in a study in contrasts, all driven by one goal. Hayley, struggling between her determination and her insecurities as a result of the holes Travis Starcroft cut into in her natural confidence. He'd been more than just her employer, he had the power to cut off her access to the little girl she'd grown to love. Bright colors, that was Hayley since she'd been out of work. Today, red crop pants with a snug fresh top in the narrowest of stripes, piled on with reds and oranges and yellows. Today her hair was pulled back with a headband and left to explode into its wild curls.

Under other circumstances, Melinda would never think to find her in Maureen's company—a woman withdrawn into herself, hidden behind a pastel short-sleeved camp shirt with tidy buttons up the front and a stiff neat collar, a bridle leather belt fastened just so over pleated pants, her purse a constrained and featureless item held snugly against her body, her wavy hair tamed back into something severe. The only sign of a breakout personality came at the edges of her sleeves and shirt placket, where tiny pale violet flowers were sprinkled against white.

And there was Melinda in the middle of them, feeling older than both of them and younger than both of them at the same time. A lifetime of experience she had with this . . . yet she hadn't been the one to lose Eileen, and she wasn't the one fighting the influence of Travis Starcroft. True enough, she'd done without a father, watched him walk away and never understood it; she'd done with a mother who fought every moment of her own abilities, never mind her daughter's. But she'd had her grandmother, oh yes she had. And she had Jim—believing in her, listening to her. And now she stood between bright Hayley and stricken Maureen, grounding them both with her confidence and glad she'd gone for the quietly personable look of the day with the gauzy tunic and sharp slacks and sandals with just enough personality to snap.

Their unlikeliness, she thought, might well work for them. They'd certainly had no trouble getting into the ER—rushing in alongside an ambulance gurney with a car accident victim on board and one of the Driscoll County paramedics at the helm. He'd given her a look, but in the end had done no more than exchange quick greetings. He was coming off shift, she knew that much—tired from a long night and more than willing to let his curiosity drop.

Once inside, she left Hayley and Maureen to sit off to the side of the waiting room—rows of chairs enclosed by bench-lined walls and full enough so they wouldn't stand out. "Sit close, keep up a conversation," she advised them—and went on an ostensible mission to scope out the vending machines, which just happened to be in the hallway leading to the hospital proper. It meant buying something sticky and full of more preservatives than food, and she fussed with the packaging as she scanned the hallway.

Nothing like the PICU, these hallways. Off-white and beige, strictly utilitarian, with colored lines on the floor to match the unit designations listed on the wall. Follow the blue to be dumped out in the Main Lobby, follow the red to get to Radiology, follow the yellow to Outpatient Surgery . . .

All normal enough, if she didn't count the red-striped sawhorse barricade just down the hall, and the RESTRICTED AREA sign taped to it. A hasty-looking sign, made up by someone trying to look official but caught off guard by the situation.

Hmm. Well, she'd been around this hospital often enough . . . visiting, working. Taking care of earthbound spirits. On occasion, finding herself on the receiving end of care. On rare occasion, which was far too often, rushing in because Jim had been battered around on the job. She knew a long way or two around . . .

"Miss," said a woman from behind her, voice sharp with tension, "you can't go down there."

Melinda whirled, didn't hide her startled response. "Oh!" she said. "Sorry, I was just looking at the sign. I mean, mostly I was trying to get this"—she gestured with the package of trans fats and chemicals—"open." And she tugged ineffectively at the packaging to illustrate.

The woman—a stethoscope slung over her shoulders, her scrubs a no-nonsense blue, and her hair scraped back into a ponytail that was losing the battle of an obvious all-nighter—took a few brisk steps and took the package, opening it with an expert twist. When Melinda reacted with surprise, she only ruefully shook her head. "That tells you far too much about what I eat around here, I'm sure. But best to stay away from that end of the hallway. Things are a little tense around here right now."

"I understand," Melinda told her. "And I will." *Because I have another way in mind.* Or two. Whichever worked.

She headed back for the other women, neatly depositing the opened package in the trash along the way. Hayley gave her a startled look. "Did you just—?"

"Oh, *please*," Melinda said. "If I'm going to indulge, I'm going to do it right." She glanced at her watch, decided against calling Delia just yet, and drummed her fingers against her own leg, pondering their options. *A hallway to the stairs. Or grab a chance at the staff elevator before reaching the stairs.* Both meant perfect timing. Both would do best if they had some sort of distraction.

Which . . . they totally didn't have. A glance around revealed the area unusually light on ghosts, and those who were here had an annoyed, scowly look about them. Not the time to go asking for favors. That was best done with a ghost who was already curious about her and the fact that she could quite clearly see them all.

Not that she blamed them for their irritated lack of interest. If they'd been listening to the pied-piper ghost all night . . . And that ghost was still here, all right, her increasingly fractured song wending through the hallways and ever-present in the background, just enough to set Melinda's teeth on edge.

But no longer, she realized with surprise, enough to lure her in. Perhaps because she was an adult, perhaps because the song had never been aimed at her in the first place, perhaps because she'd been so thoroughly rejected . . . whatever it was still doing to the children of this town, it now only battered against Melinda's nerves.

It would be too much to hope that it would break apart so much that it no longer held sway even over the young girls. *But even if it does . . . what of the girls already affected?*

"What're we going to do?" Hayley asked, her voice low.

"We're going to have to find a way past the restrictions," Melinda said frankly, an eye toward Maureen. "They're pretty tense about what's going on. They've got a blockade in the main hallway, but I know a few other ways in from here."

"A blockade?" Maureen tightened her hold on her purse. "This won't do any good if we upset everyone for no good reason. And I still don't truly understand how you think I can help at all."

Inwardly, Melinda winced. Given more time to think, Maureen would back out entirely. Melinda had to get them moving, get Maureen immersed in the middle of it before she had a chance to talk herself out of what good she could do, or even what she was experiencing.

"A blockade?" Hayley echoed. "Oh, *please*. They couldn't really think it was *catching*, could they? An infectious disease, restricting itself to little girls of a certain age? That would be like saying only twelve-year-old boys could catch the measles."

"They may still believe it's coincidence," Melinda

said, although certainly that must be a stretch by now. "The stairs, I think. And . . . a distraction in the bathroom." She pondered the possibilities, deciding against any actual mess making. These people had enough to deal with. It would no doubt be enough to burst out of the facility while *exclaiming* about something—someone sick, explosive plumbing . . .

"Mel!"

She whirled at the sound of Jim's voice and found him striding over from the intake area, where his partner, Bobby, hovered beside a propped-up gurney and its small occupant, dividing his attention between the child and the distraught mother beside them. "Wow," she said. "You didn't waste any time getting a first call in."

"Pretty much the moment I walked in the door," he said, coming right up close . . . tipping his head the way he did when it was just between him and her, no matter how many other people were around. In the background, Hayley nudged Maureen and murmured something, and they backed away a step—but not so far they couldn't still hear, Melinda noticed with absent amusement. "Listen," Jim said, his gaze taking her attention back to his new arrivals. "We only have a moment; they'll probably take her right back, because—"

"She's one of them," Melinda finished quietly.

"But she's not gone, not yet. And I thought, if there's anything you can do . . ."

Melinda caught Hayley's eye, found her eavesdropping, indeed, and ready to go—while Maureen looked like a deer in headlights. "It may not be what you signed up for," Melinda told her, "but I think you need to see this. To be part of it."

"She does," Hayley said firmly, taking Maureen's arm. Maureen looked startled—for the first time, perhaps, truly comprehending that she was no longer Hayley's employer and would no longer be treated as one—but didn't resist beyond an initial reluctance to move.

Melinda was already following Jim back to the gurney, where Bobby was patting the cheeks of a droopy-eyed little girl in Little Mermaid pajamas. "Come on, darlin'," he said. "Don't go anywhere on us."

"Mrs. Vega," Jim said, "this is my wife, Melinda. She's been working with this situation."

Bobby looked up, surprised at that, but Mrs. Vega didn't hesitate. "Please," she said, clutching tightly at a worn stuffed lobster, her black hair in morning disarray and her face without makeup; she wore a baggy T-shirt over sweatpants, clearly caught out in the early stages of her morning routine. "Can you help her? Please tell me I got her here on time, that there's something you can do! The news reports make it sound like there's nothing anyone can do, not even the experts!"

Maureen bit her lip and turned away, and while

Hayley put a quick, steadying hand on her arm, she nonetheless went straight to the little girl and began singing—"The Hokey-Pokey" this time— and she took the girl's slack hands from her lap and laced them with her own, encouraging her to join in with the song's gestures.

"I don't—" the girl's mother said, confused. "What are you—"

"She's helping," Melinda said quickly. Hayley hadn't done this long enough to realize it was no help at all if things moved so quickly that no one could accept it. "She's counteracting what your daughter is hearing. Has she said anything about it, these past couple of days? About the song she's been hearing?"

Dazed, pulled between Melinda and her daughter, the woman said, "We all get things stuck in our head . . . things that won't go away. That's what I told her. But she kept complaining about it. She said she didn't know this song, not until the woman sang it to her. She said . . . she said it was a voice she'd never heard before. She said that it came to her in her sleep, that it woke her up and kept her from playing her letters in school. I told her . . . I told her . . ." Her voice grew strangled and small. "I told her it was her imagination."

Melinda winced. "Children deserve to be believed," she said, as gently as she could. "Their experience of this world isn't always our experience, but that doesn't make it any less valid."

"Mel," Jim said, his voice so low as to barely be heard . . . understanding, but still a hint of question there. *Is this the time?*

She spared him a glance. "This isn't about me," she told him, knowing where his thoughts had gone—knowing he understood how strongly she felt about the matter—about what she'd been through as a child, from the time she'd seen her first ghost to the more recent hurts, just as deep, from disbelieving friends. At least Delia was up front about her struggle to accept Melinda's gifts, her difficulty in facing elements of a world she'd never believed existed until her entanglement in Melinda's life had exposed her to more than she'd ever imagined. At least she still looked at Melinda as if she was a friend, as if she was *Melinda,* and not as if she was something to laugh at or scorn or whisper about behind her back.

That hadn't always been the case.

So yes, she understood what it was like for these children to face the pied piper while the adults around them denied the existence of anything but imaginary friends and earworms, and maybe she understood better than most. That didn't mean it was *wrong* to take their part in this . . . or that this girl's mother didn't deserve matter-of-fact truth.

On the other hand, it didn't mean this was the time to get stuck on it, either.

But her gentle tone seemed to have done the trick, for the girl's mother only said, somewhat distant in reminiscence, "When I was her age, I saw someone looking in my bedroom window. It only happened once, and no one ever believed me. . . . I should have remembered what that felt like. . . ." And oddly, it seemed to have calmed her. "It happens to us all, doesn't it?"

"I'm afraid it does." Melinda gave her a rueful smile.

"My Carmen . . . I didn't even think. But last night after she was in bed, I saw the news story, and they said one of the symptoms was . . . well, they said *hearing things*. And then when she couldn't really wake up this morning . . ."

"You did the right thing to bring her here," Melinda said.

The woman searched her eyes. "But you don't agree with them. You think she *is* hearing something."

"I know she is," Melinda said. "Because I can hear it, too."

Maureen gasped, turning on her. "Eileen?" she cried. "You heard it then?"

Melinda nodded, as firmly as she could. "Yes."

Those fragile hands were full of strength as they grasped Melinda's shoulder, heedless of the bruises already there. She couldn't help a small cry of pain as Maureen said, "Even before she got sick? Before she *died*? What do you know, Melinda? Tell me what you know!"

"Hey, there," Jim said, moving in with all his experience, his strength restrained and replaced by precision as he deftly slipped in his fingers to break Maureen's grip and fold her hands closed, holding them within his own as she jerked away, wild-eyed at his sudden intrusion and teetering on the brink of striking out in reaction—grieving, angry, confused.

"We gonna have a problem here?" Bobby asked, moving closer—his eyes on Maureen but the question directed at Jim.

"No," Melinda said, hasty with wishful thinking. Because she still needed this woman—they *all* still needed this woman. Melinda had no illusions; in the end, she would be the one confronting the pied piper, trying to end this siege on the children of this town. But to get the ghost's attention in the first place—

"Mama?"

The girl's mother made an inarticulate noise, a mix of joy and disbelief; she threw herself toward the gurney. "Carmen! My baby girl!"

The girl wrinkled her nose. "I'm not a *baby*."

"You're *my* baby," the woman said, and kissed plump olive brown cheeks, one after the other, and then the sleep-rumpled black hair. But Melinda winced—for the dissonance of the pied piper's music grew suddenly louder, stronger.

From the other side of the girl, Hayley looked up at Melinda and grinned. "We won one!"

"I can't believe it," Maureen said. "You really did it." She looked at Melinda. "What you told us to do the first time you saw us . . . the day Eileen died . . . it might have worked?"

"I think," Melinda said, so gently, "that it might have been too late for Eileen already. I'm so sorry. I'd only just realized what was happening, and what might help."

"But I don't under*stand*." Maureen's voice rose; she made a visible effort to lower it. Not so the pied piper, who wailed her song in the background. "What *is* happening?"

Carmen looked at her mother and frowned—childish frustration, expressed vividly on her features. "But I can still hear her, Mama. Make her go away!"

Her mother cast a quick, panicked look at Melinda, who nodded. "I'm afraid so. The problem isn't within Carmen, you see—we haven't *cured* her of anything. Hayley's song just interfered with what she heard." Hayley had already started humming the "Bingo" song, gathering Carmen's attention again. Carmen, in the easy and natural way of little girls everywhere, reached out to pet Hayley's wild curls, her gestures in time with the music. "That's what you'll need to do, anytime she gets that look in her eyes. Her favorite sing-alongs—especially the ones with the gestures and dances that go with them."

"For how long?" the woman asked in horror. "She'll have to sleep *some*time, surely!"

But Maureen had reached her limit of going without answers. "Melinda!" she cried in frustration, reaching again to grasp Melinda's arm—but with a glance at Jim, reluctantly letting her hand fall away.

Melinda looked at Carmen's mother . . . looked at Maureen. She exchanged a glance with Jim, who shrugged, a look that said, *You've got to tell her sometime*—right before he grabbed Bobby's attention and nodded at the intake station. "Paperwork," he said.

Bobby gave him a wry little look that made it perfectly clear he knew he was being dragged away so the ladies could talk, but since the girl was stable, he'd let it happen. "Paperwork," he muttered on his way past Melinda—but it was a good-natured grumble, and she made up her mind to pack extra muffins up for him for their next shift, even if he did turn right to Jim with an obvious what-the-hell-is-going-on-here? expression behind the words she couldn't hear. Jim would handle it, in that she had confidence.

"Melinda . . ." Hayley said, a strange echo of Maureen's demand but full of uncertainty. *How are you going to tell her that's what that tone meant? How are you going to tell her and still get her to come with us and help?*

Melinda started with a deep breath—not unaware of the strange intimacy of these surroundings, out in the wide intake hallway of the ER, well back away from the entrance and yet adjacent to the waiting room. Not really private at all, except in the way that people made room for one another in these strained, forced public encounters. Seeing one another and pretending to have invisible shields; seeing everyone's most extreme emotions and strain and grief and pretending not to see anything at all. Still, she moved in close, and she lowered her voice. "There's a woman," she said, and winced again at the noise in her head, one hand going to her temple as she forced herself to think past it. "I think she's lost her daughter, and she's looking for her."

"She sings," Carmen said wisely, although she'd not been paying any apparent attention at all, and had, in fact, taken to what was probably meant to be braiding a section of Hayley's hair, her hands moving in time to "Bingo," which must still have been humming in her thoughts. "But not very well."

"Yes, that's right," Melinda said. "She sings a

very old lullaby. It's Welsh, in fact—I looked it up."

"How could you have?" Maureen said, eyes narrowing. Resistant, even though she already knew the answer, because Melinda had already told her.

"I heard it, remember?" And because she knew that wouldn't be enough, Melinda sang a few careful phrases of it—in synch with the ghost's now barely recognizable song.

Carmen gave her a startled look. "You know the song!" And then she added, "You sing it lots better than she does."

Hayley gave her an equally startled look, and Melinda said, "Right now, that's true. It wasn't before. She's changing . . . her song is changing. I think that's why you were able to reach Carmen at all . . . why she was only half in that place, instead of completely affected." Then she added for Hayley alone, "But I think the . . . woman . . . is reacting to what we're doing here. She's angry—"

"An invisible singing woman," Maureen scoffed.

But Carmen's mother knew. Just looking at her eyes widen, Melinda could see that. And Carmen's mother believed, too. Where she hadn't believed her daughter, she did believe in ghosts, probably always had. Perhaps she, too, had had a special grandmother. Melinda fought the instant impulse to ask for her help—but no. Not with Carmen here, needing constant attention. Not even if they might well have a better chance of success with someone who *believed*.

Assuming they could even reach the PICU. That they could even get the ghost's attention in the first place. That they could somehow pull her away from the havoc she caused.

"No," Melinda said to Maureen's sarcasm, steady enough only through dint of long practice, "not an invisible singing woman. A ghost."

Maureen recoiled from her—looked at the pure belief from Carmen's mother and recoiled from her, too, and then sent a blast of accusation at Hayley. "You brought me here for *this*? You're making me relive my child's last days for *this*? This . . . this . . . *fantasy*?"

"It's *true*," Hayley said. "It's why I met her in the first place—she heard the song the first time Eileen did. She was already trying to find this . . . ghost . . . when I went to her after Eileen passed away. I wouldn't have believed it, either, but I walked in on a conversation, and this friend of hers just spilled it. He's a professor at the university, and he totally believes her. And her wrist? That was another ghost—"

"Someone confused," Melinda said quickly, defensive of Angie's spirit. "I'm still working with her. She died violently, so . . . that can be hard on them."

"Oh, *really*," Maureen said, cold words from a woman so battered by grief and so constrained in life by her husband. "And I'm supposed to believe this."

Hayley threw her a look of desperation, but Melinda only shrugged. "Does it really matter?" She checked on Jim, who bent over a clipboard while Bobby juggled a handful of supplies—prepacked tubing, IV bags, and boxes that seemed determined to squirt through his grasp; he seemed to have given up on getting any response about their gathering, and was instead flirting with a nurse over the top of his handful. Jim glanced at her, and she could read it easily enough. *I can only stall as long as I can stall.*

"You know," Melinda said, rubbing her temple, "usually this is about the time someone's loved one might tell me a nickname only the other person knew, or some other meaningful secret . . . some memory I have no way of knowing. And then whoever I'm talking to starts to believe, and the healing begins. And *then* I can cross the ghost into the Light, and whoever's left behind has a new understanding of the one they lost." She lifted one shoulder, offering a rueful smile. "But I don't have that this time. I can't even get this ghost to talk to me—that's the problem. That's why I need you."

"*Why?*" Maureen said, and if it was a demand, it was a frustrated and helpless one, the protest of someone who was used to the fact that her protests didn't count at all.

"Because of what you have in common," Melinda said.

"She's a mother," Carmen's mother said, understanding. "And you say she's lost her child . . ." She looked at Maureen. "You had the first little girl, didn't you? The one they keep talking about on the news. The one who didn't make it." Her voice held sympathy and horror; her hand, all unknowing, stroked her daughter's arm. "If she'd listen to *anyone* . . ."

"Yes, exactly." Melinda flinched at a particularly fractured musical phrase even as Carmen hiccoughed a sudden sob, her fingers slack on Hayley's hair—the sleepy sound of a child crying herself to sleep. *Back to sleep. What have we done?* She didn't dare say it out loud . . . that by pulling Carmen away, they'd only made things worse for everyone, enraging the pied piper . . . driving her to further extremes. *But at the same time weaker, because she'd lost her hold on Carmen in the first place . . .* Melinda grasped at thoughts going as fractured as the pied piper's song, trying to reach Maureen. "All I can do is repeat what I said before . . . what do you have to lose? Because you don't have to believe. Not really. I just need you to say what you feel, from your heart. I need something that will reach her."

Maureen recoiled from her with something akin

to horror. "And if I *did* believe you, then . . . you're saying . . . you want me to talk to the person who killed my daughter!"

"To help *my* daughter!" Carmen's mother said fiercely. "Look at her! How long do you think we can fight this?"

Melinda took a step back from them, over-whelmed by the noise within her head; she pressed the heels of both hands against her forehead, knowing their conversation had become too loud. They were getting looks from people in the adjacent waiting room, those unable to maintain the pretense of the privacy bubble any longer. And a desperate glance at Jim showed her he wasn't looking in their direction at all, nor was Bobby—in spite of the commotion they'd turned into. No, both Jim and Bobby eavesdropped with intense and open interest on the phone call the nurse had taken—an interest she invited by exchanging grim looks with both.

*What now?*

She didn't have long to wait. The nurse hung up, exchanged a few terse words with Jim and Bobby, and went to touch the shoulders of others at the intake station, bringing them up to speed on whatever she'd learned as Jim shoved the clipboard back and spun on his heel, heading back to them.

Maureen had fallen silent—so had Carmen's mother, both of them now aware of the renewed tension at the intake area. There was only Hayley's singing, low and growing desperate—and clashing with the shout of song in Melinda's mind. Jim outpaced Bobby on the way back to them and reached Mel. "You okay?"

She realized she still pressed her hands to her forehead; she let them drop. "I'm good," she said. But she made a face at his patent disbelief and said, "I'm managing, okay? What's going on?"

"That was a pediatrician's office on the phone. They just got three call-ins from frantic mothers . . . they're sending them straight here. Mel, you're running out of time. Whatever you're going to do—"

*No, no, no. Not* more *of them.*

"We've got to get past that barrier," she said desperately. Either Maureen was coming or she wasn't—Melinda had done what she could. Now she had to go *do* what she could, whatever she had to work with. But she knew better than to gesture toward the secondary route, toward the stairs and the staff elevator; she sent only her gaze that way, and when she looked back, she knew he understood.

"Get ready, then," he said. "But you'll have to move fast. I don't have a lot to work with here."

"Move fast," she said. "I can do that." She gave him a quick kiss. "You're the best."

He grinned, the sudden, one-sided grin that always shot straight through to her heart. "Don't forget that when everyone's talking about your clumsy husband."

"My. . . ?" *What?*

But he was off and away, even as Bobby, on the approach, lost his grip on half the supplies in his arms from turning too fast, clearly in complete bafflement as Jim backed away from him, hand up in a hold-on gesture. "No problem," he said, a little more loudly than strictly necessary. "I'll get it." Still backing away, the hasty strides of someone getting ready for trouble coming—but who hadn't, as it happened, turned around to see trouble right on his heels.

*He knows that cart is there.* And so rather than calling a warning—and glad to see that Bobby only watched openmouthed, well aware that his partner *ought* to know that cart was there— Melinda turned to Hayley. "We've got to go," she said. "*Now.*"

"But—" Hayley glanced at Carmen, whose half-mast eyes reflected the pied piper's renewed efforts.

"Her mother can sing with her," Melinda said. "Hayley, I need you." She looked at Maureen. "And I need you, too, but I can't wait for you to make up your mind, and I can't spend any more time convincing you."

"I—" Maureen hesitated, torn between her reactive emotions and the imminent potential of being left behind as she, too, realized the limitations of Jim's strategy.

Melinda didn't pause, not for either of them. She headed across the waiting room, without haste and without any gesture so furtive as looking back to check on Jim or on her erstwhile team . . . at least, not until the startling collision-and-crash noise that made her whirl back—if only for an instant—and there was Jim, tangling with the cart, his expression surprised and convincing and embarrassed all at once, except for that brief instant when his gaze met hers across the room and his unspoken pride and love and not a little *get a move on!* came through loud and clear.

She got a move on. From the waiting room to the long, seldom-used side hallway with stairs at the end and a staff-only elevator along the way. A glance behind her showed Hayley quickly catching up and Maureen belatedly trotting along behind, scooting across the open area with such a furtive step that she drew curious glances from anyone who wasn't completely drawn up in Jim's noisy distraction. Melinda allowed herself both an instant of relief and a wince, and bypassed the elevator to head straight for the stairs. She knew these stairs; they might be seldom used by patients and visitors, but they weren't off limits, and she found them useful for the occasional private conversation.

But this time, when she reached out with confidence to yank back on the door, it didn't budge. Instead, her shoulder took the brunt of it, and she made a little involuntary noise of surprise as her fingers slipped from the metal handle. *Locked!*

"That's a fire exit!" Hayley said indignantly.

Melinda was already turning back the other way, heading for the elevator. "It's probably open from the inside . . . that's all that matters on this floor." Chancy, to go for the elevator . . . push the button, hang around, hope no one had noticed their precipitous departure or realized their intent.

"Hey! You three! Stop!"

And there, at the other end of the hallway, was chance run out—a big beefy security guard, overworked on this day of restrictions and CDC invasion and highly annoyed with them for adding another thing to the mix. Maureen gasped; Hayley cursed in a low voice that was somewhat filled with awe.

"Run," Melinda said, and then louder, looking back at them, "Run for it!" And she headed for the elevator, knowing they could never make it anyway, not when they had yet to push the button—except maybe, just maybe, the car would be waiting. Maybe there wouldn't be much delay after all. Maybe they could just barely make it.

The security guard, seeing her intent, cursed in a much louder voice than Hayley had done; he, too, broke into a run. Too big to be agile, too much muscle to be quick, his hand clamped over his copious keys to keep them from bouncing right off his belt.

"Mel!" That was Jim, not a cry for her to stop, not a warning to run faster—just reaching out because he couldn't help himself. And someone in the waiting room who had apparently been waiting just a little too long shouted, "Run, girl, run!"

And Melinda ran, oh yes, hand outstretched and reaching for that button, footsteps of her cohorts behind her, the waiting room shouts rising in the background and almost overcoming the noise of the pied piper herself. The security guard pounded closer, close enough to see that his eyes were blue and furious, his arm already stretched out to block them.

*Not going to make it. Not going to make it—*

The elevator doors *whoosh*ed open on their own. Much faster than any elevator doors should ever open, but Melinda didn't hesitate to question it, just threw herself into the oversize car, making room for the other two as Hayley barreled in behind her and Maureen skittered in with a little shriek of disbelief at her own temerity. And still the security guard came on, filling the doors—

Which slammed shut just as improbably fast as they'd opened. And stayed that way, in spite of the obvious pounding the man gave the call button on the other side. Maureen stared wide-eyed, only squeaking faintly once at a particularly loud bang, and Hayley said, "Wow," and Melinda straightened her clothing, crossed her arms, and gave the empty corner an expectant look.

"*You're spozed to say* thank you," the boy said, appearing in his hospital gown and otherwise the full bloom of happily mischievous health—complete with hair.

"Thank you," Melinda said, dutifully if not without a wry bite, even breathless. "You're off your turf, aren't you?"

"*Hey, they're* all *mine. I just have my favorites.*" He scowled. "*Usually. But* she's *making a mess of things. I want her gone. You can do that, right?*"

"Who. . . ?" Maureen asked, and didn't finish, apparently deciding she didn't want to know.

"Oh, I know!" Hayley said. "Whoever messed with the elevator the last time we were on it!"

Melinda nodded, keeping her eyes on the boy. "Would you care to take us to the PICU floor, or shall I press the buttons?"

"*My elevator,*" he said, completely unaffected by the noise outside—the first guard joined by a second, and their obvious bafflement over the behavior of the mechanism. "*My buttons.*"

The car shifted; Maureen grabbed at the rail as if she'd never been in an elevator before.

"It's all right," Melinda said, as reassuring as she could be while she was still catching her breath.

"But . . . the numbers . . ."

A glance over the door revealed that the first-floor circle remained lit. The boy laughed, delighted. "*So they don't know where you are.*"

"You *are* clever," she told him, and told the other two, "He's doing it on purpose, so they won't know where we're going."

"But who . . . ?" Maureen asked again, her gaze searching the corner where Melinda had directed her comments.

"Oh, he's beside you now." Just to play with her, Melinda suspected, and she gave him a mildly admonishing look. "He's someone I met when I was first coming to see you. The hospital is . . . well, it's a busy place for me." To the boy, she said, "Play nice, okay? I need her help, and if you scare her, I might not have it."

"*She's already scared,*" the boy said, perceptive as all children could be. And then he looked directly at Melinda, and suddenly his hair was gone beneath his baseball cap, his face turned pale and gaunt, his arms thin and chest skinny beneath the gown. "*She's smart to be scared. You should be scared, too.*" And he disappeared.

"Oh, I am," Melinda breathed. "No question about that."

The elevator slowed . . . came to an appropriate and polite stop. The doors didn't open. *Our choice,* Melinda decided. She said, "There shouldn't be anyone outside this door. I hope. What we need to do is find the first empty room—there aren't likely to be any empty patient rooms, but a storage room, a bathroom . . . even one of the family rooms. She's here somewhere, I know it. . . ." Obvious enough, with that contorted song scouring her head from the inside out—but muted enough so she knew better than even to try reaching the pied piper from this elevator. The boy's influence was too strong here—for now.

And when it ran out, she realized, there was no telling how suddenly they'd be carried back down to the first floor. They'd better move.

"What if—" Maureen started.

Melinda didn't even let her get near the end of that thought. "As long as we're on this floor, we're trying to reach her. Hayley, if we need interference—"

"That's me," Hayley said, a determination in her eye that Travis Starcroft had probably never seen. "Interference."

"Here goes, then." Melinda hit the Open button; the elevator doors opened in the most normal fashion, clunky and slow, jerking in their tracks. A quick, cautious look showed her a twin to the hallway below—except here, there was carpeting instead of linoleum, and here there was a different quality to the mutter of noise in the background—a quiet tension, a murmur of desperation . . . all nearly obliterated by the song. She shrank back slightly, palms pressed to her head at the onslaught. "It's not about me," she murmured to herself. And that meant whatever she heard, the children heard so much more deeply.

"Melinda?" Hayley reached out to the Open button, this time holding it down—stopping the doors just before they would have closed again. "Are you—"

"I'm good," Melinda said. "Let's go. An empty room, and then Maureen can call her." But she pulled off her sandals first, and used them to keep the elevator door from closing all the way. Someone might find them regardless, but they wouldn't come up from this elevator. She thought she heard a childish giggle echo up the elevator shaft as she straightened, and knew at least one person approved.

They moved forward with caution, with Melinda leading the way and checking the first door they came to—locked, as was the second, and the third. Storage rooms, meeting rooms . . . if protocols for their security were ever relaxed, this wasn't the day for it. But then they came to the first patient room, around the corner from a view of the nurse's station, and Hayley drew Melinda back, hope on her face. "This is where the Rolands are," she said. "Their daughter came in after Saiyesha— I came to see them while you were gone that last weekend. They know me; they might let us use the room, if I tell them we're working on a cure."

"Oh?" Maureen said. "And are you going to tell them we'll disturb their daughter so we can talk to a *ghost*?"

Melinda gave her a patient look. "Actually, I suspect they'd be glad for anything that might disturb their daughter at all," she said. "Wouldn't you have been?"

Maureen recoiled. "You don't mince words, do you?"

"I don't have *time* to mince words," Melinda told her. "And I think the people I'm trying to help—both the dead and the living—deserve better than dancing around the truth. All that nodding, all that soothing and saying the expected thing . . . people stop listening, don't you think?"

"I—" Maureen stopped; she clutched her purse a little more tightly. "Yes," she admitted, without looking happy about it. "I guess so." And then she gave Melinda her own frank appraisal and added, "Though somehow I doubt you ever quite say the expected thing."

"There doesn't seem to be a lot of opportunity," she admitted.

"*Well?*" Hayley said, impatient. "Should I go in? Should I ask them? What should I say?"

Melinda hesitated. An empty patient room, that was one thing. A room with someone in it . . .

there was no telling what the pied piper might do. Or when the next hospital staff member or even someone from the CDC would be in to check on the child.

"The stairs," Maureen said, just as impatiently as Hayley. "They should be unlocked up here, right? Fire exit?"

The stairs. Not as private, but immediately accessible. And they'd been out in this hallway long enough. "Let's go," Melinda agreed, but she hesitated on the way past the elevator and reluctantly snagged her sandals.

"But—" Hayley said.

Maureen got it; she nodded. "It's a hospital," she said. "They need it. It's a chance we'll have to take."

"Try to watch for us?" Melinda asked the empty elevator interior as the doors jerked closed.

"*Try . . .*" A faint voice, fading before the word had barely been said, and disappearing into the pied piper's wailing song.

"He's very young," Melinda told the others. "I don't think we should count on him."

"Then we'd better hurry," Maureen said briskly. "Even if I'm faking this, I don't want to get caught in the middle of it. No, I take that back. *Especially* if I'm faking it."

"Someone's coming!" Hayley shot an alarmed look down the hallway, where two voices rose in volume—one voice full of jargon-speak and words like *PET scan, EEG,* and *cytokines,* the other saying *fungus* and *parasites* and *we didn't know about* Pfiesteria *before the late eighties, either—think outside the box!*

*Further outside the box than either of you are likely to manage.* But they ran, all three of them; Melinda didn't bother with her shoes until they'd reached the stairwell—until they'd slipped inside, one-two-three, and closed the door behind them as quietly as possible. Melinda peered out the wire-reinforced square of glass in the center of the door and saw them then, X-ray envelopes and clipboards and folders in hand, coming around the corner to one of the locked rooms. They unlocked and entered it; light flickered on, visible for only a moment as the door closed.

She pivoted to put her back to the door, leaning against it with momentary relief. They hadn't been heard; hadn't been noticed. Just quickly run out of luck on a busy floor.

"Now what?" Maureen asked grimly. "What do you want me to do?"

Melinda pushed her feet into the sandals, tugging the heel straps into place. "She might not be real to you, but she's real to me and to all these children. She's singing right now—only her song has become frantic, somehow. She's not accomplishing whatever it is she wants to do—not finding what she wants—and now she's felt at least one child slip out of her grasp. *And please, let it stay that way. Let Carmen's mother keep her awake, at least for a little while longer.* "Just talk to her. Call her—as if she was just out of sight. If my friend Delia is right . . . if she truly doesn't understand the consequences of what she's doing . . . then she *needs* to understand. And she needs to know I'll help her, if she'll only talk to me."

"And if she doesn't listen to *me?*" Maureen said drily. "Just because I'm a mother? Just because I'm the mother of the child you say she killed?"

"Then I hope at least you'll have drawn enough of her attention so I can engage her," Melinda said.

"What am I doing?" Hayley asked, looking entirely out of place in this institutionalized stairwell, her bright colors and her flying-wild hair still holding the twisted little braid Carmen had placed in the front section of it.

Melinda glanced back out the door. "You're our lookout?"

"Shoot, yes," Hayley said. "I can do that." She took up position on the other side of the window, where she, too, could peer out.

And they both looked at Maureen.

"I—" She closed her eyes, turned away from them.

"Maureen," Melinda said, "this isn't about what

your husband will think, or about the trouble we're going to get in when we're caught—because I think our chances of being caught before we get out of here are pretty high. That's the price of what we're doing, and it's worth paying. So none of that matters." She moved up to Maureen, close enough that she couldn't be ignored—close enough so it was obvious she'd just keep putting herself there, even if Maureen turned away again. "This is for Eileen. This is for the children who deserve a chance to live, just like she did. Just pretend she's up that set of stairs, just out of your sight. *Hey! I need to talk to you!*"

"Hey," Maureen said, though not with any volume.

"*Hey!*" Melinda said, fast and hard.

"Hey!" Maureen said, annoyed now. *Good.* "I need to talk to you!"

"I know you're here, and I need to talk to you," Melinda prompted her. "Think of Eileen. Think of what you'd say to any living woman who tried to hurt her."

"I know you're here!" Maureen said, her back straightening noticeably.

But the song never faltered. The pied piper didn't care.

"Sing this," Melinda told her.

Hayley shifted restlessly by the window, stiffened, and then relaxed. "Into the elevator," she updated them, and then shifted her attention to sounds in the stairwell above them—a door opening, closing again. A few quiet words, voices raising, and then the doors—two people apparently choosing the stairwell for a few private words, just as they had.

Maureen looked at Melinda in despair. "Sing?"

"*Sleep, my child, and peace attend thee . . .*"

Maureen stared at her in surprise. "Why . . . that's beautiful! Don't tell me that's the song—"

Melinda nodded. "Sing it," she said. "With me. It doesn't matter—it's your voice that will matter." She took a deep breath, started strong—never mind that she completely overshadowed Maureen at first, her voice a sweet contralto. She sang a phrase, let Maureen repeat it, sang another—and soon enough Maureen's volume grew. "*Soft, the drowsy hours are creeping, hill and vale in slumber sleeping—*"

That's how far they got, before Maureen's face flushed with sudden anger. "You and your song!" she shouted, and the stairwell rang with it. "You're hurting our children, and I won't have it! You killed my daughter!"

"Whoa," Hayley muttered, unheard by Maureen and barely heard by Melinda. "You go, girl!"

Barely heard, because the pied piper shrieked up several scales in anger, and Melinda's arms tingled with the intensity of the spiritual energy, the pinpricks of miniature lightning racing along her skin and up her shoulders to meet at her spine, gathering there to build in her head as the stairwell darkened around her.

"What?" Maureen said, suddenly uncertain again, her freckles stark against her pale skin even as she faded into that darkness. "Do you . . . is that—?"

"You got her attention," Melinda said, putting one hand on the ceramic-faced cement block wall to keep her bearings. "Talk to her. I'll hear anything she says to you. Ask her what she's looking for . . . ask her what she needs."

"I don't care what she—"

"*Ask* her!" Melinda closed her eyes against the darkness, looking for that familiar white silhouette. Even her own voice came to her dimly through the noise of the angry ghost, shrieking her unrecognizable song. "She's not doing this out of malice, Maureen"—*I don't think*—"she *needs* something, and she doesn't know how to find it. Until I can help her with that, she's not going to stop. She's not going to cross into the light. So just *ask* her."

"Voices," Hayley said. "Below us. Not sure—"

"I know you're here," Maureen said, not quite as convincing as before. "Tell me what you're looking for."

"No," Melinda whispered as the darkness lifted

slightly, the oppressive winds of energy easing from her skin. "We're losing her."

Hayley stepped forward. "Eileen was five," she said loudly. "She was opinionated and sassy and even a little spoiled. She struggled with her numbers, but she loved to read. She thought Smurf ice cream was the best *ever*. She had freckles like her mother, and she had her father's chin and eyes. She had the best smile you've ever seen—it took over her whole face and made you smile back, no matter what you had going on. She had pudgy little arms that knew how to hug really hard, and we miss her so very much. You took her from us, and *you owe us some answers.*"

Tears ran freely down Maureen's face; she took Hayley's hand. "She was my *baby*!" she said. "Purple was her favorite color. She had a kitten named Smudge and a gerbil named Mac, and she couldn't really understand why they wouldn't be best friends. She was my baby, and we buried her yesterday, and *you owe us some answers!*"

Hayley said something then, but Melinda couldn't hear her; she heard only the wailing, a series of barbed-wire notes twisting through her mind as darkness settled around her. She tried to say something and couldn't—or maybe she did say something and just couldn't tell. She barely felt hands on her arms, supporting her . . . keeping her upright. *Barely.* "I know you're here," she said,

which had to be the understatement of the year—
and she wasn't sure if she said that out loud, or just
inside her own head. "Please, tell me what you
need. What you're looking for. I want to help you."

Hostility washed over her, and determination,
and the sense that no one, *no one* was going to
stop this song—no one would be allowed to interfere.

"I do want to stop you," Melinda admitted. "I
*have* to stop you. You've already killed one child.
I'll do whatever it takes to keep you from killing
another. But we can still find what you need! We
just have to do it a different way. You've been all
alone; you haven't had anyone to help you. Now
you've got me, and if you can just trust me, we
can—"

*Fury and disbelief and spiraling power—*

"We can work together!" Melinda cried. "Don't
tell me you want to kill these children. I can't believe it. Not with the gentleness of your song when
it started. That song held love, not harm."

The merest of hesitations in that onslaught—
the angry winds of energy, the prickles of spiritual
fury. The darkness pulsed around her.

"I knew it!" Melinda pushed forward into that
hesitation. "It *was* love. Your love, and your loss. I
can help you, I swear I can. We can do this a different way, a way that doesn't leave more children
like Eileen—"

Denial at that—resentment and *I would never* and *How dare you—!*

Melinda winced; she braced herself. Delia had been right . . . this spirit not only hadn't meant to hurt Eileen, she couldn't even bear the thought that it might have happened at all.

But she wasn't going to stop what she was doing unless she understood the consequences.

Melinda braced herself, leaning into the gusting emotions, battered by darkness. Determined. She couldn't back down, not this time. She wouldn't get another chance . . . not until it was far too late, with children in various stages of fading away from this life throughout this hospital. "I *do* dare," she said. "Because I've been watching it happen. Children falling asleep . . . children not waking up. I saw Eileen die. And her spirit *was already gone.* Now, you act like the loving mother you once were and you pull yourself together and talk to—"

Fingers tightened around her arm, yanking her back to the world in which the stairwell flickered with fluorescent light, and the ghost's anger stirred her hair and set goose bumps on her arms. Maureen, flushed and wild-eyed, held her from one side. But it was Hayley who'd snatched her away from that precious private conversation, and Melinda cried, "*Why?*" and "I have to go to her," but then she heard it—pounding steps on the stairs from below.

Purposeful, fast-moving . . .

"They know we're here!" Maureen said, her whisper strained.

"Or they're guessing." Melinda glanced up. They could go up a floor, try their luck . . . maybe get into an empty patient room above a room on this floor. It'd be just as close as anything on this floor. *Hindsight. Should have tried that first.* "Up," she said, pointing.

"But—" Hayley didn't get it; Maureen didn't get it. And when Melinda drew breath to say it again, all too aware of the flickering light and impossible indoor breeze and the looming presence of the pied piper, the stairwell door quite suddenly slammed open—hard enough to hit the wall behind it and bounce back, barely missing the three of them.

They cried out in startled fear, all of them, and recoiling from the two men barging through in their security blues. And though Melinda was the first to react, she was also the closest to the door, the easiest to snatch. "Over the rooms!" she cried to Hayley. "Run!"

Hayley sprinted away like a startled young deer, flashing red and bright stripes and flying hair. Melinda shouted, "Keep talking to her!" because she wasn't about to let this opportunity get away, not even with the guards from the ER pounding into sight on the landing below them, red-faced and, yeah, really unhappy about running up the stairs at all. And because really, even if the four guards were brusque and a little rough as they shoved her and Maureen onto the PICU, wasn't that exactly where she wanted to be?

"Ow, ow, ow!" she said, a protest as well as a cry of pain when one of the men clamped down just a little too hard on her arm after all, still bruised at that. He glanced at her braced wrist, glanced at his rough grip, looked abashed . . . but not a whole lot. Only enough to move his hand to her shoulder.

"You three have caused a whole lot of trouble," he said. "We've got a hospital in crisis, and you're playing games? Not cool, lady."

"We're not anything near *playing games*," Melinda told him, offended.

"What about the third one?" One of the guards from the ER lingered in the doorway, still panting—quite obviously hoping to let Hayley go for now.

"Wait until we get a sighting," the other ER guard said, and the man holding Melinda nodded. None of them seemed to notice Maureen's tremulous tears; none of them seemed to notice the flickering lights—not just in the stairwell, but in the hallway as well. "Let's go."

"Where are you taking us?" Maureen asked, her voice tight and thin.

"Security office," the man said—he seemed to be in charge, or at least the most likely to talk.

"The elevator, I damned well hope," one of the ER guards said.

"Four of you," Melinda said, thinking only that she somehow had to stay on this floor. *Somehow.* Hoping that Hayley had better luck upstairs than they'd had here. "You'd think this was a slow day."

"Don't be smart." The hold on her shoulder tightened. "You're in enough trouble."

"You don't understand—I'm trying to help—"

"Yeah?" The man snorted. "You're doing it wrong."

Maybe. Maybe there had been another way. Maybe there'd been another way days ago, when she hadn't been able to get the pied piper to talk to her. Maybe she'd missed something . . . maybe she'd gone the wrong direction.

Then again, not a whole lot of clues around here to go on. She still didn't have a name, still didn't know what had killed the woman, or when she'd died. She knew only what Delia surmised—that she was a mother—and what she'd guessed: that the ghost was searching for something. *Someone.*

The lights flickered. One of the guards muttered, "Just what we need." And another said impatiently, "Let's just take care of this," and they hurry-marched Melinda around the corner, where they ran smack into Saiyesha's family. Drawn, worn . . . losing hope. Her mother and her aunt, with her father not in evidence.

"Melinda?" Saiyesha's mother said, startled.

"Maureen?" said one of the women at the nurses' station, equally startled. "*You're* the intruder we were warned about? What are you doing here?"

"I needed—" Maureen started, and ran out of words. "I just needed—"

"You know these women?" said the most vocal of the guards.

"She helped us," Saiyesha's mother said. "She helped my daughter. Saiyesha hasn't lost ground nearly as quickly as . . ." She glanced at Maureen and away; she must have been familiar with the name. "As some. And we've shared what you told us. Listen . . ."

They all did, for that moment—even the guards, in an automatic reaction. Up and down this main hallway, from within the rooms, came the sound of straggling music. Off-tune, worn voices . . . tired voices. But determined voices, singing children's songs. Clashing CD players muttered in the background, mixing "Bingo" with "The Hokey-Pokey" with "Five Little Fishes" with songs too mingled to identify.

"Oh my God," Melinda said. "*That's* what happened. That's what triggered her off—" What changed her song, sending her into fierce overdrive. The resistance—a resistance that had spread as quickly as the children had come in, and the children had started coming in sooner and sooner in the cycle, before they'd even fully fallen into the pied piper's spell. She raised her voice. "Do you see? If you want what you need, you'll *have* to come to me, because these people won't let you have their children!"

"Maureen?" A wary note entered the voice of the nurse behind the desk.

Maureen opened her mouth to respond, but had no words; she only shook her head.

And that's when the lights went out. Abruptly, no warning. One of the guards cursed; the one who held Melinda clamped down on her, sparks flew from the darkened lights overhead, and Melinda thought, *Hayley,* and *She's done it,* and then almost instantly went to the delicate electrical equipment monitoring these children, helping to keep some of them alive.

She wasn't the only one. "Where's the generator?" The nurse demanded of the guards. "What's going on?"

"Check it out," the guard demanded, and someone seemed to know who and what he meant, because amid the pitch-black chaos, one of the men shifted and clicked and spoke into his radio microphone—and then shouted in surprise as the whole thing spewed a hail of sparks, lighting his features as he flung the mike away.

"Oh, just *stop it*!" Melinda cried at the ghost. "Can't you see who you're hurting the most? It's not me, and it's not these people—it's the children! Is that really what you want? Is that how you want to be remembered? And what about *your* family, your child or children? Is this the legacy you would leave?"

One of the security guards muttered a profoundly rude assessment of her sanity—words that would have turned Jim on him in an instant.

As if she hadn't heard it all before.

"Talk to me! Whatever you *really* want, we'll find a way to make it happen!"

"Do you know who's doing this?" the guard demanded.

"Yes!" she said. "I told you—"

"You—!" Maureen screamed into the darkness. "You selfish—! Maybe you didn't know what you were doing before, but now we're *telling* you!"

"Hey!" Her escort shouted in surprise; flickering sparks revealed Maureen torn from his grip and heading down the hall.

"Keep singing to them!" she called into the patient rooms. "Don't let them go! Keep singing!" And then, shouting into the hallway, her face lifted and gleaming wet in the spark light, "You can't have them! No more!"

"There!" Melinda said, pointing at the hard white glare of a figure at the end of the hall. "There she is!"

"Where? *Who?*"

The guard beside her held tight with a grip full of frustration, but Melinda didn't need physical freedom to step up to this ghost. "Do you see, now? What you've been doing will no longer work. We're not giving up our children so freely. Whatever you need, you'll have to talk to me to get it— and I *want* to help you. It's far past time for you to cross over into the Light."

Anger lashed back at her, howling in sound— tearing through her mind with razor claws. Anger that they would interfere, fury that they would accuse her of such horrifying things. She barely heard it when the guard said, "Whoa, she's going down!" and still there was Maureen in the background and the darkness and then someone softening her fall to the floor, lowering her with unfamiliar hands. And then she couldn't hear or feel those things at all, just the anger and denial and deep, thrumming sorrow, all so tangled with her own thoughts that she couldn't even begin to think through the chaos.

*Silence.* She needed silence. She needed a space for her voice to be heard.

*Silence.*

She'd done it once—made a single slice of silence in the pied piper's gripping cacophony. She could do it again. Not to escape, this time . . . but to create the room for conversation. To stop this violence and start the communication.

*Go away,* she'd thought before. Not this time. But the same purity of *want,* so hard to find with her mind twisting and writhing under such vast twining reverberation of emotion and sound. *Silencesilencesilencesilence,* and she tried to find the same place, the same intensity . . . the same *feel* that she'd been in the night before, when she'd finally done the thing that had reached this spirit, however briefly.

Oh—*there*! Blessed flicker of a soundless moment, followed head-on by astonishment. Another, and Melinda lifted her head, found the ghost in the corner, her stark nuclear-white presence dimming slightly. Another, and she made it to her knees, never slacking in her focus . . . not even when she asked gently, "Who is the lullaby for?"

*Tap, tap, tap.* A little girl's voice shrieked out into the silence. *"No, Mummy! No, watch out!"* And shrieking brakes, shriller than the fractured song. The sound of impact, metal against flesh, and the ghost flickered wildly; sparks cascaded, peeling out from every wire overhead.

Not enough to follow . . . not quite yet. Not without more than sound to go on. So she kept talking. "It wasn't Eileen. We know that much, because you didn't stop looking. And it wasn't Saiyesha, or the little girl after that, or any of these others. And yet you don't want us interfering to recover them."

That same puzzlement . . . the anger and denial and *"No, Mummy!"* and deep, deep yearning . . . more than that. Protectiveness.

"You're not protecting these children, whatever you think," Melinda said. "You're killing them. But you don't understand that, do you? For you it's all about the one child. She's trying to warn you? Did you die in an accident?" The shriek of tires and brakes as Jim stepped out into the street at the store . . . this is where they had come from. This woman, becoming aware of herself.

*Tap, tap, tap.* Familiar, that sound. Confusing, as though her two most needy spirits had mixed their signals. And then the ghost began to fade completely. Not the slight dimming she'd shown before, the one which, if completed, would have allowed her features to show through—but a departure. "No!" Melinda took several swift steps in her direction. If the guards or the nurse had anything to say about it, she couldn't hear them. Only the ghost and the hallway around them . . . not the frightened parents, not Maureen, not anyone else who might have arrived on the scene. "You have to see that we can stop you now! *I* can stop you. You're growing weaker, and you haven't found what you want, what you *need*. But I can help you do that!" She stopped, held out a beseeching hand. "Show me," she said. "Can you do that?"

She wasn't expecting the sudden slice of dark,

dark humor she felt. Or the sudden immersion into not-quite-complete darkness, a world of dim and shadowy figures, only the barest difference between light and darkness. The *tap, tap, tap* suddenly came through to her palm; she carried a stick.

*A cane.*

Before she could voice her understanding, she found herself walking forward, caught up in the inexorable pull toward death . . . confident tapping, familiar ground. Stopping at the curb of the suburban street, ready to cross to the park with her daughter lagging behind, tugging at their joined hands . . . disobedient. Listening for car engines at this crosswalk, hearing nothing. Taking that first step, the second—and losing her grip on her daughter. Turning . . . looking for her . . . hands outstretched and patting the air . . .

Only dimly hearing the engine of the speeding car. Hearing more acutely her terrified daughter. "*No, Mummy! No, watch out!*" Hearing the sound of a terrible, terrible impact.

Hearing nothing.

Melinda gasped—she flailed for her bearings, here in the darkness. Her braced wrist struck a wall; she clung to it a moment, drawing herself upright. "You can't see," she said, realizing it. "You're looking for a child you never saw . . . one you can't find by sight."

*Sorrow, sorrow, sorrow.*

"That doesn't matter now, you know," Melinda

told her. "Whatever limitations you had in life . . . those aren't part of you now. They don't *have* to be, anyway. It's your choice—whether you know you're making the choice or not." The pied piper might have dimmed a little more, become less blinding, her features just barely peeking through like a photo so overexposed it washed out all detail. But no more than that, and Melinda suddenly understood. "But what's the point, right? Because you can't recognize her by sight, whether you can see or not. It'd just be distracting. So . . . you're singing to her. And . . . what, examining the souls of the little girls you draw to you? Because that's what's happening, you know. Eileen's spirit . . . it never left her body. That's because it was already gone, wasn't it? Why didn't you just let it go when you saw it wasn't your daughter?"

But in order to respond, the woman would have to stop singing. And she wouldn't. Or couldn't.

Or either way, wasn't.

Now, as Melinda let the song back into her head, it no longer scraped along her thoughts . . . instead, it wailed in sorrow, throbbing with loss and desperation. Now it wrapped itself around her very heart, so she understood. It was more than reunion this woman sought. She'd been resting, unaware of herself—and then torn from that rest by a mother's sudden need to protect her endangered child.

"Talk to me," she said. "Talk to me, and I'll help

you find her. Tell me who you are; tell me when you died and where. I can help you find her. I can help you find peace so you can let go of these children and go into the Light."

Blind desperation, blinder than any loss of sight. *Tap, tap, tap.*

*She'd been resting.*

How long? How many years?

Her endangered child . . . a daughter . . .

How long?

Just because she was looking for five- and six-year-olds now didn't mean her daughter was still that age.

*She'd been resting, and torn from it by her child's need.*

Just because she'd left her daughter alive didn't mean she was still alive now.

"Angie," she said. "Your daughter's name is Angie. And I know where we can find her . . . if you let these children go."

# 15

MELINDA GAZED OUT on the familiar Otigwa Lake overlook and shivered, even if she tried to hide it from him. Bright sunshine, birds flitting in the fresh foliage, faint breeze rustling up the underside of the leaves . . . pure bright spring day, and still the shiver. "Thanks for coming."

"You can't think I'd let you come back up here alone." He cut the engine, gave her a sideways glance and defensive hands. "I know, I know— You do what you have to do. But in this case . . . I stand by that. Not alone. Not after what happened before." Not that it hadn't taken some fancy footwork to get his shift covered . . . and he'd be cooking meals at the fire station for a month.

But worth it.

"Hey, no argument here. I don't want to be anywhere near the wheel of a car when it comes to this overlook. I mean, I think Angie's gotten past that, but . . . if I'd had to park miles down the road and walk up here, that's what I'd have done." She looked at him, smiled. "This way is much better. Besides, look at the great company I got to keep on the drive."

"There *is* that," he said, as if his ego was really that big. But it made her smile again, and it covered his worry. And it kept the conversation away from the car pulling in beside them—Maureen Starcroft and Hayley, with the noticeable absence of Travis Starcroft.

Travis Starcroft, Jim thought, was likely to be noticeably absent for some time. Not smart of the man, to show up at the hospital in the aftermath of the excitement and lay the law down to Maureen. Not smart to try to wrest back control of his un-controllable life by sending her home, by forbidding her further contact with Hayley and Melinda. Not that he ever saw the woman as hitting the BFF category with either of them, but . . .

No, not the smart thing to do. Not to a woman who had just conquered all her own insecurities, crossing the line of her own beliefs to confront the spirit who had taken her daughter. Not to mention the whole *defiance of authority* that had gotten them up to the PICU in the first place.

And so Travis Starcroft had moved to an apartment in town until individual and couples counseling took hold . . . or didn't.

Hayley, too, seemed to have found a new freedom in her ability to take action in spite of the odds—Jim no longer saw her wavering from confident to uncertain, and Melinda had remarked on the same.

Totally worth a little ribbing from Bobby about his clumsy moment with the equipment cart. *Totally* worth it.

The aftermath at the hospital . . . something else again. Trying to pretend that he was caught up in picking up his mess . . . trying to pretend that he didn't know exactly what was going on, or that the woman he loved was involved. From the moment the elevator doors snapped shut so unnaturally to the moment security had given up on their various override procedures and gotten their vague PICU sighting to go pounding up the stairs . . . then everyone there had been interested; then he hadn't had to pretend. Though by the time anyone understood what had happened—the mysterious power outage in PICU, the inexplicable events that left security closedmouthed and the CDC speechless, and no one at all offering any explanations for an entire ward of children suddenly emerged from various coma states—it was good and done with.

As for how she'd walked away from security . . .

"It was dark," Melinda had told him. "And I had a blind woman to guide us." For it hadn't taken much to scoop up Maureen along the way . . . and then to hesitate in the stairwell, where they'd met up with Hayley, as the lights came back on and the children began to wake, eliciting astonished celebration from the entire floor.

They'd emerged from the stairwell into ER with tears still flowing, but Jim knew joy when he saw it.

He'd also known to hustle them on out of there before security found their way back down, and he hadn't thought to question the quick open-and-shut salute the elevator doors offered them on the way by, or Melinda's quick, "Scott! I'll be back for you!" outside in the parking lot.

But Melinda had a bargain left to fulfill . . . and Maureen and Hayley wanted to see it through. So here they were, on a warming spring day, the noon sun shining down on the overlook and not leaving much to the imagination when it came to the mangled guardrail or the smashed foliage below.

"Anyone here?" Jim asked, unbuckling his seat belt.

Melinda's fingers twitched toward hers, but stilled. They'd agreed on that before coming—he'd be at the door before she unbuckled; he'd twine his arm through hers even as she got out. "Humor me," he'd said, and it must have shown on his face—the memory of the last time they'd been here.

"Nothing so far," she told him, and she waited as he disembarked and went around. "But I think I know how to get them." She slipped from the Outlook with much more grace than he ever had to hand and took his arm, turning it into a cozy gesture.

"You sure?" he asked, with an eye toward the overlook as she gazed in that direction.

She shook her head. "You've got me. And . . . Angie's been quiet since she came to me the other night. I think she's frightened by what she did . . . to herself, to her foster mother . . . even to me."

He stepped behind her, wrapping his arms around hers at her waist, resting his chin on her head. "I've got you, all right." She leaned back into him, as if to say that was perfectly all right with her.

Maureen and Hayley joined them, offering matching expressions of inquiry; Melinda shook her head slightly beneath his chin. "But I bet they're not far." She smiled—he couldn't see it, but he knew that tilt of her head. "Let's see if I'm right."

He knew the moment before she started singing what she was going to do—felt the expansion of her slender torso, the inhalation of air. He closed his eyes as she sang out to the overlook, her voice gentle and sweet and confident.

*Sleep, my child, and peace attend thee,*
*All through the night*
*Guardian angels God will send thee,*
*All through the night . . .*

And by then Hayley had joined her, her alto reaching a little to find Melinda's natural range, and Maureen—her voice thinner, less certain, but knowing the song. They couldn't help but know the song.

*Soft the drowsy hours are creeping*
*Hill and vale in slumber sleeping*
*I my loving vigil keeping,*
*All through the night.*

"Ah," Melinda said then—looking off to the side, where Jim could see nothing at all, nothing but deep tire tracks in the soft dirt leading over the edge, where tires never should have gone at all. "Angie. I thought you might remember that song." She straightened slightly, turning—but didn't try to move out of Jim's grip. Good thing, too—as if he would have let her.

"That?" Melinda smiled again, at what only she could see. "That's your mother."

Angie looked dumbfounded. A slender, colt-legged girl with fair skin and even fairer hair, she stood in midair just past the edge of the overlook. She showed none of the injuries that had caused her death, but her eyes had no color at all. Filled with unfathomable darkness, endlessly deep . . . Melinda sensed rather than saw that the girl looked at her, but the remainder of her expression showed clearly enough. *"Mummy?"* she whispered.

The pied piper was as ever—a glaring white silhouette, even in this daylight expanse—her edges limned with deepest black to match her child's eyes. It was barely possible to see her stiffen, to see by the change in her facial outline that she'd opened her mouth . . . but she'd been singing so long, she didn't seem to know what to do with actual words.

*"Mummy, you came for me? Even after what I did? What I've . . . done?"*

"That wasn't your fault," Melinda said, and her heart went out to the confusion holding this young girl back. "That woman was supposed to take care of you, not take advantage of you. And thanks to you, a friend of mine has already made a call to the authorities, and the man who took those photos . . . he'll be found. He'll be stopped, and he'll pay for what he's done. I'm so sorry that everyone let you down, that no one helped in time to stop what you experienced . . . but no one else will ever face his camera."

She straightened a little. *"That's good,"* she said,

but her attention never left the other spirit. Waiting for understanding . . . waiting for forgiveness there, too, her eyes full and black and shimmering.

"Your mother is confused," Melinda said gently. "She's been sleeping, in a way." Held here, Melinda suspected, by her daughter's very presence . . . but not aware, not watching. Not realizing. "She doesn't realize how much time has passed. What's her name, can you tell me?"

*"Pam,"* the girl said uncertainly. She wavered slightly, as if she might run, as if her mother's failure to respond to her was too much to absorb.

"Give her a moment, Angie. Let me see if I can help." Melinda beckoned to her, as carefully as if Angie had been a shy young deer. "Come stand with me. You don't have to be alone any longer, not even while you wait for your mother to understand." Angie shifted slightly, her head tipping up, and Melinda laughed. "Don't worry about him," she said. "He's with me. He can't see you. He's here because he loves me." Jim's arms tightened slightly around her, but he took his cue from her soothing voice and didn't speak up. "And my other two friends . . . they're here because they loved a little girl a lot like you."

Angie shifted like wispy smoke, leaving an imprint of herself behind . . . not quite committing to her new position on solid ground, close to these adults she didn't know. Melinda had the impression she would snap back like a rubber band at the first sign of trouble, and she couldn't blame the girl. So she was careful when she moved within Jim's arms, turning slightly to face the wavering bright silhouette. "Pam, after your accident . . . you lost some time. But your daughter didn't . . . your beautiful daughter continued to grow. Until she had an accident of her own . . . and that's what woke you, and made you so frantic to find her. But you were looking among the living in Grandview . . . and Angie was here, in Otigwa. And like you, she's no longer alive. But now you've found her, and you know she's as safe as she can be—and you can cross into the Light together."

The featureless cutout of light of Pam's spirit fluctuated, full of confusion . . . trying to understand so many things at once. Melinda felt her emotions—whirlwinds of shock and sorrow and disbelief, as cyclonic as the windstorm she'd created in the hospital hallway. Her hand—a mere flutter of light and dark—lifted, reaching out toward Angie, but briefly, ever so briefly, before it fell back and disappeared into the generic whiteness of her overall form. Angie hiccoughed a heartbroken sob and began to fade; Melinda bit her lip in dismay.

"What?" Hayley asked, a mere whisper. "What is it?"

Jim shook his head, a gesture felt rather than

seen. "I don't think it's going well. The singing ghost . . . it's a lot for her."

*The singing ghost.* Her own singing had brought them both here, but Pam might not have realized that—might have answered the call without knowing what had brought her, *or* her daughter. So . . . "Sing," she told the woman. "This one last time. Sing for your daughter."

And after a moment, Pam sang.

She sang as it had been when she started, as it was meant to be. A lullaby full of love and heart. Not the familiar opening phrase, but words from the final verse, particularly fitting . . . particularly poignant. "*'Though sad fate our lives may sever, parting will not last forever . . .'*"

Angie didn't hesitate. She firmed up, filling in, her liquid eyes pulsing with the music and her sweet little girl's voice. "*'There's a hope that leaves me never, all through the night.'*"

Melinda gasped, backing into Jim's firm grasp, as Pam exploded into champagne sparks that spiraled up and down her form to strip away the glaring white coat of her silhouette. Melinda could only hold her breath, squinting against a shower so bright that it burned itself against her eyes in flashbulb blind spots, waiting . . .

Blinking furiously and waiting . . .

While Angie shifted from one foot to another, her hands gripping the hem of her shirt and tugging, giving away her youth and her fears, waiting . . .

"Ah," Melinda said, her hands tightening over Jim's. "She can see, now."

Pam looked down at herself . . . casual stay-at-home-mom suit, a light, soft sweater over jeans. She looked at her hands, opening and closing them; she looked at her body, patting herself with those hands as if she needed to see the one touch the other in order to believe it.

*"Mummy?"*

Pam jerked her head up. She saw Angie and her face crumpled; she held out her arms. *"Blue,"* she whispered. *"I knew blue would look just like your eyes."*

And Angie's eyes were indeed suddenly blue, a soft sky blue to match her fair hair and girl-fresh complexion. She sobbed and ran full tilt for her mother, wrapping her arms tightly around her waist. *"You came for me; you came for me!"*

And Pam, while she stroked her daughter's hair and rubbed between her shoulder blades, looked over at Melinda. *"I didn't know,"* she said. *"I only knew to call for her, and to examine those who came. I didn't realize that those who came to me were so deeply called that they never left. I couldn't even feel them any longer."*

"She's together with her daughter," Melinda

said, sagging slightly in relief. Jim knew how to interpret that—she felt his relief in turn. She looked at Maureen, at Hayley—knew what they needed to know most. "She didn't realize that her call was so strong that even when she'd seen enough of a child to know it wasn't hers, she hadn't actually let her go. She didn't know what she was doing to any of them with her song."

"And Eileen?" Hayley was the one to ask it, with Maureen gripping her hand so very tightly, urging her on. "You said you didn't see her when she passed. Her spirit. That . . . it was already gone."

"I think she was still caught up by Pam's song—trapped with Pam, somehow," Melinda said. "I had hoped to see her when Pam stopped singing at the hospital, but . . . since we haven't, we can hope she's already passed into the Light. She was very young, without much to keep her here."

Pam lifted her head, catching Melinda's eye—and while she didn't remove her soothing hands from her daughter, her nod was enough to take Melinda's gaze to the right spot. To the little girl standing on the other side of Maureen, patting her mother's hip with the proprietary air of a bossy little girl just now going puzzled. "Ah," Melinda said. "She did stay with you."

"*Not that I knew it. I truly was blind, to everything but that which I sought. It was no wonder that my physical limitations lingered.*" She smiled, sad and small and wry. *"But she must have been so lost . . . she had no idea where else to go."*

And by now Maureen was brushing at her side as one might brush away an insect, until Melinda said, "Maureen," and smiled and looked down at Eileen. "Do you remember me?"

Maureen gasped. "Eileen!" she cried. "Eileen!"

But Eileen was no multitasker; she looked back at Melinda, happy enough to ignore her mother now that she was clinging to her. *"You were at the park,"* Eileen said. *"Last week."*

"Not long ago," Melinda agreed. "Would you like to say good-bye to your mommy and Hayley?"

*"Daddy?"*

Tight sadness constricted Melinda's throat. "You can tell me your good-byes to your daddy. I promise I'll tell him exactly what you say."

*"I can do that,"* Eileen declared, and proceeded to give her a lengthy list while Melinda's eyes widened and Maureen and Hayley exchanged knowing glances. *"And he has to lock the door at night, and feed my kitty her special treats, and . . . maybe that's all. And I love him."*

"I think maybe that last part is the most important, don't you?"

*"Of course!"* Eileen tossed her head and her curly hair, every bit the princess in her hospital gown as she'd been sitting on the park bench and expecting

ice cream to come her way. *"But he knows that. Daddies do."*

"You're pretty smart," Melinda told her. "And how about your mommy? I can tell her everything you say."

*"Oh, no, I don't need to say anything to Mommy,"* Eileen declared, and Melinda's surprise must have shown; Maureen guessed the worst and bit her lip and swiped away a tear—but barely had time to do it before Eileen ran at her and threw her arms around Maureen's thighs—and then, a whirlwind, went straight to Hayley to do the same. Hayley staggered back slightly, her eyes widened, her hand tightly wrapped around Maureen's, as Eileen flung herself away with just as much energy. *"Good-bye, Mommy! Good-bye, Hayley! I love and love you!"*

Pam kissed her daughter's head and held out her hand to Eileen, who skipped up to take it. *"I brought her this far,"* she said. *"Tell her mother I'll see her safely to the other side."*

*I will,* Melinda said with her nod.

Just as soon as she could find her voice again.

# 16

Rick Payne stood just a little too close and managed to whisper just a little too loudly. "No kidding. You made a Cone of Silence? And that worked?"

"I hadn't thought of it in those terms," Melinda murmured, watching Hayley gesture expansively from the small portable platform that made up the stage at Tiny Hearts Pre-K School. As brightly dressed as ever, her hair gathered into a high ponytail that all but exploded behind her head and a happy flush on her caramel cheeks, Hayley returned her hands to the acoustic guitar strapped over her shoulders and strummed the final chorus of the song in which she led the class, tipping her ear toward them as though she couldn't hear them at all—which of course led to enthusiastic singing that could more properly be called shouting.

"And you took on the security guards? Boy, I'd

have given anything to be a fly on the wall for that one. And just what's going on here exactly? That you thought I'd want to see?"

"If I'm right, a farewell to some new friends," she said, and glanced at him. "You know, you really need to get out of your office more often, if watching that whole mess at the hospital is your idea of fun."

"Well, not fun, exactly." He shifted away from her slightly as Jim gave him a no-kidding look. "So what's our story? We're here to cheer on the debut of your colorful friend?"

Melinda spoke through lightly gritted teeth. "We *are* here to cheer on Hayley's debut." Her first job in children's entertainment, even if it was a volunteer gig. Her days were mostly taken up working with Saiyesha, who had come out of her coma with some special needs. She'd recover, the doctors said, given time . . . but for now, she required someone to take her to physical and cognitive therapy, and to work with her on the cognitive exercises at home. And while her doting parents did those things as best they could, they wanted the best for Saiyesha while they were at work. And so even now, Saiyesha sat in the hollow made by one of the Tiny Hearts' teacher's crossed legs, singing just as loudly as the rest of them, her clapping slightly off time.

"Oh, hey—" Payne pulled out a folded newspaper, tapping the front-page story about the up-state child porn ring, and the anonymous tipster who had broken the case several days earlier. "See? That's me!"

Melinda snorted softly. "Strictly speaking, that's me."

"*Hey.* Did you or did you not wake me up in the middle of the night to ask me to do this?"

Okay, points to him. She turned her head, low-ered her voice even more, and hoped he'd get the hint. "Well, you're right. I needed your help, and I appreciate it. Angie appreciated it, too."

Fortunately, the conversation didn't seem to be bothering the children at all, and it certainly wasn't bothering Hayley—flushed with success, delighted at the children's responsiveness. All the same, Melinda was glad they'd chosen to linger in the back of the room, near the door—although she couldn't deny she'd be amused at the sight of Jim folding himself up to sit on one of the avail-able lilliputian chairs. But if Payne got any louder, she figured she could just push him right on out.

It was a thought that didn't last long, startled out of existence by Delia's appearance in the door-way—tiptoeing with exaggeration, Ned trailing at her heels. "Delia!" she whispered. "What . . . ?"

Hayley started a new song—one last song, she told them—getting all the children to their feet and coaching them in the clapping and *ooh!* and *ahh!* noises of punctuation that they would make on cue.

"I wanted to cheer Hayley on," Delia whispered back. "It's so neat that she got into this because of . . . well, you know."

"Right," Melinda said, barely suppressing a smile. Back to not saying things out loud, they were. "And Ned?"

"We thought he could pick up some pointers on the whole Teen Reader Leader thing," Delia said. "This is supposed to be one of the best programs in town."

"Ah," Melinda said, not quite convinced. "Well, he's just in time to help hand out cupcakes when Hayley is done, anyway."

Ned slunk around in front of her to claim a piece of wall on the other side of Jim. On the way by, he muttered, "Are you kidding? I figured something was up." Always a little more interested in the ghostly side of things than Delia would prefer, that was Ned . . . and he'd come to have a pretty good instinct for those moments Melinda was multitasking between worlds.

"And if we're lucky, you're right," Melinda told him, though not without a quick glance at Delia to find her engrossed in watching Hayley and the children, her eyes bright and fully immersed in mom mode—not to mention a little probable memory mode going on there.

And then she looked past Jim, past Payne and Ned, to the foursome waiting impatiently in the corner. "Come with me this afternoon," she'd invited them, after getting their attention with the simple lift of a vintage turntable needle to scratchy fifties vinyl. They'd been quiet since the pied piper had gone . . . singing in the shadows, humming in the background, but gone sad and a little wistful. In a way they'd all been players in the larger whole, and now they were left behind, still unfulfilled, still unable to articulate just what they needed.

She hoped she'd figured it out. That it was as simple as that, after all.

Hayley finished the song with enthusiastic applause for the children and led them in clapping for each other, too—and then asked them to keep their seats while she passed out cupcakes and milk, a specially approved treat. As she pulled her guitar strap over her head, she caught Melinda's eye and nodded slightly.

"You're on, fellows," Melinda murmured to them—and like that, they appeared on the little stage, perfectly placed and aligned, and in a spotlight, to boot. Their eyes twinkled, their suits were pressed, their straw boaters had not a single smudge; their red bow ties were exactly straight. As one, they took breath; as one their expressions lit and they began to sing. Not one of their bawdy songs, thank goodness, and not one of the seriously sentimental tunes, either, but a lively, engaging song that filled the room with enthusiastic, exacting harmony.

> *Pack up your troubles in your old kit-bag*
> *And smile, smile, smile.*
> *Don't let your joy and laughter hear the*
>    *snag*
> *Smile, boys, that's the style!*

Melinda couldn't help it—she nodded with the music. The children stopped their chatter and turned to the stage, mesmerized; one little girl stood up and bounced in time to the music.

"They all hear it, don't they?" Payne said, fascinated. "They *see* it." And then he frowned. "That isn't at all fair."

Melinda smiled. "They've been sensitized," she said. "A week from now, two weeks . . . who knows how many of them would perceive what's happening. But for now . . . the guys have an audience. And I think that's what they've wanted all along."

"You're kidding," Delia said. "You're talking about the barbershop singers, right? You brought them *here*?"

Melinda made a keep-it-down gesture. "I did," she said. "I thought it would be good for all of them. As well as possibly solving the whole crossing-the-guys-over situation." She shook her head at Delia's expression. "It's not a big deal for the children, Delia. As long as we don't make it one. Do they look happy?"

"They look delighted," Delia had to admit. And there was Ned in the middle of them, handing out little sippie cups of milk, and looking back at Melinda as if to say, *I know there's something going on here.*

Payne tipped his head in his skeptical, smarter-than-everyone way. Which generally speaking, he was, but at the moment? Definitely floundering. "What makes you even think—"

"Oh, come on," Melinda said. "I didn't get it at first. I was trying for something too complicated, trying to understand what four of them could need and why they couldn't talk . . . why they could only sing. But what does any of us want? What did I want, as a kid? I wanted the people who were important to me to hear me, to believe me. What did Angie want? She was being abused, and wanted to be heard—she *died* to be heard. What did her mother want? For Angie to hear her. So what do four guys, all dressed up to perform—four guys who would have made that performance if they hadn't been caught up in their usual preconcert jitters and running off with arguments so meaningless they haven't been able to talk since—want most?"

They finished their cheerful little song to the scattered applause and cheers of the children, mostly ignored by teachers who had learned to take such things in stride of late. The spotlight dimmed slightly; their faces grew more solemn. They tipped their boater hats at Melinda and put them over their hearts.

> *I'll leave the nighttime to the dreamers*
> *I'll leave the songbirds to the blind;*
> *I'll leave the moon above*
> *To those in love*
> *When I leave the world behind . . .*

And by the last word they'd faded away, along with their beautifully spun harmony.

"Right," Melinda said, and smiled through happy tears. "What anybody wants. To be heard."

# Not sure what to read next?

## Visit Pocket Books online at
## www.simonsays.com

Reading suggestions for
you and your reading group
New release news
Author appearances
Online chats with your favorite writers
Special offers
Order books online
And much, much more!